This DCI Jack Harris murder mystery can be enjoyed on its own or as part of a series. Look out for the first book, Dead Hill, and the second, The Vixen's Scream, both available on Kindle and in paperback.

TO DIE ALONE

A gripping British detective murder mystery

JOHN DEAN

THE
BOOK
FOLKS

Paperback published by The Book Folks

London, 2017

© John Dean

ISBN 978-1-5215-9813-9

www.thebookfolks.com

Chapter one

As the rain lashed the hills and the wind shrieked high and wild, Trevor Meredith walked through the copse, his breathing coming hard and fast. Constantly aware of the groaning and creaking sounds around him, he shot anxious glances at the trees as they rocked in the storm, which had raged all night and showed little signs of abating with the arrival of the grey shades of day. Meredith was acutely aware of the dangers: on his trek along the valley that morning, he had seen numerous newly-uprooted trees sprawled across the slopes. One had slipped thirty metres to form a makeshift bridge across the stream: Meredith had used the trunk to cross normally quiet waters, which were now a torrent after thirty-six hours of relentless summer rain.

Slipping on the damp moss beneath his walking boots, Meredith reached the fringes of the copse, wearily slipped his rucksack off his shoulders and dropped the bag to let it rest against a rock. Feeling suddenly very tired, he let his eyes range across the slopes below him and, spotting movement in among the bracken, gave a smile followed by a couple of low clicks of the tongue. A wet and bedraggled collie emerged from the undergrowth and bounded towards him.

'You're a good lad, Robbie,' said Meredith, patting the dog's head as the animal nestled at his feet. 'At least there's someone I can trust.'

Meredith reached into his bag and produced a plastic bag of digestive biscuits, one of which he gave to the animal. Watching the dog gulp the biscuit down, Meredith chuckled and passed him another one before taking one himself and turning his attention once more to his surroundings. He considered his situation. Throughout his walk he had sought high ground and from his vantage point half-way up the slope, now had a wide view of the valley. His position allowed him to look across the stream and up at the ridge, the top all but obscured by the low cloud that had shrouded the hills all morning. He could also look to his right, along to where the valley gradually flattened out and opened up onto heather moorland. Meredith concluded his perusal with a glance left, back in the direction from which he had come.

Survey finished, Meredith heaved a sigh of relief when he saw no movement through the gloom, other than the occasional sheep trying to shelter from the driving rain behind one of the drystone walls that criss-crossed the landscape. There had been times during his walk when Meredith fancied that he *had* seen shapes in the distance, admittedly figures glimpsed but fleetingly through the low cloud before they disappeared from view, but figures all the same. Or were they? He tossed another biscuit to the dog and gave a little shake of the head as he remembered what Jasmine had said the day before – that it was all in his mind. What was the word she had used? A breakdown, she had said, tears in her eyes. He was having a breakdown. Meredith scowled at the memory and bit down on another biscuit. Jasmine was wrong: this was not his imagination.

He glanced once more to his left, half expecting to see the figures again, but there was no one there. Clearly, the rapid pace he had set that morning had left them far behind. Perhaps, thought Meredith, he would get away with this after all. No one, surely, would be crazy enough to keep going after him in this weather. Perhaps they had set off in pursuit but been forced to abandon the chase as the conditions worsened, he thought, as a particularly ferocious gust of wind battered the copse. After all, they weren't hill people, he was sure of that; perhaps it had all proved too much for them.

Despite the reassuring thought, Meredith still found himself reluctant to leave the protection of the copse. He allowed himself a few more moments to gather his strength: even though he was a fit forty-two-year-old, he had still found the going hard as he battled all morning against the winds. The pause allowed him to consider his options. Heading right and out onto the moors would bring him once again into the clear view of his pursuers. The alternative, the one he had so far selected, was to pick a partially-concealed route through the sporadic woodland ranged along the valley side, then make his way up onto the moor and move quickly towards the welcome cover of the large forestry plantation less than a mile and a half away. Glancing down at Robbie, who was sitting waiting for another biscuit, Meredith estimated that they would be able to easily reach the trees inside an hour.

Cursing once again the snapped fan belt that had forced him to leave his car back on the road, Meredith glanced at his watch, which told him that it was just before 10.30am. He had abandoned the stricken vehicle with no plan in mind, except a vague idea that, if he could reach one of the tiny villages high in the hills, he could seek help. He knew people there. However, he knew that even if he did catch a bus or hitch a lift with a farmer – Trevor Meredith had long since acknowledged that he had no alternative but to flee the area he had come to love – there was the strong possibility that he would be seen.

With a heavy sigh, he reached down for his bag and hoisted it onto his shoulders, pausing before setting off again to fish his handkerchief out of the trouser pocket of his waterproofs. Fastidiously, he wiped the rain off his spectacles, replaced the handkerchief and started walking, still unsure as to the route he would take. After a couple of paces, he paused and gave a final, longing glance back at the darkness of the wood. The temptation to sit out the storm was a strong one, yet he realised that the gale that had made his progress so tortuous was also the one thing that offered him a chance of escaping with his life.

Yet still he hesitated.

'Pull yourself together, man,' he muttered. 'You've been in tighter spots than this.'

Noticing his dog watching him expectantly, Meredith gave a clicking sound and started walking, but he had only gone a few paces when he heard, behind him, the death throes of one of the large trees in the heart of the copse. He swivelled to watch in wide-eyed fascination as it teetered for a few moments before, with a final tearing of mighty roots, it was sent crashing, heavy and thunderous, to the ground, landing less than twenty metres from where Meredith was standing. He felt the earth shake beneath his feet and noticed that several other trees, having caught glancing blows by the collapsing giant, were swaying like boxers caught by punches. At least one of them looked as if it would be brought down as well, and Meredith heard a creaking sound as it tilted at an alarming angle. Recovering from his shock, he gazed in anxious silence at the scene. To his relief, the tree remained standing but, as the wind reached a new crescendo, it seemed as if the entire copse was dancing to the gale's tune.

'Too close,' murmured Meredith. 'Too close.'

Deciding to gamble on the rain-swept moor, Trevor Meredith set out again, this time firm of step and strong of resolve. He had only gone a few paces when he realised that Robbie was not following him. Turning back,

Meredith saw the dog cowering low to the ground and emitting a low growling sound as it fixed its stare on something several hundred metres away, down towards the stream. Following the animal's gaze, Meredith saw a figure picking its way along the bank.

* * *

Jasmine Riley stood on the virtually deserted railway platform at Levton Bridge station and watched in silence as the train lumbered out of the mid-morning gloom. Having weaved its way through the hills for the best part of an hour and a half, stopping at several tiny stations en route, the train's three coaches still only contained a handful of passengers. After Levton Bridge, it was due to continue its sedate journey eastwards towards what the more ironic of the locals termed 'the outside world'.

If the passengers remained on board until the journey's end, they would reach the flatlands at the bottom of the valley and trundle into Roxham, the area's largest town. The service terminated at Roxham and there the passengers could, if they so wished, catch the mainline services and head south for Manchester and Liverpool, north up to Glasgow or east across to Newcastle. So important was the rail service that many people in the valley referred to it as a 'lifeline'. For Jasmine Riley that morning, the word could not have been more apt; the knowledge made her nervous, more nervous than she could ever recall feeling.

As the train approached the platform, Jasmine glanced round at the other people waiting for its arrival: two elderly women clutching shopping bags and a teenager too engrossed in the music playing through his earphones to pay much attention to anyone else. Looking behind her, she saw to her relief that the ticket office area remained deserted, the rail worker behind the grille concentrating on his newspaper. He did not seem to have even noticed her, the pencil in his hand and the fact that his tongue was protruding from the side of his mouth suggested to Jasmine that he was doing the crossword. In other circumstances, she would have laughed at the faintly ridiculous sight but this time was different. Now her only thought was 'such normality'. Not so long ago, it had been her normality and she felt a deep sadness as she recalled such carefree days. Feeling tears coming again, she cheered herself up with the reassuring thought that it would be her normality again soon – all she had to do was travel to Roxham, catch the connecting service out to Newcastle and arrive at the agreed rendezvous with Trevor. A nice little riverside pub, he had said. She would like it, he had said. Jasmine smiled at the thought.

Despite attempts to reassure herself, Jasmine Riley still watched nervously to see who got out of the carriages as the train pulled to a halt with a groaning of its brakes. There was only one person, a smartly-dressed businessman carrying a briefcase. He glanced at his watch and hurried past without even looking at her. Jasmine picked up her overnight bag and boarded the end carriage; she had had some wild idea of being able to jump to safety if danger threatened, rather like they did in those old cowboy movies that she and Trevor so enjoyed watching. She knew it was a deeply impractical notion but somehow the idea made her feel more confident. She even allowed herself a little chuckle as she took her seat at the back, nearest the doors.

Once she was settled, she looked round the carriage in as natural a manner as possible, recalling Trevor's final words before their parting. 'Don't draw attention to yourself', he had said, 'just act natural. Do that and you'll be ok.' Jasmine was relieved to see that the carriage was almost empty but for a retired gentleman reading The Guardian, a bored young mother staring out the window while her small child munched his way through a packet of crisps and a middle-aged man engrossed in a paperback book. Jasmine watched him for a few moments. Was he the one following her? No, he had been on the train when she got on, she was sure of that.

That had been the problem over recent days: living with Trevor Meredith had made her paranoid, jumping at every strange sound, freezing whenever the phone rang. Noticing that the man had glanced up at her, Jasmine looked away quickly, returned her attention to the window and tried to appear relaxed while inwardly rebuking herself. This was ridiculous, she thought, she was the one who told Trevor he was imagining everything. For his part, the man let his eyes rest on her for a few moments more, intrigued by what could possibly have so alarmed the bespectacled young woman with the mousy appearance. Seeing her slide another glance his way, the man felt a skip of the heart and instinctively ran a hand through his hair.

When no one else appeared on the platform, the guard blew his whistle and the train started to pull slowly out of Levton Bridge, struggling on the gradient as it reached the edge of the town, passing the Victorian primary school building half-way up the hill before leaving behind the final row of cottages. As the train gathered pace, Jasmine slid a furtive look across at the middle-aged man again. He was still engrossed in his book and she gave the slightest shake of the head. No, not him. He was just some ordinary Joe heading down into Roxham. Maybe, she mused, he was going there for some shopping, or perhaps to visit someone who lived there. Normality, she thought wistfully, always normality.

Returning her attention to the window as the train trundled across the rain-swept moorland, she wondered where Trevor was. She had not heard from him since he left the cottage early that morning but she was not worried, that had been the plan. Safer that way, he had said. Stick to the plan, always stick to the plan. These people could pick up on locations using GPS if phones were used, he had said. Jasmine recalled his final words before they parted; noticing her anxious look, he had given her a slight smile and, mimicking one of their favourite television shows, had said 'smoke me a kipper, babe, I'll see you for breakfast.' She had laughed, then he had kissed her gently on the forehead, foraged round in his pocket for his car key and walked out into the wan light. Recalling the moment, Jasmine gave a half-smile. Perhaps, she thought as the train rattled across the moors, Trevor was right, perhaps they would laugh about this one day.

She did not know about the man sitting in the next carriage, the man who had watched her from the shadows of the station before sprinting across the platform to jump onto the train just as it was about to leave. The man who now hid behind his newspaper and waited for Roxham.

Chapter two

'So, what do you think, Hawk?' asked Bob Crowther as he unscrewed the lid of his flask and poured out a cup of steaming tea. 'Is he up here?'

Crowther, the leader of Levton Bridge search and rescue team for more than fifteen years, glanced over at his companion, a large man who stood on the edge of the copse. Chewing on a chocolate bar as he looked silently out over the valley, Detective Chief Inspector Jack Harris did not appear to have heard the question and, for a few moments, the only sound was the insistent patter of the rain on the swathe of bracken stretching down to the stream. Bob Crowther, well attuned to his friend's silences after so many years, took a couple of sips of tea and glanced behind him. He frowned at the sight of his fellow team members sheltering among the trees, appreciating the rest after the afternoon's battles against the gale. The realisation that their search was getting them nowhere prompted him to try again with his friend.

'I mean,' said Crowther, 'if Meredith was out here, I would have expected us to have found him by now. Or at least turned up something to suggest which way he went.'

'Indeed.' Harris did not turn around.

'It would not have been the first time we'd searched the hills for someone who had been sitting at home watching Countdown, would it? Remember that bloke who turned up at the b. & b. in…?'

'He's here.'

'Yes, but…'

'He's here,' repeated Harris in a firm voice that brooked no argument as he finally turned round and looked his friend in the eye. His voice softened slightly. 'He's here, Bob. I can feel it.'

Crowther inclined his head slightly and Harris stared out over the valley again. He had been experiencing a growing sense of unease as the afternoon had worn on, a sense, as he and the team trudged through the rain-swept hills, that something was badly wrong beneath the brooding North Pennine skies. Jack Harris had never been able to explain his instincts but always maintained that they stretched back to his days as a soldier when his life relied on a sixth sense, the sudden feeling that made you turn around without knowing why. Harris had seen comrades die because they didn't turn round and the experience had heightened his awareness of the world around him. That's what he had said on the very few occasions when he would talk about his life before the police.

On this occasion, he had been struggling for several hours to rationalise exactly what he was feeling. He tried once more. Danger? Was it danger? No, not danger, too strong a word; rather an uneasy feeling nagging away at the back of his mind, a growing concern that whatever had threatened Meredith – and he was convinced that something was threatening him – may still be out there. He also had a feeling that whatever *it* was, was close. Very close. Perhaps, thought Harris grimly, danger was the word after all.

'I don't suppose,' ventured Crowther after watching him for a few moments, 'that your instincts happened to tell you where he is?'

'Sorry, Bob. They're never that specific.'

'I guessed as much.' Crowther sighed. 'Well, whatever has happened to him, I keep coming to the same question: why would he head across the hills when his car broke down? He's lived up here long enough to know that if he'd gone back on the road, he could have been in Levton Bridge in an hour or so.'

'Indeed so.'

'And where was he going anyway? If it's right that he told his office that he was going to an appointment at Ramsgill, whichever route you take, it's north. And Trevor Meredith was driving east. Towards Roxham.'

'He was,' said Harris, finishing his chocolate and stuffing the wrapper into his backpack.

'So, what you thinking?'

'I'm thinking how dangerous complacency can be.'

'You can't keep beating yourself up about it. These things can catch us all out.'

'Yes, but we lost precious time,' said Harris with a shake of the head. 'I tell you, Bob, I've got a bad feeling about this one.'

It had been, he recalled, the opposite scenario earlier in the day. A detective chief inspector in the market town of Levton Bridge, Jack Harris had been in a rare cheerful mood as he passed the Control Room in the Victorian house that served as divisional headquarters. The previous Friday, he had been in Carlisle Crown Court to see three travelling criminals from Merseyside jailed for stealing £95,000 of quad bikes from farms in his area. One incident had seen a farmer threatened with a baseball bat, the man subsequently suffering a mild stroke and now unable to work, his farm still on the market the best part of a year later. Acutely aware that the raids had sent fear rippling through the area's hill communities, Harris and his team had been after the gang for months and they had all received a judge's commendation at the conclusion of the trial. Not that Jack Harris put much store by commendations but it was nice to be recognised.

Outside the court building when the trial ended, the inspector had given several media interviews, during which he went out of his way to warn other gangs considering coming into the area that Levton Bridge Police were waiting for them. He had even looked into the television camera, pointing a finger somewhat dramatically into the lens and revealing that he was already well advanced in the planning of the next operation. Given that he wasn't planning anything of the sort, Harris had spent the weekend coming up with ways to thwart the gangs and by the Sunday evening, he was satisfied that he had enough in place to divert any awkward questions from the top brass when he returned to work the next morning.

But there hadn't been any awkward questions and Harris had spent the first hour of the day going through all the weekend newspaper reports, delighting in headlines that made for good reading. Never a great politician, Jack Harris was nevertheless shrewd enough to know that things like this played well at headquarters down in Roxham. He knew the high-ups would be reading the same articles, basking in the reflected glory, and Harris had already pinned the best of the cuttings up on the CID room wall to encourage his small team of detectives. HR would like that, he reckoned. Staff motivation, that's what they were always banging on about in their memos.

Now, staring over the valley and gloomily turning the events of the day over and over in his mind, the inspector realised that his good mood had coloured his reaction when the alert came in about Trevor Meredith shortly before lunchtime. He knew that he should have immediately sensed that something was amiss. The call had come from one of Trevor Meredith's concerned fellow workers at the town's dog sanctuary, reporting that he had not turned up that morning, that there was no sign of him at his home and that he was not answering his mobile phone, that he was a conscientious man and that such behaviour was all out of character.

The inspector, who happened to be passing the Control Room at the time, stepped in to listen in on the conversation, his initial instinct being to take no action. Jack Harris had long regarded it as a man's inalienable right to be able to disappear for a few hours if he so wished. He had spent enough years concocting spurious inquiries as an excuse for heading out into the hills to think any different, and everyone at Levton Bridge Police Station knew it. A man was entitled, he had announced as he left the room, to walk his dog without having half the police force out looking for him. The control operators had smiled at the comment – they knew to take advantage of a good Jack Harris mood.

The inspector's viewpoint changed when his desk phone rang some time later. His mouth full of ham sandwich, he had taken the call to be told by Control that a traffic officer heading along the moorland road between Levton Bridge and Roxham had spotted Trevor Meredith's estate car. There was no sign of the driver and no note on the windscreen indicating where he had been gone. A quick check had revealed a broken fan belt. A quick call to Jasmine Riley's workplace revealed that she had taken a day off, citing a family emergency. On hearing the news, Harris instinctively sensed that something was wrong. He had cursed, then telephoned his old friend Crowther. The inspector, who had been a member of the search and rescue team ever since his return to the area several years previously, knew how dangerous the hills could be, especially in brutal weather like the storm battering his office window. Within minutes, the volunteers were leaving their jobs and heading for the organisation's hut on the edge of a small patch of open grass behind the police station, Harris among them, struggling into his waterproofs as he went.

Once out on the hills, Crowther divided them into teams to cover as much distance as possible, meticulously re-tracing Meredith's possible routes. The teams – Crowther's working their way along the wooded valleys, a second one crossing the moor and the third moving their way steadily along the ridge – had been searching for more than three hours now but had produced little to suggest Meredith's whereabouts. Few people were out on the hills and none of those the team had encountered – a shepherd and a couple on a hiking holiday – had seen him, except for one vague report of a man with a dog, seen in the distance for a fleeting moment or two before they disappeared into the mist.

As late afternoon arrived, the winds had dropped slightly and Crowther had called a short halt as the searchers entered the copse. As the volunteers sat and talked in low tones over snacks and hot tea, their mood continued to darken: they were starting to suspect that they would not find Trevor Meredith. Everyone knew that the forecast was for the storm to renew its energies as the evening wore on. Several of the rescue team were already allowing their gaze to wander to the new batch of dark clouds gathering on the horizon.

'I think we have to face facts,' said Crowther, mindful of their mutterings, 'instinct or not, he was never here. What if his girlfriend picked him up when the car broke down?'

'Then why did he not leave a note?'

'Maybe he forgot. And she still hasn't turned up, has she?'

Before the DCI could reply, his mobile phone rang. Fishing it out of his pocket, he glanced at the name on the screen: *Gallagher*.

'Perhaps our resident Cockney can shed some light on the proceedings,' said the inspector. Matty Gallagher was the detective sergeant at Levton Bridge.

'Hope so.'

'Matty, lad,' said the inspector, 'I do hope you're not going to tell me that we've got wet-through for nothing and that Meredith and his young lady have been enjoying a cream tea in Roxham?'

'Now that,' said Gallagher's voice, 'sounds nice. Better than the muck they served in the canteen at lunchtime. No, we have not found them. The name and address in Meredith's diary for the appointment turns out to be fake.'

'Jasmine Riley still missing?'

'Yeah, but we've tracked down her elderly mum in Chester. The story Jasmine told her workmates on the phone this morning? Absolute cobblers. Fabrication from start to finish. Mum does not have cancer – in fact, she is really upset that her daughter would tell anyone she had – and she has not been rushed to hospital. What's more, she hasn't heard from her daughter for the best part of a week and was starting to get concerned.'

'Intriguing.'

'Well, if you think that's intriguing, get this. You know I said no one at Levton Bridge railway station had seen Jasmine? Well, we tracked down a bloke who got off further down the line at Maltby – he was visiting his grandmother – and he remembers someone who looked like Jasmine sitting in the same carriage. Caught her staring at him a couple of times. Wondered if she fancied him, the arrogant git. According to Butterfield, he's no oil painting.'

'We can assume that Jasmine was on her way to Roxham then. It's the next stop.'

'And his car *was* found on the Roxham road, remember.'

'Indeed it was,' said Harris. 'Look, are we 100 per cent sure they weren't travelling together?'

'The witness did not see anyone else with her. The train got into Roxham just as the Manchester service arrived so the station was busy but no one among the platform staff remembers seeing them either. I've got the

Roxham plods checking things out but they've not turned up anything yet. Not sure they will now.'

There was a brief silence.

'What you thinking?' asked Gallagher.

'I don't know, but whatever it is, it's not good. I take it there's still no word from the chopper? We could do with some help.'

'Control talked to them an hour ago – they reckon it's still far too bad to fly.'

'Try again, will you? Everything else quiet?'

'Not the word I would use. Uniform have been called twice to punch-ups at The King's Head. There's a load of locals in for a sesh by the looks of it. Been there since opening time.'

'Anyone hurt?'

'Na, it's all been a bit handbags.'

'What are the fights about?'

'Uniform are not sure. I'm keeping out of it, to be honest, we've got enough to do compiling those bloody burglary statistics that the super wants for his meeting. See you wheedled yourself out of that one.'

'Sometimes it's ok to pull rank.'

'So it would seem. Oh, some old gadgy called Harry Galbraith has been on for you three times. He's getting all aerated, says it's urgent. Who is he?'

'The Farmwatch guy. Lives up at Sneets Edge. I rang him over the weekend to suggest we do an op tonight.'

'Why?'

'Thought it would play well after my comments about travelling gangs after the case on Friday. We were going to put a press release out about it later in the week. Show that I was not talking hogwash.'

'As if,' said Gallagher. 'What do you want me to tell him?'

'Well there's no way I can do it now. Ask uniform if they can spare a couple of bodies. All they need to do is park up somewhere in case the farmers need them.

Shouldn't happen, mind – they're not supposed to get out of their cars. All they have to do is take registration numbers.'

'I'll ask but don't hold your breath.'

'In which case, make sure that Galbraith does not go out on his own if we haven't got anyone available.'

'Surely he knows that.'

'Yeah, but he tends to get a bit over-enthusiastic. Give him a walkie-talkie and he thinks he's Rambo. Daft bastard even asked me if we should be blacked up and if I had any spare camouflage trousers. It's all rather Cockleshell Heroes.'

The inspector heard Gallagher's low laugh at the other end. Noticing that Crowther was talking on his radio, the inspector finished the call, replaced his phone in his pocket and waited until his friend completed his conversation.

'That was Mike Ganton up on the ridge,' said Crowther. 'They've just been talking to a shepherd who saw a man with a dog shortly after nine.'

'That confirms the other report we had then. Meredith *is* up here.'

''Fraid not. Mike reckons this was some kind of bull terrier. Nasty looking thing, apparently. It had had half its ear ripped off at some point. The owner wasn't exactly a barrel of laughs either. Shaven-headed bloke. I'm starting to share your misgivings about this if characters like that are wandering across the moors.'

Crowther looked up at the leaden sky and scowled: it was past five and, whereas there would normally have been several more hours of summer daylight remaining, the storm had changed everything and it was already starting to grow dark beneath the heavy rain clouds.

'If Meredith is up here,' he said grimly, 'he's going to be in trouble soon because I reckon we'll lose the light by half seven. Eight if we're really lucky. And we both know the weather forecast for tonight. This is the lull before.'

'So, what do you want to do?'

'Give it another hour or so, then think again. Too early to consider calling it off.'

Harris nodded his approval.

'But if he is up here,' said Crowther, glancing back at his men, a couple of whom had already started to push on through the copse, 'we have to find him pretty damn quick. Not sure Meredith can handle a night on the hills.'

'He's a fit lad, mind. Does a lot of fell running. Keen walker as well.'

'So how come you know him so well?' said Crowther, tossing the dregs of his tea onto the ground and replacing the flask in his bag. 'He a friend?'

'I meet him out walking the dog sometimes. And he was the one I dealt with when I went to get Scoot.'

Harris gestured to the black Labrador rooting around in the vegetation a little further down the valley side.

'So, what was he like?'

'Very good. House-trained and the previous owner had been pretty good when it came to using a...'

'Trevor Meredith, not the blessed dog!' exclaimed Crowther, a broad grin spreading across his face. 'Bloody typical.'

'Bob!'

The cry came from the far side of the copse and they sprinted to where, ten metres beyond a large up-ended tree, two of their orange-clad colleagues were staring down at the body of a man. Nobody spoke for a few moments – no one liked bringing down dead bodies from the hills. Police officer's instincts taking over, Harris crouched down by the corpse and stared into the face.

'Is it him?' asked Crowther.

'Yeah, it's him.'

Harris bent down further to examine the ugly wound on the side of Meredith's head, the blood having flowed across the right cheek and dribbled down to stain his blue waterproof jacket, before being washed away by the rain.

'I take it he's dead?' asked Crowther, peering over the inspector's shoulder.

'As the proverbial.'

Cursory examination complete, the inspector straightened up and walked over to stare thoughtfully at the felled tree, whose roots had been torn from the ground during the gale.

'You thinking that did for him?' asked Crowther.

'Maybe.'

'There's certainly been plenty come down.' Crowther glanced at the other rescuers and shook his head. 'Bye, that's bad luck, that is.'

'Assuming he *was* hit by the tree,' said the inspector, patting the trunk which, to the others, seemed a strangely affectionate gesture. 'What a waste.'

'Yeah, he was a decent bloke by all accounts,' said Crowther.

'Actually, I was thinking of the tree. Must be a good forty years old.'

Crowther allowed himself a smile. 'So how come you're not sure it was the tree?' asked one of the other volunteers.

'I would have expected more extensive injuries.'

'Not necessarily,' said the man. 'Remember that guy who took a header off Langton Crag three years ago? Not a bloody mark on him. I've had worse injuries shaving.'

'Yeah,' said Crowther, looking down at the corpse, 'maybe the tree only struck him a glancing blow. Besides, look at his arm, Hawk, that doesn't look too clever. And his right hand looks pretty badly smashed up.'

'Then why's he lying over by you? Why not here, next to the tree?'

As Harris spoke, he glanced to his left, stopped and stared for a few moments at a small area of flattened undergrowth and a patch of disturbed mud. Letting his eyes roam a few paces, Harris noted a large rock. He walked over and peered down at the side furthest away from him, the side concealed from view. The green moss was tinged with streaks of blood.

'I think this is where they struggled,' he said.

'Who struggled?' asked Crowther.

'Meredith and the man who killed him.'

'What, up here?' said Crowther, unable to conceal the scepticism in his voice.

'Why not?' said Harris, walking back to stand next to Crowther. 'Maybe his attacker left him for dead – perhaps he dragged himself over here before dying.'

'Sorry, Hawk,' said Crowther as he watched the inspector crouch down by the body once more, his face so low it almost touched the damp earth, 'I still reckon he was hit by the tree.'

He glanced at the others for support; several of the men nodded.

'In which case,' said Harris, 'I am sure one of you can explain how it came to be carrying a knife.'

He half-turned Meredith's body and pointed to a bloodied mark in the side, initially concealed from view because he had been lying on his back.

'Jesus,' exclaimed Crowther, 'is that a stab wound?'

'Certainly is.' Harris turned to look at the others. 'Sorry guys, but this has just turned into a crime scene. Can we all move back, please?'

The rescue team members shuffled away but Crowther did not move.

'You ok, Bob?' asked Harris, looking at his friend.

'You know,' said Crowther quietly, 'it doesn't matter how many times we find a dead one, I always think the same thing – what must it feel like to die alone up here?'

'But he wasn't alone, was he?' said Harris with sudden energy, walking quickly over to the edge of the copse to scan the slopes. 'His dog was with him, wasn't he? So where is he?'

'Maybe he got scared and ran off. I used to have a dog that got spooked when I turned the television on.'

'No,' said Harris, with a vigorous shake of the head, 'Robbie would have stayed with his master.'

Thoughts turning to his own dog, the inspector stared to where he had last seen Scoot rooting through the bracken a little further down the slope. Harris tensed – body rigid, the Labrador was staring down at something hidden among the leaves. The inspector could see that the dog's teeth were bared and that his hackles were up. Harris could hear his low growls even from where he was standing.

'What the…?' exclaimed the inspector.

He sprinted to where Scoot was standing. After gently moving the trembling Labrador out of the way, the inspector knelt by the blood-soaked remains of a black and white dog. Looking closer, he could see that the animal's throat had been ripped out, part of its muzzle had been torn off and one ear was smeared with blood. Harris felt the tears glistening in his eyes as he surveyed the injuries. Hearing the others approaching, he quickly wiped his eyes with the back of his hand and took a deep breath to compose himself.

'What the hell is that?' breathed Crowther.

'I am afraid, that it's poor old Robbie,' said Harris quietly, reaching out to gently stroke the dead animal's flank. 'Or what's left of him.'

'You reckon he was killed by the bloke who did for Meredith?' asked Crowther in an appalled voice.

'No, these kinds of injuries were inflicted by an animal. A dog, presumably.'

'Yeah, but surely no dog is capable of inflicting injuries like that?' exclaimed Crowther.

'Depends what they are trained to do.'

'Trained?'

'You can train a dog to do whatever you want,' nodded Harris, looking up at the others with a grim expression on his face. 'And this one, gentlemen, is a dangerous as they come.'

The rescuers digested the information for a few moments, then Bob Crowther glanced nervously along the valley.

'Bloody hell, Hawk,' he said, 'you don't think that it's still…?'

His voice tailed off. Everyone knew what he was thinking.

Chapter three

'What a mess,' said Matty Gallagher, looking down at the body of Trevor Meredith's pet lying among the bracken. 'That's some dog done that.'

'Which is why he's here,' replied the inspector, nodding at the uniformed officer standing nearby on the slope who was constantly scanning the valley, a marksman's rifle in his hand.

'I'd be happier if he had a bazooka.'

'It's a dog not a bleeding elephant,' said Harris.

It was shortly after six thirty and a break in the weather had allowed a helicopter to take off from the RAF base further down the valley, bringing with it Gallagher, a forensics officer, the Home Office pathologist and the sharpshooter from the force's firearms unit. After hovering for several minutes, debating the safety of a landing, the pilot had finally been able to set down on a flat patch of grass out on the moor but, with the light fading and the wind starting to lift again, he had warned all on board that they had less than an hour. The pilot made no secret of his unease at the situation in which he found himself – he was already regretting making the landing – and now twenty-five minutes later, he was eager to depart.

In the copse, the forensic investigator and the pathologist, conscious that time was short, were working quickly to complete their initial findings: neither wanted to be left behind on the hillside, particularly not with a dangerous dog on the loose. Besides, with the rain starting to fall harder again, they knew that every drop wiped away what evidence there was. The decision having been taken to airlift Meredith to the mortuary at Roxham General Hospital, most of the search and rescue team had already started the trek back to their vehicles parked on the road several miles away, each man nervously scanning the landscape for any signs of the animal. Only Bob Crowther and his deputy, Mike Ganton, had remained at the scene and they were now standing in the copse, awaiting their instructions as they shot anxious glances across to the helicopter standing on the moor. Although neither man had said anything, each knew that, sharpshooter or not, the other was calculating how quickly they could sprint to the aircraft if the animal reappeared.

'So do you think the dog *will* come back?' asked Gallagher, unable to conceal the unease from his voice.

'You should be more concerned about the nutter that did for Trevor Meredith.'

'Yeah, I know that,' said Gallagher and looked nonplussed for a few moments. 'It's just that... I dunno, there's something about the thought of a dog doing something like that...'

He looked at the inspector but Harris had turned to stare across the darkening valley and did not reply. It was almost as if he had not heard. The ensuing silence allowed Gallagher to survey his boss. They were different in just about every way and few places brought out those differences more than the northern hills. Jack Harris, in his mid-forties, tall and muscular, face strong-jawed, blue eyes piercing and thick brown hair without a hint of grey, was at home in the valleys and the moors. A man not given to conversation, Harris sought out every possible opportunity to spend in the hills, revelling in their silence and their solitude.

Gallagher hated silence and solitude. A decade younger, he was stocky, black hair starting to go bald and displaying the first flecks of grey, giving him the appearance, a colleague had once said, of an ageing monk. More sociable and open than the inspector, Gallagher loved to talk, so had always struggled with his colleague's reluctance to elaborate on what he was thinking. During his time in the Metropolitan Police, before heading north to work in Levton Bridge, the sergeant had been used to detectives who discussed their theories in cases but getting Jack Harris to explain anything had always been a difficult task. And now, there, on that rain-swept hill beneath those thunderous skies, Matty Gallagher was surprised to discover that what he needed now, what he really did *need*, was for Jack Harris to talk to him, to offer some kind of explanation, to offer some kind of reassurance. Suddenly, the sergeant felt very small.

Noticing his sergeant's uneasy demeanour, Harris smiled at him. The gesture took Gallagher by surprise as it always did on the rare occasions that the inspector displayed warmth to another human being.

'Don't worry, Matty lad, even if it does return, Scoot will smell him a mile off.' Harris nodded at his dog, who was rooting through the bracken down by the stream, apparently now unconcerned by what had happened. 'You any good at climbing trees? Did they have them in London?'

Gallagher stared at him – you never knew when the inspector was joking, usually because he wasn't – then gave a rueful grin when Harris winked. After enjoying the rare joke, the sergeant's expression grew serious again as he looked back down at Robbie, the blood matted on his fur.

'So, what kind of a dog did this, do you think?' he asked.

'One that was specially trained.'

'The thought had occurred,' nodded Gallagher. 'You ever been to a dog fight?'

'Unfortunately, I have,' said Harris. 'It was back in Manchester. I'd not long been a DI…'

Even from where they were standing, the officers could hear the baying of the crowd from inside the warehouse as they watched the bull terriers tearing each other to shreds in the makeshift ring, its floor stained with blood. Jack Harris felt his stomach churning as he heard through the darkness the agonised shriek of one of the animals and the cries of triumph from the crowd. It was shortly after 11pm and four RSPCA officers, supported by more than fifty uniformed police officers and detectives, were standing on the edge of an industrial estate on the eastern fringes of Manchester, amidst workshops – most of which were dark and boarded up.

Looking across to the warehouse, the officers saw, illuminated by dim lights shining through grimy windows, the vague shapes of men waving their hands in the air as they urged on the fighting dogs. Not that the officers needed to see inside to know that the place was crowded: outside the building was parked a fleet of 4x4 vehicles. A computer check had already revealed that some of them belonged to a number of well-known local villains. At least one of the vehicles was stolen.

Trying to blot out the sounds of the fight, the detective inspector's mind went back to the reason for his presence there. An RSPCA inspector called Ged Maynard, a wiry man in his mid-thirties, had requested police back-up for a raid which would mark the culmination of a protracted investigation by the organisation into dog fighting in the area. Jack Harris had been given the task of co-ordinating the police support. His knowledge of the kind of people involved meant that he was not in the mood to take risks – among the police contingent were armed officers under orders to shoot the bull terriers if need be. Jack Harris knew the effect that bloodlust could have on an animal.

A particularly loud roar from the crowd in the warehouse dragged the detective's mind back to the job in hand.

'I think,' he said, looking at Maynard, 'that we have heard enough. Time we put an end to this sick little game.'

'I want Radford,' said Maynard.

'Only if I don't get to him first,' said Harris.

Maynard nodded and the officers moved quietly forward, tension etched into their faces, expressions that mixed apprehension with disgust at what they would find.

'Ok,' said Harris as the raiding party started to fan out to secure the perimeter of the warehouse, 'let's get this done.'

With raucous shouts of warning, the uniformed officers barged their way through the doors and poured into the building. For a few minutes, all was chaos as men hollered in anger and lashed out at the police while others tried to escape, only to be apprehended, some wrestled to the ground, arms wrenched behind their backs to be handcuffed. Jack Harris had a sudden sense of danger and whirled round to see a large man running towards him, holding an iron bar above his head.

'Drop it!' shouted the inspector.

The man kept on coming and Harris, moving rapidly and instinctively, a legacy of Army training, swayed to one side and brought his knee up hard and fast into the man's midriff. With hardly a sound, the man sunk to the floor, the blood drained from his face and the metal bar clattered to the ground.

As some sort of peace returned, and those arrested ceased struggling, while those who had managed to escape the building melted into the shadows, Jack Harris stepped forward towards the ring that had been created in the middle of the floor. Heart pounding and stomach turning again, he hardly dared look and momentarily he closed his eyes. Eventually, he forced himself to open them and gave a small sigh at what he saw: lying amid the bloodstained dust on the floor was a bull terrier that had suffered horrendous wounds. It was obvious even from several feet away that it was dead. Harris turned a heavy gaze at the other dog, which stood on the far side of the ring, eying the inspector balefully, slavering as it did so. Bloodstained and trembling, a livid fire in its eyes, foam flecking its mouth, the animal snarled as it saw Harris move towards it.

'Give it up, fella,' said the inspector quietly, holding out a hand. 'Your fighting days are over.'

The dog eyed him uncertainly for a few moments then lunged forward, teeth bared. A single shot rang out and the animal jerked backwards, its legs giving way as it sunk to the floor. For a couple of seconds, it struggled to stand before keeling over again, this time lying still. Tears in his eyes, Jack Harris walked over and knelt down beside the animal. Battling his emotions, the inspector reached out a hand and gently stroked its flank, which moved ever so slightly. With the slightest of sighs, the dog breathed its last. Jack Harris closed his eyes for a moment then turned and looked up at the marksman.

'Sorry, Jack,' the man said. 'I know how you didn't want to... I mean, you did say...'

'I know,' nodded Harris wearily. 'I know.'

Consumed by fury, and with the shrieks of the dogs still ringing in his ears, the inspector jumped to his feet and, spotting a familiar face among the arrested men being taken out to the police vans, he strode rapidly outside.

'Wait a minute,' he said to one of the uniformed officers, pointing at a burly dark-haired man in his late thirties. 'I want to talk to this one.'

Harris walked up to the man until their faces were but inches apart.

'Gerry Radford,' he said in a soft voice laced with menace, 'I am going to make sure you wish you were never born.'

'No wonder he's such a mess,' said Gallagher after listening to the story and glancing down at Robbie. 'They're crazy, those dogs.'

'Yeah, but only because people make them that way.'

'I guess so.'

The sergeant looked up towards the copse, where the pathologist and the forensics officer were deep in conversation with the rescue team leaders – Gallagher assumed it was about moving Trevor Meredith. Taking a few steps down the slope and glancing to his right, along to where the valley opened out onto moorland, Gallagher

30

saw one of the helicopter aircrew tapping his watch then holding up five fingers. The sergeant gave the thumbs-up signal.

'Running out of time, guv,' said Gallagher. 'So, are we safe to assume that the owner of the dog that killed Robbie was the bloke who did for Meredith?'

'Not sure there's any other possibility.'

'Boy, he must have fought like a tiger to protect his master,' said the sergeant, perusing the dog's injuries again. 'Gives a new meaning to man's best friend.'

'Didn't have you down as a dog man,' said the inspector approvingly.

'We had a dog when I was kid in East London.' Gallagher hesitated as if struggling with something. After a few moments, he continued. 'One night, I took him for a walk and some youths approached me, wanted my money.'

'What happened?'

'When I said I didn't have any, the biggest lad said he would knife me.' Gallagher shook his head at the memory. 'I was absolutely terrified. That's when Jake – that's what we called our dog, Jakey-boy – he stepped between the two of us and growled. Showed his teeth, the works. The big lad went for him with the knife.'

'And?'

'Jake bit him. Kid howled like a stuck pig. Next thing I know, they were legging it off down the street.'

Harris smiled at the image but the sergeant's expression remained solemn.

'Thing is,' he said, 'the next night the same gang jumped a kid from the next street and he wasn't so lucky. Ended up on a life-support machine. I often wondered, you know…'

He did not finish the sentence and there was a moment's silence.

'Anyway,' said Gallagher, suddenly embarrassed and eager to move on, 'that's my theory about why Robbie…'

His voice tailed off as he noticed Crowther and Ganton emerge from the woodland, carrying the stretcher bearing Meredith's corpse. Crowther looked over to them and nodded in the direction of the helicopter.

'Something tells me that they've called our flight,' said Harris.

The detectives fell in behind the stretcher as the rescue leaders bore it down the slope. As they approached the aircraft, one of the crew walked across to meet them.

'He ok to fly?' he asked, glancing at Scoot who had appeared from the bracken.

'He'll be fine,' said Harris. 'Can we take the dead one as well?'

'Not sure about that,' said the crewman dubiously. 'From what I saw, it's a bit of a mess. Can't you pick him up in the morning? It's only a dog, after all.'

'But one that is now evidence. I've arranged for a vet to check him over tonight. Besides…' Harris looked at the crewman, 'I think Robbie deserves a bit of respect after what he did for his master, don't you?'

The crewman gave a slight smile and nodded.

'I'll get a blanket,' he said.

Five minutes later, the helicopter was flying fast and low across the moors as the gathering gloom began to shroud the hills in darkness once more.

Chapter four

'This is ridiculous,' said Alison Butterfield, glancing across the table at the veterinary surgeon as he examined the remains of Trevor Meredith's pet. 'A complete waste of time.'

'What is?' asked James Thornycroft, peering up at the young detective constable over his spectacles.

'This is,' said Butterfield, unable to conceal her disgust. 'We get a murder and what do I end up with? A post-mortem on a dog. There's more important things to worry about than what happened to some mutt.'

'They deserve as much respect as humans.'

'You sound like my governor. I mean, if I'd wanted to work with the sodding RSPCA....' Butterfield left the sentence unfinished.

'Perhaps,' said the vet quietly as he looked up at her, 'such views would be better kept to yourself, Constable.'

Butterfield looked at him coldly but did not say anything – if she was honest, the same thought had occurred to her the moment she opened her mouth. She knew only too well how rapidly words travelled in the hill communities of the North Pennines and it would not have been the first time that her language had landed her in trouble.

It was approaching nine o'clock and they were standing in the examination room of the vet's practice in Levton Bridge, which was housed in a modern flat-roofed building in a side street off the market place. As she watched the vet continue with his work, Butterfield realised that she hardly knew him, an unusual phenomenon in the town. James Thornycroft had only recently moved to Levton Bridge, having purchased the business when the previous owner took early retirement. Local rumour suggested that the old man had drunk most of the profits and had no option but to sell up. She recalled that at the time the sale went through, there had been some talk of an urban vet taking over a rural practice – a few derogatory comments from the older farmers, her father included, about his lack of knowledge of the community, but she had not taken much notice. When you lived in a place like Levton Bridge, such talk was background noise. Butterfield wished she had listened harder now because she was not sure to whom, if anyone, James Thornycroft confided his thoughts; to whom her intemperate words would be conveyed. First rule of living in a tight-knit community, she thought bleakly, find out who talks to whom. Watching the vet working now, the detective constable wondered if her comments would get back to Harris.

They were in the examination room because, earlier in the evening, the constable had received a call from Harris on his mobile, ordering her to meet him at the playing field near Levton Bridge's primary school. When the helicopter arrived, he had instructed her to take the remains of Meredith's dog to the surgery. The inspector said he would be with her in a few minutes. Irked by what she saw as a menial task, Butterfield had seethed on the journey back into the town centre. Now, she and Thornycroft had been at the surgery for twenty minutes.

Silence settled on the room as he continued his examination and, for the first time, Butterfield turned her attention away from her own frustrations and looked at the body of the dog. The constable found herself watching with a growing, morbid fascination as the silence lengthened and the vet worked, the sweat glistening on his balding pate as he probed the remains of Robbie, occasionally tutting to himself at the extent of the wounds, seemingly oblivious to her presence. Butterfield found herself surprised to feel her irritation replaced by something deeper, something darker, something that had been buried for years, something that she had tried to push to the back of her mind, a dark childhood memory that stirred now. The constable gave the slightest shakes of the head, as if the motion would banish it from her thoughts.

'He looks pretty badly mauled,' she said instinctively. The sound of her voice surprised her. She did not even realise that she had spoken.

'How observant,' said Thornycroft, giving her a sly look. 'I can see why you became a detective.'

Butterfield cursed herself silently: it was tough enough being a female police officer in Levton Bridge without making it worse with stupid pronouncements. Noticing her discomfort, Thornycroft allowed himself a slight smile and carried on with his work. Silence settled on the room again until, finally, he gave a grunt, straightened up and walked over to the sink.

'Are you even remotely interested in my findings?' he asked, turning on the tap and beginning to wash the blood off his hands. 'Or would I be wasting your precious time?'

'All I'm saying,' said Butterfield, irritation returning at his sarcastic tone, 'is that I don't know why we're wasting time on the dog when we've got a man in the morgue. He's more important.'

Thornycroft turned round and glanced towards the door, so briefly as for it to be hardly noticeable.

'Meaning?' he asked, walking back to the examination table.

'Well, it's a question of priorities and I think we have got them wrong this time.'

'I shouldn't let your chief inspector hear you talking like that. He loves his dogs, does Jack Harris.'

'I don't care if he does – this is a murder inquiry and if all we can do is worry about…'

'All we can do is worry about what?' asked Harris.

Butterfield whirled round in horror as the inspector walked into the room.

'I didn't hear you come in,' she gasped.

'Clearly.'

'I did,' said Thornycroft.

Butterfield glared at him.

'Well?' said Harris, fixing her with a stern look, 'what were you saying about the inquiry, Constable? Another one of your illuminating insights into my policing methods, no doubt? I have half a mind to suggest that you become DCI in my place.'

She hesitated.

'I'm waiting, Constable.' The voice was harder now.

'I was just saying,' mumbled Butterfield, 'that what with Meredith's body being taken down to Roxham, I thought we should be at the post-mortem.'

'Oooh, I would not have thought to do that. Oh, no, hang on, perhaps I checked after all. And perhaps the pathologist can't do the full examination until tomorrow morning. Maybe you would like to call him to discuss it? I'm sure he would appreciate your input. After all, Professor Michaels has only been in the job twenty-seven years.'

Butterfield shook her head meekly – her impetuous comments had put her on the wrong side of the inspector's sharp tongue too many times since her transfer to CID and she could not risk another confrontation.

Could not risk being sent back into uniform. Butterfield tried not to meet the inspector's gaze as he looked at her.

'And as for poor old Robbie here,' added the inspector, switching his attention to the remains of the dog, 'you might not think he is important but find the dog that did this and the odds are we will find the man who murdered Trevor Meredith. Satisfied?'

Butterfield nodded dumbly and watched in glum silence as Harris examined the corpse. As she looked closer at the body again, the childhood memory forced its way back to the front of her mind once more. A farmer's daughter, she had been brought up not to regard dogs with any kind of sentimentality and yet... and yet...

'So, what have we got?' asked the inspector, looking at Thornycroft expectantly.

'One well-mangled dog, Hawk.'

Butterfield sighed – so the men were friends. Only friends were allowed to call him Hawk.

'It seems remarkable to me,' continued the vet, 'that a dog could be capable of something like this. I mean, I've never seen injuries quite like this.'

'I have,' said Butterfield suddenly, the memory finally forcing itself to the fore.

'I very much doubt that, Constable,' said Thornycroft, looking at her sceptically. 'I've been working with animals for years and...'

'But you're in the country now, Mr Thornycroft. Things are different up here,' said Butterfield.

Thornycroft looked as if he was about to dispute the comment, and turned to Harris for support. He was to be disappointed.

'Her dad runs the farm up past Leygill,' said Harris. 'He's had his fair share of trouble with sheep worrying down the years. If Constable Butterfield says that she has seen injuries like this, then she has.'

Butterfield looked at the inspector gratefully.

'I'm sorry,' said Thornycroft, inclining his head slightly, the realisation that the farm could be a client prompting him to adopt a more respectful tone. 'Still learning these things. Sorry, Constable, didn't recognise the surname.'

'No reason why you should have,' replied Butterfield with a slight smile. 'Dad doesn't use you. Says you don't know one end of a bullock from the other.'

'Thank you for those few kind words,' murmured Thornycroft, acutely conscious that Jack Harris had given a low laugh. 'So when did you see injuries like this?'

'I was only a kid. We had a flock attacked by a Labrador.' Butterfield nodded at Scoot, who had just wandered into the room and slumped heavily beneath one of the benches. 'Like him.'

Now it was the inspector's time to be irritated but he said nothing, instead marvelling in silence at the constable's ability to say the wrong thing time after time.

'Its owners had let it off the lead,' continued Butterfield. 'When it came into our top field, it went berserk. Chased the sheep all over. Caught two of them and ripped their throats out.'

The others watched in silence as she brushed a hand across her short-cropped blonde hair, as if trying to wipe away the memory.

'One of the ewes was pregnant.' Her voice dropped to little more than a whisper. 'It was the only time I ever saw my father cry.'

'And the dog?' asked Thornycroft.

'Dad put a bullet into it.'

'Ah.'

'Like she said, James,' commented Harris dryly. 'People do things differently up here.'

'So it would seem.'

'Trouble is,' said Harris, laying a hand gently on the dog's head, 'poor Robbie was not a sheep, was he? And I can only think of one thing that would make a dog attack

38

another one in such a savage way. I assume you know about dog fighting, James?'

'Come on, Hawk, you're surely not suggesting that something like that is happening here?'

'There've been rumours,' said Harris. 'The local RSPCA lad reckons there was a plan for an empty barn on Jenner's farm. I am wondering if Trevor Meredith had got himself involved in some way.'

'He was certainly a somewhat naïve man at times,' said Thornycroft and clapped a hand to his mouth. 'Sorry, should not speak ill of the dead.'

'I take it you knew him fairly well then?'

'Not really. That is, a bit. We were not close or anything like that, mind.' The vet noticed both officers staring at him and sighed. 'I guess you will find out anyway but I did not get on with Trevor Meredith – or rather, he did not get on with me.'

The detectives exchanged glances.

'It's nothing sinister,' said the vet quickly. 'My predecessor had treated dogs from the sanctuary for free – even paid for some of the drugs, I understand. I think he saw it as some sort of social service. I am afraid I cannot afford to be such a philanthropic soul.'

Harris raised an eyebrow.

'Don't look at me like that, Hawk,' said Thornycroft. 'When I took the business over, my accountant said that there was no way such a state of affairs could continue – it was costing the business a lot of money. I had no alternative but to stop it.'

'Community spirit indeed,' murmured Butterfield.

'Business is business, Constable. Trevor Meredith understood.' The vet noticed their sceptical looks. 'He did. Honest he did.'

'If you say so,' said the inspector. 'After all, we can hardly ask him now, can we?'

Thornycroft looked at him anxiously.

'Look, I hope this does not get me involved in your inquiry,' he said.

'I am sure that it has no bearing on what happened,' said Harris. 'What does have a bearing, though, if there's a link between what happened to Meredith and dog fighting. What kind of dog did this to Robbie, do you think?'

'I'd need to do casts of the bite marks and send them off for analysis to be 100 per cent sure,' said the vet, pursing his lips. 'Somehow I don't imagine that your Superintendent Curtis will stump up for that.'

Harris nodded gloomily. He knew how Philip Curtis reacted to anything to do with animals. In addition to his work as a detective, Harris was a wildlife liaison officer, a role which had over the years turned him into a national figure much in demand to address conferences and to give television and radio interviews. Curtis, the recently-arrived superintendent at Levton Bridge, had made it clear that he did not like the amount of time Harris lavished on such affairs or the publicity it engendered. 'Not proper policing,' was a phrase he had been heard to utter but never within earshot of the inspector.

Not that the mutual dislike was all about wildlife: part of it was connected with one of the superintendent's first decisions on arriving at Levton Bridge. Detesting the fact that Scoot accompanied the inspector wherever he went, Curtis saw an early opportunity to establish his superiority as divisional commander. He issued a memo banishing the dog from the divisional headquarters, a decision he was forced to reverse in the force of highly vocal protests from many of the staff, everyone from grizzled old constables to bright-faced young secretaries who had all been feeding Scoot titbits for years. Philip Curtis had resented the humiliation ever since.

'So,' continued the inspector, 'assuming that my beloved superintendent decides not to sanction the expenditure, would you care to hazard a guess?'

'I dunno, some kind of terrier? Maybe a pit bull?'

'I thought that was what you would say,' murmured Harris, his mind going back to the reports earlier in the day of the man and his dog on the hills. 'Mind, I haven't heard of one like that in the area. Have you?'

For the second time in a minute, James Thornycroft hesitated. Harris looked at him.

'Well?' he said. 'Have you?'

'Not really.'

The answer came a little too quickly and, looking at the vet, the inspector sensed a change in his demeanour, a caution that had not been there a few moments previously. Harris also noticed that Thornycroft had stared to sweat again.

'That does not sound very definite,' said the inspector.

'Well it is.' This time, the reply sounded defensive.

'What about injuries like this then?' asked Butterfield, picking up on the change in mood and gesturing to Robbie. 'Are you sure you haven't seen anything like this since you came here?'

'I only took the practice over four months ago.'

'That wasn't the constable's question,' said Harris.

Thornycroft looked at the detectives for a moment or two, anxiety flitting across his face before he regained his composure.

'No,' he said, his voice firmer. 'No, I have not seen injuries like this since I came here.'

Butterfield was about to say something when a look from Harris silenced her.

'Ok, James,' he said briskly, heading for the door, 'not sure there is much else we can do here so we'll leave you to it. Thanks for all your help. It is much appreciated.'

'No problem,' murmured the vet.

Chapter five

Darkness had begun to fall and the wind had started to build again, driving rain into the detectives' faces as they stepped out of the front door of the surgery onto the glistening pavement. As they began to walk, Butterfield waited respectfully for the inspector to explain their sudden departure.

'The weathermen said it would have a second blast,' said Harris instead, glancing up at the heavy clouds. 'Something tells me it is going to be one of those nights.'

'Guv?'

'This kind of weather does funny things to people, Constable. Funny things.'

'Jack Harris!' came a shrill cry from behind them. 'I want a word with you!'

'See what I mean,' murmured Harris, turning and staring without enthusiasm at the rapidly approaching figure. 'When's the election again?'

Butterfield chuckled. Striding down the street towards them was the slightly balding figure of Barry Ramsden, who in addition to running an optician's shop in the town centre, was the parish council chairman. He and Jack

Harris had known each other since schooldays – it had not always been an easy relationship.

'How can I help, Barry?' asked the inspector, trying to sound courteous as the councillor reached them.

'There's rumours of a crazed dog on the hills. I'm getting phone calls.'

'Now there's a surprise.'

'What can I tell them, Jack?' Ramsden sounded genuinely concerned. 'I mean, folks are frightened. They've heard what happened up there.'

'Tell them not to worry. I am pretty sure that the animal is well away from here by now.'

'I assume it has got something to do with the death of Trevor Meredith?'

'No comment,' said Harris and started walking again. He had only gone a few paces when a thought struck him and he turned round. 'Oh, while I remember. Am I right in thinking that you are one of the directors of the dog sanctuary?'

'Chairman actually,' said Ramsden. 'My father was one of the founders of the place.'

'Can you think of any reason why anyone would want to kill Trevor?'

'No. The man was a saint as far as I was concerned. Loved dogs, really loved them. The idea that a dog owner could be the one who ki…'

'This talk of you closing down a few months ago,' said Harris, cutting across him. 'Was there anything in that?'

'Gossip, Jack,' said Ramsden, with a shake of the head. 'All pub talk. You know what people are like up here. God knows where these rumours begin.'

Harris nodded and without another word, walked away, leaving the councillor standing in the street. It was not long before the detectives emerged into the market place where they headed towards the inspector's white Land Rover parked close to the Town Cross. Harris glanced across to the far side of the square, where two drunks in their late twenties were arguing outside the darkened Co-op store.

'What's the betting they've been at the King's Head?' he said.

'Been like this all day apparently,' said Butterfield, following his gaze. 'Uniform have been called there three times. Every time they get things calmed down, it flares up again.'

She glanced at the inspector. Although desperate to ask about the encounter with James Thornycroft, the constable nevertheless resisted the temptation to raise the subject: you never knew where you were with Jack Harris and she realised that, having irked him earlier, she had to choose her words carefully. Her short experience of working with the DCI had taught her that only when he was ready would Jack Harris talk.

'So, what do you think about James Thornycroft?' asked Harris as they reached the vehicle and he fished in his jacket pocket for his keys.

Butterfield looked at him with relief: it was so often the way with Harris, his moods blew over so quickly, and to be excluded from the murder inquiry would have been a major disappointment for the ambitious young officer. Nevertheless, she resolved to proceed with care.

'Look,' she said, trying to sound respectful, 'I know that you are friends with the guy and all that…'

'What on earth gave you that idea?'

'Well, he called you Hawk for a start…'

'Yeah,' said Harris darkly, 'and if he does it again, I may be forced to rip his oily little head off his oily little shoulders.'

'So you're not friends then?'

'Of course we're not,' said Harris. 'I mean, give me some credit, Constable. The man's a deeply unpleasant individual. I would like to think that I display a little more judgement when selecting my friends.'

'In which case,' said Butterfield, realising not for the first time that she did not really know who the inspector's friends were, 'I would say that James Thornycroft is lying through his teeth.'

'I agree,' said the inspector. He stopped walking and looked hard at her. 'And I would hope that even if he was my best friend you would still tell me if he was wrong'un.'

'Of course I would.'

'Good. And you are right, he was certainly acting strangely,' said Harris, starting to walk again and nodding across at the drunks who were now squaring up to each other. 'He's not the only one, though, mind. Isn't that Len Radley and Charlie Myles? I thought they were good friends?'

'Thick as thieves, guv.'

'Like I said, this weather does funny things to people,' said the inspector, unlocking the vehicle's door and gesturing for Scoot to jump into the passenger seat. 'I'm going to see Matty, he's over at Meredith's cottage. Can you go back to the station and do some discreet checking on James Thornycroft?'

'Be a pleasure.'

'Discreet, remember.'

'You know me, guv.'

'Exactly,' he said, pausing half way into the vehicle. 'Look, I'm serious, don't talk to anyone up here, you know how fast word gets round. That's why I didn't pursue it back there – let's keep this nice and quiet. Let's just see if there's any intelligence on him first. I seem to recall someone saying that his last practice was in Bolton so you might ring the local cops, see if they can dig up anything.'

'What are we looking for?'

'Not sure,' said the inspector, clambering into the vehicle. 'Anything that links Thornycroft to Meredith or dog fighting, I suppose.'

'But Thornycroft is a vet.'

'And Harold Shipman was a doctor,' said Harris, reaching down to start the engine.

'Good point,' said Butterfield, looking over at the drunks. 'Do you want me to sort them out first?'

'No, leave them to it. They're too pissed to do any serious harm.'

One of the drunks gave a cry of pain and staggered backwards, clutching his bloodied nose.

'On the other hand,' grinned the inspector, jumping out of the Land Rover. 'You see how Charlie is, I'll stop Len doing something he'll regret in the morning. Assuming he can remember it.'

The officers moved swiftly across the market square as Len Radley lurched forward again, his fist still bunched. He was about to deliver a second blow when Jack Harris intervened, knocking his arm to one side. Radley gave him a stupid, drunken look.

'Go home, Len,' said Harris calmly, 'or else I'll have to nick you – and you know how I hate paperwork.'

Len Radley considered the comment for a few moments then nodded and started to weave his way along the pavement.

'Good boy,' said Harris and turned to look at the injured man, who was sitting on the ground, clutching his nose and being tended to by the constable.

The inspector sensed a presence behind him and, without turning round, casually flicking his bunched fist backwards. He gave a smile of satisfaction as he heard Len's pained grunt. The inspector turned to see the drunk sway for a few moments before sinking to his knees and clutching his face. Butterfield gave a little shake of the head: how had Harris known what Radley was about to do, she thought?

'I should do you for police brutality,' slurred Radley, glaring up at him. 'You could have broken my nose.'

'Believe me, Len, if I had wanted to break your nose I would have done so. Now get out of here or you can spend a night in the cells, paperwork or not.'

The drunk hauled himself to his feet and appeared about to challenge the instruction but a single, menacing step forward from the inspector was all it took and with a final glare, Len Radley weaved his way out of the market place, staggering several times as the rain lashed down ever harder and the wind started a low moan. Harris watched him disappear round the corner then gave a shake of the head and returned his attention to the man on the ground.

'So, what's this about, Charlie?' he asked. 'Not like you two to fall out.'

'We'd had a skinful, Mr Harris.'

'Tell me something I don't know,' said the inspector, helping him to his feet. 'I assume you were in the King's Head?'

Myles nodded.

'What's kicking things off?' asked the inspector.

Charlie Myles did not reply.

'Alright,' said Harris, 'if that's the way you want to play it. Go on, get yourself home. Might I suggest you take the long way, though. Just in case Len fancies another go.'

'Thanks,' said Myles, producing from his trouser pocket a grubby handkerchief with which he dabbed his nose. 'You saved me from a right pasting, I reckon, Mr Harris.'

'Yeah, I'm all heart. Go on, get out of here.'

Myles hesitated.

'Something you want to tell me?' asked Harris.

'Look, I ain't going to tell what me and Len were fighting about – that were personal – but maybe I can still help you.'

'Not sure quite how in your state,' said Harris and winked at the grinning Butterfield. 'Unless you are going to buy me a drink then I would have to decline your kind offer because I've got a particularly pleasant single malt waiting for me – assuming I ever get home, that is.'

'I heard that fellow from the dog place were found dead on the hills today.'

'You knew him?' said Harris sharply.

'Yeah,' and Charlie Myles glanced nervously around the deserted market place as if fearful that someone was watching their conversation. 'I mean, just to look at, like. Folks in the pub were saying that his dog were killed as well. Folks reckon it were another dog as did it.'

'It was.'

'Is it still up there?'

'You said you had something to tell me,' said Harris, ignoring the question.

Harris looked round but Len Radley had vanished and the only movement in the deserted square was a cat skulking in the shadows in front of the darkened Co-op. The inspector glanced back to the Land Rover where Scoot had sat up in the passenger seat, his ears pricked as he watched the cat make its way past the store. The dog noticed his master's expression and lay down with a disappointed expression on his face.

'Go on, Charlie,' said Harris. 'There's no one can hear you. Tell me what you know about Trevor Meredith.'

'You got to promise me that it won't go no further, Mr Harris. I don't want people thinking I'm a snitch.'

'You know me, Charlie.'

'Aye, Mr Harris, I imagine I do. It were six or seven weeks ago – about midnight. I were up by Jenner's Farm…'

'And what, pray, were you doing there?' asked the inspector, glancing across at Butterfield with a slight smile.

'Out for a walk,' said Charlie evasively. 'It were a nice night.'

'Nice night for conies, more like. Look, I've warned you before about poaching,' said Harris sternly. 'Anyway, I'll let you off this time. I take it you saw something?'

'Aye. There's an old barn up there – George Jenner used to keep his silage in it but the roof started leaking. He ain't used it since last winter.'

'I know it,' nodded Harris; he and Scoot had passed it many times in recent weeks on their walks. 'But I have never seen Trevor Meredith up there if that's what you are trying to tell me.'

'That's exactly what I'm saying, Mr Harris – he were snooping round like he were looking for something.'

'Any idea what?'

'All I know is that when he saw me, he walked off quick like in the other direction. It were right suspicious.'

'Is there any chance that…?' began Harris but Charlie shook his head quickly.

'I ain't saying nowt else, Mr Harris. I've probably said too much. You know what folks are like round here.'

'Sometimes,' murmured Harris as, without a further word, Charlie Myles headed unsteadily across the market place and disappeared from view, 'I wonder if I do.'

'There's definitely something weird going off tonight,' nodded Butterfield.

'Well, hopefully tomorrow we can make sense of it all,' said Harris walking back to his vehicle and climbing back into the Land Rover, 'and who knows, I might even remember to attend Trevor Meredith's post-mortem.'

Butterfield could see him laughing as he edged the vehicle past her and out onto the main road through the town centre. She grinned ruefully.

* * *

Tidying up the examination room as he prepared to head for home, James Thornycroft tensed as he heard a sound from the reception area.

'That you, Hawk?' he called.

There was no answer. Trying to stay calm, he walked out of the room and into the reception area to be confronted by a large shaven-headed man.

'What the hell are you doing here?' asked Thornycroft nervously, glancing past the man. 'And where's the dog?'

'Don't worry about the dog, what have you been telling Jack Harris and his little bimbo friend?'

'I did as I was told,' said Thornycroft, trying to stop his voice trembling. 'I told them nothing.'

'That had better be the truth.'

Thornycroft saw the flash of steel as a knife appeared in the man's hand.

'For Christ's sake!' he exclaimed. 'I told them nothing!'

The man walked up to him, leaning so close that Thornycroft could smell his fetid breath and feel the chill of the knife's blade against his neck.

'Keep it that way,' said the man and walked out into the night.

Chapter six

Jasmine Riley sat on the bed in her Roxham guest house room and stared down at the mobile phone in her hand. Why did Trevor not ring? He had said he would ring. Promised he would ring. Promised that they would arrange where to meet up again once they were both safely out of the valley; said he would give her the name of the pub in Newcastle. Trevor had impressed upon her the importance of not ringing him: if anything happened to him, he had said, the last thing he wanted was his phone falling into the wrong hands. GPS, he had said for the umpteenth time, these people could do wonders with GPS. You had to be careful when dealing with these people, he had said, had to keep one step ahead of the game, make sure you gave them no way of tracking you down. She had often wondered how he knew these things, where he had learned to speak in such a way. Don't worry, he had said with a reassuring smile just before leaving the cottage that morning, he would ring.

But he hadn't.

Jasmine Riley looked down at the phone for a few more moments then up at the clock. 10pm it said. She sighed.

'Sorry, love,' she said and dialled Trevor Meredith's number.

High up in the dark hills, lying among bracken in a valley swept with rain, Trevor Meredith's mobile phone rang and rang and rang.

* * *

Ten miles north of Levton Bridge, a battered old red pick-up drove slowly along the road as it wound its way like a ribbon through the bottom of the valley. The vehicle's headlights, one much dimmer than the other, were the only illumination in the darkness and showed up flecks of driving rain. The vehicle slowed next to the entrance to one of the small fields that patchworked the hillside and the passenger, a man with a flat cap jammed over his shock of white hair, got out and walked, bow-legged and stooped, to open the gate. The job done, Harry Galbraith walked back to the vehicle where the driver, Dennis Soames, a stocky farmer in his thirties, wound down the window.

'Well?' he asked.

'Should be alright,' said Galbraith.

The pick-up reversed slowly into the entrance and drew to a halt, its bonnet hardly noticeable from the road. Soames cut the lights then waited for Galbraith to re-join him. Sitting there with their windows down, the two men listened to the sounds of the night: the patter of rain on the vehicle's windscreen, the whining of the wind across the rock escarpment far above them and, occasionally, the plaintive sound of a sheep bleating as it sheltered from the storm behind one of the drystone walls.

'Old Man Jenner alright with us parking here?' asked Soames.

'Aye, as long as he doesn't have to do no work, he'll be fine.'

Both men laughed and Harry Galbraith rooted around in his canvas bag before producing two tin-foil packages and handing one of them to Soames.

'Ham,' he said.

'Grand.'

Galbraith rummaged around a bit more and produced a flask and two plastic cups.

'Tea,' he announced.

'Even better.'

Galbraith reached into the bag again and produced a small Tupperware box.

'Cake,' he said. 'Home-made.'

'Your Elsie knows how to look after us, Harry.'

For a few moments, the only sound in the vehicle was the munching of sandwiches then Soames looked at his friend.

'Are you going to try the police again, Harry?'

'No need.'

'I'm not so sure.' Soames looked anxious. 'I mean, we're out here on our own. Jack Harris did say that we should only do it with the police around and we've heard nowt from them since you talked to that Gallagher chap.'

'Relax,' said Galbraith, reaching into a glove compartment and producing a radio. 'We've got this if we need them. Which reminds me, we better have a codename for tonight. How about something…?'

'I'd still feel better if…'

'Don't fret,' said Galbraith, noticing his friend's increasingly anxious expression. He unscrewed the lid from the flask. 'Tea?'

Three miles further down the road, back towards Levton Bridge, the lights of a black saloon car cut through the darkness.

Chapter seven

'Nothing!' exclaimed Matty Gallagher, glancing across the living room from the bureau he had been searching. 'We've been through this place with a fine toothcomb and there is absolutely nothing to suggest why anyone would want to kill Trevor Meredith.'

Jack Harris, crouching by a bookcase in the corner of the room, did not reply. It was shortly before 10pm and the detectives were in the small cottage on the edge of Levton Bridge which had been Meredith's home for a decade. The house was like the man, tidy and unremarkable, and the officers has been searching it for the best part of an hour, speaking little as they went through drawers and files, seeking something which would cast light on Trevor Meredith's death. As their labours continued to prove fruitless, the sergeant had grown increasingly frustrated.

'I mean,' he said, holding up a sheet of paper in disgust, 'he's not even behind with his gas bill. It'd be easier to see why someone would want to murder Mother Teresa.'

'She local then?' asked Harris, not looking up.

'You know the new Indian on the corner of Wesley Street? She works in the kitchens. Cooks a mean rogan josh, I can tell you.'

Gallagher grinned with delight at his quip then sighed as Jack Harris gave no sign that he had heard.

'Wasted,' said the sergeant gloomily, 'that's what I am.'

Harris said nothing but, looking down so that Gallagher could not see his face in the shadows behind the sofa, he allowed himself a smile.

'Talking of the Indian,' said the sergeant, looking up at the clock above the fireplace, 'if we get finished here in time, I quite fancy a curry and they open late on a Monday night. You on for that?'

Again Harris did not reply. Gallagher sighed – he knew the answer anyway. The sergeant returned to his inspection of the bureau but could not concentrate, he kept thinking about his favourite curry house back in London. A little back street job. Nothing to look at from the outside but chapattis to die for. Matty Gallagher sighed. God, he'd tried, he thought, he really had tried to settle in the North, but in recent weeks he had found himself thinking more and more about the old places. With an effort, he dragged his mind back to the task in hand.

'I tell you something weird,' he said, looking round the room. 'It's been bugging me ever since we got here. There is nothing of the man.'

'What do you mean?'

'Well, think of a normal house. There'd be pictures for a start – parents' golden wedding anniversary, grandkids, being presented with the golf trophy, that sort of thing. I bet even you have got pictures around your gaff, the day you and Scoot got married, that kind of thing.'

The inspector chuckled and glanced across at Scoot, who was sitting in a corner watching the two men work.

Then the inspector looked at the pictures on the wall: two nondescript prints of landscapes which could have hung in any house in the country. He wondered why he had not noticed the absence of the personal touch himself and looked approvingly at his sergeant.

'What's more,' said Gallagher, flicking through some papers on the bureau. 'There's nothing here either. We've got a little desk like this at home and it's crammed with personal things but this guy? It's like he's a non-person.'

Both officers looked up as a forensics officer clumped down the stairs and entered the living room.

'Anything?' asked Gallagher hopefully.

'Not really.'

Gallagher nodded gloomily and the forensics officer walked out into the hallway and left the cottage.

'Maybe this is a waste of time,' said the sergeant. 'Maybe we're looking for a connection that doesn't exist. Maybe it's a good old-fashioned loony out to kill the first person he sees. Wrong time, wrong place.'

'You're the second person to have said that today.'

'There you are then.'

'And you're both wrong.'

'Ah.'

'This feels deliberate,' said the inspector, replacing the book on the shelf and walking over to stare out of the window. 'Someone was out to get Trevor Meredith.'

'I don't suppose that you have any evidence to support the theory, by any chance?'

'Don't complicate things.'

Gallagher surveyed the back of the inspector's head for a moment; in the year since he had reluctantly forsaken his beloved London to set up home with his fiancée in Levton Bridge, the sergeant had struggled to come to terms with much about his new life. At times, the silence of the hills themselves threatened to stifle the life out of Matty Gallagher after the bustle of the capital – he sometimes thought that he would kill to hear a car horn in the middle of the night – but the thing which most exercised his mind was the difficulty he experienced in reading Jack Harris. Wondering now if the inspector was joking – everyone knew that Harris was perfectly capable of cutting corners – the sergeant eyed the DCI uncertainly.

The inspector walked over to sit on the settee. Feeling strangely weary, he remembered that he had not eaten anything apart from a chocolate bar up on the moors. Maybe, he thought, looking over at the sergeant, who had now returned his attention to the bureau, a curry might not be a bad idea after all. It was time the inspector bought a pint for the sergeant.

'So where do we go now then?' asked Gallagher, lifting up some of the papers before letting them drop haphazardly – several floated onto the carpet. 'We've got nothing here.'

'Let's go through what we do have then.'

'That shouldn't take long,' said the sergeant, settling down in one of the armchairs and flicking through his notebook. 'Trevor Meredith, 42, 43 next month. Manager, and also a director, of Levton Bridge Dog Sanctuary, a not-for-profit company largely dependent on grants and donations.'

'I gave them fifty quid when I got Scoot there,' nodded Harris, gesturing to his dog whose ears pricked when he heard his name.

'Then you will know that it's hardly the kind of place where murderous tensions run high. And nothing we hear about Meredith makes me think anything else. If he did have a secret life, he sure as hell kept it well hidden.'

'I imagine that's why it was a secret life.'

'You know what I mean.'

'What else do we know about Meredith?'

'Precious little. He came to Levton Bridge ten years ago – looks like he moved here when he got the manager's job,' said the sergeant, flicking over a page of his notebook. 'Here it is – he started work on 9th October,

57

1999. He was made a director three years ago. A reward for loyal service – they'd had four managers in three years before that because the pay was so poor and they were delighted that he had stayed.'

'Where had he been before he came here?'

'The staff reckon he'd been travelling for a few years.'

'Travelling where?'

Gallagher looked up as Butterfield walked into the room.

'Ask the lady yourself,' he said.

'They didn't know,' said the constable, sitting down in the only vacant armchair and stretching out her legs. 'One of them reckoned it might have been Europe.'

'It's a big place,' said Harris. 'Couldn't they be any more specific?'

'Not sure anyone was interested, guv.'

'Doesn't that strike you as odd?' said Harris.

'You know what this place does to people.'

'Yeah,' said Gallagher with a sly smile. 'Half of them get nose bleeds going to Roxham. I pass them sprawled out on the roadside when I drive home. It's a truly pitiful sight. I stop to help them but what can you do?'

Harris looked as if he was about to remonstrate with his sergeant: Gallagher's disparaging comments about life in the hills had often been known to irritate people. Harris knew this only too well, having fielded several complaints from irate townsfolk and eventually, following acerbic comments from Superintendent Curtis, the inspector had found himself warning his sergeant to be more sensitive; but only half-heartedly. Jack Harris appreciated from personal experience how claustrophobic life could be in the division's hill communities.

'Surely,' said Harris, suddenly aware that the others were looking at him for some kind of response, 'we must be able to find something. What about his CV, there must be something in there?'

'What CV?' asked Butterfield. 'I went through every file at the dog sanctuary and there isn't any sign of a CV. His personnel docket in the filing cabinet was empty. No letters, no reports, no nothing. It's like Trevor Meredith did not exist before he came to Levton Bridge.'

'Yeah,' said Gallagher, holding up a sheet of paper. 'We know how much he paid the gas board but we know virtually nothing about Trevor Meredith the man.'

'What do we know about the girlfriend? Did she pop out of thin air as well?'

'No, there's plenty on Jasmine Riley,' said Gallagher, glancing down at his notes. 'She lived with her mum in Chester while she trained as a legal clerk. Left home when she got a job in Levton Bridge, working at the solicitors in the market place. Arrived a couple of months after Meredith turfed up.'

'Now there's a coincidence. Did she know Meredith before she came here?'

'Seems not,' said Butterfield. 'The staff at the sanctuary reckon that they met at a party. They had been together ever since.'

'Yeah,' nodded Gallagher, glancing round the room. 'Her mum said they were going to get married next spring. Jasmine moved in here not long ago.'

Harris walked over to the window again.

'So,' he said, 'if they were making all those plans, why on earth were they getting out this morning in such a hurry? And why were they travelling separately?'

'Your guess,' shrugged Gallagher.

Harris walked back over to the bookcase and reached out for the volume he had been studying earlier: a history of blood sports.

'I keep coming back to the dog fighting,' he said. 'I've got this idea that Trevor Meredith decided to do a bit of freelance investigation.'

'Well, he was damned foolhardy if he did,' said Gallagher. 'Those guys can be pretty mean. They'd kill you as easy as…'

The sergeant's voice tailed off.

'Indeed,' said Harris.

Idly, the inspector flicked through the book, giving an exclamation when a piece of paper fluttered onto the floor. Reaching down, he turned it over and read the mobile phone number written on it in what he assumed to be Meredith's hand, neat and tidy like the man. After showing them the piece of paper, and receiving blank looks, Harris started to dial the number.

'Are you sure that's wise?' said Gallagher dubiously. 'I mean, what if it's…?'

Harris waved the protest away and listened for only a fleeting moment then hurriedly hit the cancel button. He looked at the piece of paper in bemusement.

'Now why,' he asked softly, 'would a man who wasn't even late with his gas bill, have the phone number of Gerry Radford?'

'Who's he?' asked Gallagher.

'One of Manchester gangland's finest. He and I go way back.'

'Brilliant,' breathed Butterfield, eyes gleaming as they always did when Jack Harris talked about his experiences with major league criminals; it was, the young detective had always thought, what you joined the police for.

'So,' asked Harris thoughtfully, 'on whose side was Trevor Meredith, do we reckon?'

Chapter eight

The two farmers in the pick-up saw the black car's lights cutting through the night long before the vehicle came into view. Still sitting in the passenger seat, Harry Galbraith reached for his notebook in the glove compartment.

'About ruddy time,' he said. 'Thought we weren't going to see owt tonight. Have a look at its registration number as it goes past, lad.'

As the car finally appeared round the corner, its headlights illuminated the pick-up truck, dazzling the farmers for a few seconds. The vehicle came to a halt thirty metres away.

'Do you think they saw us?' asked Soames anxiously.

The car's headlights went out.

'I reckon that answers your question,' said Harry.

'I told you we shouldn't have done this without the police.'

Harry Galbraith did not reply but his look betrayed his own anxiety. Two men got out of the car and started to walk towards the pick-up. Their shapes in the gloom suggested to the farmers that both were heavily built. The strangers took up stations either side of the vehicle and the one on the passenger side, a shaven-headed man, leant down to the window as Harry Galbraith struggled frantically to wind it up.

'And what might you be doing here?' asked the man in a quiet voice as he placed a hand on the window to prevent it being closed any further.

'We're from Levton Bridge Farmwatch,' replied Harry, trying to sound calm. 'We're working with the police.'

'Are you now?' The man gave a thin smile. 'And what exactly do you do for the police?'

'We take the registration numbers of vehicles passing through the valley and pass them on,' said Harry.

'And why would you do that?'

'We're trying to stop rural crime.'

'Well there's a thing,' said the man, glancing across the roof at his friend with a grin that revealed yellowing teeth. 'Ain't that public spirited?'

The other man made no reply.

'Well now,' said the shaven-headed man, looking back into the car, his voice suddenly hard-edged. 'It seems that we have a problem because myself and my business associate here would rather that you did not report our registration number to the police.'

'All cars get reported,' said Harry pompously, gaining in confidence a little and ignoring his friend's gestures to say nothing. 'You ain't got nothing to worry about if you ain't up to no bother.'

'Which is unfortunate,' said the man, 'because we are.'

Harry stared at him, unsure as to what to say. The shaven-headed man took advantage of his confusion, reached into the car and grabbed the farmer's notebook.

''Ere,' said Harry, 'give that back!'

The man's reply was to snap out a fist which caught the old man on the side of the face. As Harry reeled in shock, Soames glanced out of his window and saw a flash of metal as a knife appeared in the accomplice's hand.

'Bloody hell!' he exclaimed, turned on the pick-up's engine and slammed the vehicle into gear.

The pick-up lurched forward, sending the two assailants staggering backwards, the wing mirror clipping the shaven-headed man's elbow as the vehicle shot out of the field entrance. Soames glanced in his rear-view mirror to see the man give an enraged bellow and, clutching his arm, start running back to his car followed by his accomplice.

'Are they after us?' asked Harry anxiously, rubbing the side of his head and glancing down at his hand to see flecks of blood.

'I told you this was a daft idea,' said Soames, ramming his foot onto the accelerator, sending the vehicle careering down the road.

'Won't this thing go any faster?' shouted Harry as the vehicle rocked and swayed on reaching 45mph. He glanced through the side mirror and saw the other car's headlights flashing repeatedly as the vehicle set off in pursuit. 'They're after us.'

'I'm doing my best,' exclaimed Soames, hurling the vehicle round a corner, the wheels screeching as they slipped on the damp tarmac.

Turning round, Harry Galbraith saw the black car appear round the bend, closing rapidly as it gathered speed.

'Come on, come on!' he exclaimed, fear in his voice as the headlights dazzled the farmers when the car drew close.

'What were that?' cried Soames in alarm as they heard a loud metallic sound when something struck the back of the vehicle.

'Jesus! He's firing at us! He's got a gun!'

Soames threw the pick-up round a sharp left-hand bend, battling frantically with the steering wheel as the vehicle bounced off the grass verge. Glancing in the mirror again, he saw the black car fail to take the corner properly and skid, one of its headlights being extinguished amid a shower of glass as the front of the vehicle delivered a glancing blow to a drystone wall. The black car juddered to a halt and stood motionless for a few seconds. Seizing his opportunity, Soames rammed his foot even harder onto the pick-up's accelerator and sent the vehicle rocking and rolling into the night.

'It's never gone this fast!' he cried as the speedometer climbed above 65mph and he battled to control the shaking vehicle.

Harry suddenly pointed to his left, to a gap in the wall just before the road crossed a small humpbacked bridge.

'There!' he shouted. 'Put the lights out and go there!'

Plunged into darkness, the pick-up shot through an opening in a wall and onto a bumpy side track. For a few moments, Soames wrestled with the steering wheel as the pick-up entered a small sparsely wooded copse and he tried to steer it between the trees, struggling to see in the darkness. The vehicle lurched violently as it cannoned off one of the trees, a rending sound indicating that the bumper had been torn off. Galbraith looked across his friend and saw, back on the road running parallel, the single headlight of the black car pass by and continue along the main road. Soames gritted his teeth and kept the pick-up careering through the woodland, grimacing as it clipped another tree, the impact threatening to wrench the steering wheel from his shaking hands. With a sudden glistening of water, a stream appeared in front of them and Dennis Soames hit the brakes.

'No, go over it!' cried Harry Galbraith. 'Go over! They'll not be able to follow us!'

Soames nodded and gunned the engine again. For a second or two, it seemed as if the juddering vehicle would stall in the stream, then it somehow found grip, its tyres spinning on the wet rocks before the vehicle emerged on the far side. Soames hit the brakes and the pick-up slewed to a halt, its wheels sinking into muddy grass. For a few moments, neither man spoke then Harry Galbraith clapped his friend on the shoulder.

'Well done, lad!' he said. 'You should be one of them Grand Prix drivers.'

'I reckon I should be more than that, Harry,' beamed Soames. 'See, I remembered his registration number!'

'Boy, Jack Harris will be pleased with you, Dennis lad.'

And together they sat and listened to the pounding of their hearts in the silence of the night.

* * *

'Come on,' said Harris wearily, glancing at his watch and walking out of Meredith's living room into the narrow hallway. 'Not sure we can do much more tonight and I've got a nice bottle of Scotch waiting for me back home.'

'And I might just make that late curry,' said Gallagher, reaching over the back of the sofa for his overcoat and glancing at Butterfield. 'Fancy it, Alison?'

'Don't you want to get back to Roxham?'

'No point. Julie's on nights again. She's still on A&E. Besides, I really could murder a curry.'

'Yeah, so could I,' said Butterfield. 'Hey, if you want to have a couple of jars, you can kip on my floor again.'

'See how I go.' Gallagher looked at the inspector. 'You coming, guv?'

He expected the usual bland refusal but, this time, Jack Harris hesitated.

'I am sure Scoot would appreciate a bit of chicken,' said the sergeant, seizing his chance. 'I could ask Mother Theresa to sort it for you.'

Butterfield looked at him with a perplexed expression on her face and mouthed the words 'Mother Theresa?'

'Tell you later,' said a grinning Gallagher. 'What about it then, guv?'

The inspector nodded.

'Aye, go on then,' he said, heading for the front door. 'Why not? About time we did something like this. Curtis is always banging on about team spirit.'

Gallagher beamed.

'Oh, while I remember,' said the inspector, reaching for the front door handle. 'Did anyone get hold of the Farmwatch lads?'

'Damn,' exclaimed Gallagher, clapping a hand to his mouth. 'Completely forgot to tell them that, what with the goings-on at the King's Head and things here, uniform could not spare anyone for tonight.'

Harris stared at him.

'What you looking at me like that for?' said Gallagher. 'Surely, they wouldn't be daft enough to go out on their own, not when we've had a murder up on the h…' His voice tailed off as he saw the inspector's expression. 'Jesus, don't tell me they would.'

'You haven't met Harry Galbraith,' said Harris, allowing himself a slight smile despite his concerns. 'It's like Last of the Summer Wine meets The Sweeney.'

Gallagher roared with laughter but the sound died in his throat when the inspector's mobile phone rang.

'Somehow,' said the sergeant gloomily, 'that does not sound good.'

The inspector listened for a few moments before muttering a 'thank you' and ending the conversation. Placing the phone in his coat pocket, he looked at them.

'I am afraid the curry will have to wait,' he said grimly. 'That was Control. Someone's just tried to kill Harry Galbraith and his mate.'

'Jesus,' said the sergeant quietly. 'They'll have my nuts for this.'

'And mine,' said Jack Harris darkly. 'And mine, Matty lad.'

Chapter nine

'Pleased with you!' exclaimed Harris, glaring at the two farmers sitting in front of him. 'Why the fuck would I be pleased with you? I mean, don't you listen to a sodding word I say?'

Startled by the vehemence of the inspector's onslaught, Harry Galbraith and Dennis Soames stared at the floor and said nothing as he paced the room. It was just after midnight and the farmers were at one of the tables in the dimly-lit and deserted first-floor canteen at Levton Bridge Police Station, cradling mugs of steaming tea in their hands.

'I mean,' continued the furious inspector, 'I have come across some acts of crass stupidity in my time – mostly from my superintendent – but this takes the biscuit, it really does. You're morons. Fucking morons.'

'Now hang on, Jack…' began Galbraith.

'Hang on nothing, Harry. You could have got yourselves killed tonight. This isn't a bleeding game. Surely you heard that we have already had one man found dead up on the hills?'

The farmers said nothing.

'Well?' said the inspector, glaring at them as if he were a schoolmaster and they his naughty pupils. 'What do you have to say for yourselves?'

'We thought you would be pleased that we remember the car's registration number,' said Soames plaintively.

Harris glanced down at the scrap of paper that Soames had proudly handed him when the farmers arrived at the police station. The inspector looked at the hopeful expression on the young man's face and gave a sigh.

'It's a fake,' he said, his tone of voice softening as he saw Soames' crestfallen expression. 'We ran it through the PNC and it doesn't exist. They probably had the plate made up in some back-street chop shop.'

Soames looked confused.

'A chop shop?' he asked.

'Never mind. Suffice to say that the number will not lead us to the men who tried to kill you.'

Soames sunk deeper into his seat and Harris drew up a chair and sat down at the table with them.

'Look,' he said, in a much gentler tone, 'that is why I am so angry. These guys tonight were professionals. That's what we are up against. The gangs coming into our area and screwing your farms are highly organised and perfectly capable of turning nasty. I accept that these two were beyond the norm but if you want to be part of Farmwatch, you have to play by the rules. My rules.'

'We're sorry, Jack,' said Galbraith quietly, 'we really are. We didn't think. Have we got you in trouble?'

'I'll survive,' said Harris, his anger now spent. 'What worries me more is the trouble you got yourself into. Just promise me that you won't do anything daft again, eh, lads?'

The farmers nodded.

'We promise,' said Galbraith. He hesitated for a moment or two before adding anxiously, 'Does this mean we have to give our walkie talkie back?'

Harris chuckled.

'No,' he said, 'you can keep your walkie talkie.'

Galbraith looked relieved. The inspector gestured to the caked blood on the side of the old man's face.

'That looks nasty,' he said. 'Has anyone had a look at it?'

'It's only a scratch.'

'Yeah, well, don't wash it before you leave here. I've got a forensics officer on his way in and she'll take a swab – see if we can get anything from it.'

Galbraith looked confused.

'Just don't touch it,' said Harris.

A slim, dark-haired uniformed inspector walked into the room and headed for the kitchen.

'Any luck with the roadblocks, Alec?' asked Harris, walking over to join him.

'Sorry,' said Alec Hulme, reaching into a cupboard and taking down the tea caddy. 'Want a brew?'

'Aye, go on.'

'Top up lads?' asked Hulme, looking across the counter and nodding at the farmers' mugs.

'No, we're alright,' said Galbraith. 'But thank you.'

Hulme surveyed them for a moment as they sat at the table in their flat caps and scruffy overcoats.

'Are Batman and Robin ok?' he asked Harris in a voice so low that the farmers could not hear.

'I think the enormity of what happened tonight is just starting to sink in. I've been trying to impress the danger they put themselves in.'

'Yeah,' said Hulme with a smile, 'I heard your attempt at community engagement. Curtis would be proud of you. In fact, I understand he wants to include the phrase "fucking morons" in his next report to the police committee.'

'Well, what do you expect me to say?'

'Aye, maybe. Listen, talking of Curtis, he's been after you again. Probably wants to congratulate you on your services to neighbourhood watch. Who knows, perhaps he will recommend you for the QPM.'

Harris chuckled, he liked the inspector.

'I wouldn't get your hopes up about the roadblocks, mind,' said Hulme, removing a couple of mugs from another cupboard and turning his attention to the water heater mounted on the wall. 'I reckon whoever those psychos were, they're long gone. We had a call from a motorist a few minutes after the shooting and she said their car must have been doing 75 when it passed her. Damn near rammed her off the road. It'll not have taken them long to get out of the valley at that rate.'

'You alerted other forces?'

'Yeah, but what's the chance that they are still in the car?' said the inspector, stirring the mugs of tea. 'They'll probably torch the thing first chance they get.'

'I guess.'

Hulme looked across at the farmers.

'We're towing their vehicle in now,' he said, handing the inspector his tea in return for murmured thanks. 'We had a message from the vehicle examiner, though – he can't take a look until tomorrow. He's over at that double fatal RTA down past Roxham. Having said that, it won't take a genius to tell us that there is a bloody great big bullet hole in one of the rear panels.'

Hulme raised his voice so the farmers could hear.

'You got lucky tonight, lads,' he said, looking across at them. 'A couple of centimetres to the left and the bullet could easily have ruptured your petrol tank.'

'See,' said Harris as he returned to his seat, 'this isn't a game.'

'Yeah,' nodded Hulme, walking over to stand by the table, 'don't go out without us. I mean, surely you know how busy we were tonight?'

'Talking of which,' said Harris, 'I heard it was all fun and games at the King's Head?'

'It was like the Wild West in there. I half expected to see a load of horses tied up outside. I even toyed with the idea of closing the place down. Hey, talking of the King's Head, I understand you saved Charlie Myles from a beating.'

'Yeah, but it was all a bit handbags.'

'Not sure about that,' said Hulme, looking at Harris. 'When I nipped out for a fag, I saw Len Radley staggering past the police station, clutching his nose. I don't suppose that was anything to do with you?'

'Who me?' said Harris, giving him an innocent look. 'Anything else I need to know about?'

'No, but I really would ring Curtis. He has been on the phone several times. He sounded quite agitated, said he has been trying for ages. Reckons your mobile must be switched off or something.'

Harris fished it out of his pocket.

'Ooh, look,' he said. 'Six missed calls.'

The inspector raised his eyes to the ceiling.

'One day, Jack Harris,' he said as he walked out of the canteen and into the dimly-lit corridor, carrying his mug of tea. 'One day…'

Harris grinned, replaced the phone in his pocket and took a sip of his drink. Glancing across the table, he noticed Dennis Soames whispering conspiratorially to Harry Galbraith.

'Something I should know about, lads?' asked the inspector.

Soames hesitated.

'Come on, Dennis, spit it out.'

'I may be able to help you, Mister Harris.'

'You're the second person who has said that tonight and I still haven't got back to my bottle of whisky,' said the inspector. 'At least you're sober. Go on, then what do you know?'

'I don't want to get in no trouble,' said Soames, glancing over at Harry Galbraith.

'I'll keep your name out of it.'

Soames still looked unsure.

'Go on,' urged Galbraith, 'you can trust him, you know that. Besides, I reckons we owes him summat after what happened tonight.'

'Aye, ok,' nodded Soames. 'It's about Trevor Meredith. See, I knows something about him. Not sure if it is important, mind.'

'Given what I know about Meredith,' said Harris, taking a sip of tea, 'even his shoe size would be of interest. You don't happen to know his shoe size, do you?'

'Why would that be of interest?' asked Soames, looking bemused.

'Never mind. Go on, Dennis, what do you know about Trevor Meredith?'

'He likes his gambling.'

Harris sat down at the table.

'And how might you know that?' he asked.

'There's a few lads been meeting up at the King's Head for a game of poker.'

'Really?' Harris looked surprised. 'Not sure we know about that.'

Soames hesitated.

'It happens after hours,' he said eventually, prompted to reveal more information by a reassuring look from Harry Galbraith. 'It were the landlord's idea. He puts all the lights out in the bar to make it look like the pub is closed and we play in his back room. You can't see that from the street.'

'We?' said Harris. 'Does that mean you have been part of it, Dennis?'

Soames nodded.

'But you struggle with Snap!' exclaimed Harris. 'What the hell were you doing getting mixed up in something like that?'

'I didn't reckon it could do no harm.'

'It can if you don't know what you're doing.'

'I know that now,' nodded Soames. 'That's why I stopped playing.'

'A wise decision, Dennis,' said the inspector as he took a sip of his tea. 'Mind, something tells me that there would not have been much money involved.'

'I lost fifty quid one night.'

'Fifty quid! Jesus, Dennis, you can't afford that!'

Soames nodded gloomily. Silence settled on the room for a moment or two then a thought struck the inspector.

'Was the poker, by any chance, what the trouble was about at the pub tonight?' he asked. 'We saw Len Radley and Charlie Myles going at it hammer and tongs in the market square.'

'Charlie owes him a hundred quid,' nodded Soames. 'They've been arguing about it for the best part of a week.'

'And Meredith?' asked Harris. 'He was a regular player?'

Soames nodded.

'And he lost, did he?' said the inspector.

'Oh, aye. I reckon he owed various folks more than five hundred pound.'

Harris gave a low whistle.

'Mind, he weren't the worst,' said Soames, 'I reckon James Thornycroft lost more than him.'

'The vet?' asked Harris with a gleam in his eye. 'Ok, I'll need the names of everyone involved. Oh, and you can take it from me, the poker game is closed from now on.'

Soames nodded gloomily.

* * *

Ten minutes later, Jack Harris was sitting in his office, staring out into the darkness of the night and trying to make sense of the day's events. Suddenly, he felt very weary, stood up and reached for his coat.

'Come on, feller,' he said and headed for the door, glancing down to where Scoot was lying. 'I reckon it's been a long enough day.'

Scoot stood up and wagged his tail. The inspector was just about to switch the light off when his mobile phone rang. Harris glanced up at the clock on the wall: 12.30am, it said. He sighed then looked at the name on the phone's screen and smiled. It was Leckie. A uniformed constable with Greater Manchester Police, Graham Leckie was one of the inspector's closest friends in the service. They had first met at an RSPB conference more than a decade before, sitting next to each other during a seminar on birds. They had instinctively connected through their passion for the subject and discovering that they both worked for Greater Manchester Police – Harris had just taken up his first posting as a copper after leaving the Army. They met regularly after that to swap information about wildlife crime. Even when Harris moved north, they talked regularly on the phone and, Manchester being little over an hour and a half down the motorway from Levton Bridge, still met for a drink several times a year. Leckie's main job was in intelligence so he had proved a useful contact for Jack Harris on more than one occasion. And given that Leckie's speciality was gangland crime…

'Morning, Graham,' said Harris, sitting down again, tipping back in his chair and placing his boots on the desk. 'Working late.'

'You must be joking, pal. One of the lads has had his leaving down the snooker club. I think it is fair to say that drink has been taken.'

'Alright for some, matey. I still haven't got home to my bottle of whisky.'

'Not that nice one I gave you – the Dalmore?'

'Na, that went ages ago.'

'Pisspot,' said Leckie. 'Anyway, sorry it's taken me so long to get back to you. I take it you want me to solve another crime for you? Someone nicked a sheep?'

'Actually, it's a murder. Guy found on the hills.'

'Got a name?'

'Trevor Meredith,' said Harris, shifting his legs on the table. 'Ring a bell?'

'Sorry.'

'It was a long shot. I really wanted to talk to you about Gerry Radford.'

There was a silence at the other end of the phone.

'You still there, Graham?'

'Yeah, I'm still here, Hawk. What the hell do you want with Gerry Radford? He linked to your dead guy?'

'Could be. I want to know what he's up to these days.'

'Same old, same old – still trafficking, drugs, cigs, in fact, you name it, Gerry Radford has got his mitts all over it.'

'What if I want to lift him?'

Another silence.

'Graham?'

'Yeah, I heard you, Hawk. Give me an easy one, why don't you? I mean, you know the score with Gerry Radford. And let's be honest, after what happ…'

'Forget that,' said Harris, returning his chair legs to the floor, standing up and walking over to stare out of his office window. 'That's history and I really do need to interview him.'

'You'll need to persuade our Organised Crime Squad that there's something tasty in it for them as well.'

'Will you put some calls in for me?' asked Harris. 'Or maybe fix up to meet your Organised Crime guy? Who is he these days?'

'She, mate.' There was a pause. 'Annie Gorman. You remember Annie, don't you?'

'Jeez, she was only a sergeant when I…'

'Careful how you phrase it, Hawk.'

'I was going to say when I left GMP.'

'I've heard it called many things,' chuckled Leckie. 'She's on a fast-track is our Annie.'

'So it would seem. What do you reckon then, will you be able to set something up?'

'Leave it with me.'

The inspector hit the cancel button, slipped the phone into his pocket and walked over to the door. He looked around the office for a moment or two, gave a chuckle, muttered 'Annie Gorman', switched off the light and walked slowly down the deserted corridor.

Chapter ten

Dawn was only just colouring the sky the next morning when Jack Harris emerged from his home and surveyed the dim shapes of the hills. Home was a tumbledown cottage on a narrow track halfway up one of the best known local landmarks, referred to locally as the Dead Hill. Harris had purchased the house, which was obscured from the winding valley road below by a fold in the hillside, after stumbling across it while out on a walk with Scoot. The former shepherd's cottage had been in a dilapidated condition and it had taken the inspector the best part of a year to restore it to a habitable condition, doing most of the tasks himself and calling in favours for the rest. Now, it was his bolthole, close enough to Levton Bridge if he needed to get there quickly but far enough to escape the world – the nearest habitation was a farm well out of sight on the other side of the hill and Jack Harris liked the fact that he could not see anyone from his front window.

However, as his mother had always told him when he was a young man, he could escape the world but he could not escape himself and that had proved the case yet again when he had reached the cottage just a few hours previously. Having completed his conversation with Leckie, the inspector had headed out of Levton Bridge, deep in thought as he guided his Land Rover along the valley road until he took a right turn and edged the vehicle up the rocky little path leading to the cottage. On arrival, he had taken Scoot for a ten-minute walk across the hillside, the inspector turning up his collar as the wind gathered pace once more and drove the rain hard into their faces. Half way down the track, man and dog had abandoned the effort and run for the welcome warmth of home and hearth, and malt whisky.

Once back in the cottage, Scoot had wolfed down some dog biscuits and curled up in front of the crackling log fire in the living room and Harris had sat in the worn armchair, sipping his drink and trying to read a wildlife book to clear his mind. Harris usually turned to wildlife books for relaxation – the antique bookcase in the corner of the room was piled high with them, many on the brink of toppling off the shelves – but, time and time again, the breeding cycle of pelagic cormorants failed to hold his attention and he found himself dragged back to the events of the day. Eventually, he had given a sigh and let the book fall to the floor, the inspector instead sitting and staring gloomily into the flickering flames of the fire.

The revelation that a gangland figure like Gerry Radford might be involved in his investigation – Harris was convinced the gunmen were his associates – had given the inquiry an added frisson for the detective, bringing back some old memories. As he sat there, he was honest enough to admit that it was a revelation that was not completely unwelcome: Gerry Radford was unfinished business. Harris and Radford went back a long way and the inspector's mind ranged across events that he had hoped to forget, yet secretly wanted to remember. Sitting and staring out into the darkness, oblivious to the rain spattering against the window, Harris could see once again the mocking smile on Gerry Radford's face. He clenched his fist and quickly stopped, realising that he was still holding the whisky glass.

When the momentary anger had passed, Harris acknowledged to himself that there was another reason why the involvement of a man such as Gerry Radford had excited his interest. The inspector knew that part of him missed the murky world of organised crime. He had returned to work in his home town of Levton Bridge because in Manchester's urban sprawl, he had desperately missed the North Pennine hills and their solitude, had wanted to look out upon big northern skies, had craved the sound of the wind whistling across the escarpments and been desperate to stand and watch buzzards quartering the slopes in search of prey. However, Jack Harris knew that sometimes he also missed the big city, missed the challenge of gangland figures like Gerry Radford. Missed? Was 'missed' the right word? he asked himself as he sipped his whisky. It was the word he always used but, if he was honest, *needed* was a much more apt word. Even though Harris already knew this, it still surprised him each time he thought it.

After considering the involvement of Gerry Radford, Jack Harris had gone on to think about other things. Having allowed himself some pleasant recollections of Annie Gorman's charms, he focused his mind on the events that had occurred since Trevor Meredith's disappearance the previous morning. As he did so, he found himself thinking that he was missing something. At the back of his mind was the nagging conviction that he had seen something that should have triggered his instincts but had failed to do so. Something that would have unlocked one of the investigation's many secrets.

Shortly after three, after fruitlessly racking his brains for the best part of an hour and half, the inspector had given a low curse and emptied his third glass of whisky – he knew he should have stopped at two with an early start ahead of him but it was good stuff – and climbed wearily up to bed. His sleep had been short and fitful, disturbed by the noise of the storm raging outside. As he had lain there in the darkness, Scoot sprawled across the bottom of the bed, Harris had listened to the conifers swaying and creaking in the nearby copse as the gale finally reached its crescendo before blowing itself out. With each sound, the inspector's mind went back to Trevor Meredith and his poor dog lying amongst the bracken. More than once, Jack Harris reached out to the bottom of the bed and stroked the slumbering Scoot.

Morning brought a calmer, different feeling. With that thick-headed feeling that only lack of sleep and a couple of drinks too many can engender, Jack Harris stood for a few moments outside the cottage and let his gaze roam slowly around the hills as they stretched away into the distance, the green of the slopes in the early morning mist fading to blackness up at the summit; the only sounds, the bleating of sheep and the chuckling of the stream as it weaved its way past the rear of the cottage. As he gathered his wits, breathed in the fresh morning air and started to feel himself come alive, Jack Harris smiled at the ever-strengthening streaks of light which heralded the dawn of a new day. As ever, it was a view that brought calm to his mind: the view that had been with him during his Army days, wherever he had been in the world, the view that had brought him back to the valley after so many years away, the view which never failed to work its magic.

Feeling better already and light of step, he set off, followed by Scoot, for their early morning walk, over to the copse and round a couple of the fields, the inspector pausing repeatedly, as he always did, to gaze out over the valley stretching away below them, its details gradually revealed in the emerging daylight. Constitutional completed, Harris grabbed a quick bacon sandwich then man and dog climbed into the Land Rover and the inspector made the twenty-five-minute drive along the valley to Levton Bridge, allowing his mind to make the gradual transition from solitude to police station hubbub. As he approached the town, his radio crackled.

'Control here,' said a woman's voice. 'Just to let you know that the media circus has turned up. They're camped on the front step.'

'Just what we need,' said Harris. 'Is Coco the Clown in?'

'In his office.'

'Even better,' sighed the inspector.

Ten minutes later, he was driving into the town, navigating the vehicle through narrow streets, past houses with lights out and curtains still drawn. He brought the vehicle to a halt at the bottom of the hill leading to the market place, a hundred metres from the Victorian house that had acted as Levton Bridge Police Station for as long as anyone could remember. The inspector leaned his elbows on his steering wheel for a few moments and silently surveyed the scene. Gathered in front of the station was a group of journalists and Harris could see at least one television camera. He was not surprised to see them: the suspicious death of a man and his dog on the high hills had the media sensing a story. Besides, everyone knew that Jack Harris made for good copy.

Spotting the inspector's familiar white Land Rover, the journalists turned and headed down the street towards him. Harris started edging the vehicle forwards, ignoring their shouted pleas as he manoeuvred through the throng and parked it in front of the police station – ever since Curtis had issued an edict that all police vehicles be parked in the yard at the rear of the building, Jack Harris had made a point of parking at the front. Getting out of the vehicle, Scoot behind him, the inspector picked his way through the crowd and walked up the front steps of the building, conscious of the clicking cameras behind him.

'DCI Harris?' said a man's voice. 'Can you tell us the name of the dead man found on the hills yesterday yet?'

'No comment.'

'Come on, Jack,' said a young woman, 'you never do no comment.'

The inspector turned and looked at her. She was an attractive young blonde reporter who worked for the local television station. Harris had noticed her before and, perusal concluded, he gave the slightest of smiles, turned and headed back up the steps. The look was not lost on the young woman and she blushed and fell silent.

'Come on, Harris, give us a break,' said a man's voice. 'Is it still rated as suspicious or are you saying it's a murder now?'

'All in good time,' said Harris, pushing his way into the building.

'And what about this mad dog roaming the hills?' asked another reporter.

'All in good time,' repeated the inspector as the door started to close behind him.

'But my news editor says we can't really wait until your press conference.'

'What press conference?' asked the inspector, walking back outside and looking down at the young man from the top of the steps.

'Your superintendent says there'll be one at nine,' said the reporter, handing the inspector a fax. 'Reckons he'll give us all the details we need.'

'Does he indeed?'

'Yeah,' said another of the reporters, 'we assume you'll be putting something out about the other incident as well. We heard there might have been a firearm involved. Can you tell us anything about what happened? Is it true that a shot was...?'

'No comment,' said the inspector and disappeared into the station without a further word.

Once in, he walked purposefully up to the first floor and along the main corridor to the office occupied by Philip Curtis. Without knocking, the inspector entered and stood for a moment, surveying the man behind the desk with his customary distaste. Always someone who had respected rank during his military days, Harris had found that mindset challenged by the arrival of Philip Curtis. More used to senior officers who stood up for their troops, the inspector had quickly come to suspect that the superintendent's main – and probably only – priority was his own career-advancement. Everyone at Levton Bridge knew that was not the way Jack Harris approached things and it had long been apparent to everyone else in the station that their viewpoints were irreconcilable. Indeed, a scathing Harris had often used the phrase 'stuffed shirt' about the divisional commander. Curtis, for his part, confided to his few close allies within the station that he resented the lack of respect afforded to him by his head of CID.

A tall thin man, with sharply angular features and thinning dark hair, Curtis was flicking through some paperwork and glanced up with irritation when the inspector entered the room.

'How many times do I have to tell you, you should knock before...' he began but the look on the inspector's face caused him to leave the sentence unfinished. 'Ah, it's you.'

Harris gave him a dark look and the superintendent shuffled his papers into a neat pile and placed them carefully in one of the trays on his desk, all moves designed to buy himself time as he pondered how best to play the conversation. Encounters with Jack Harris were rarely easy affairs.

'A busy night then,' observed the superintendent after a few moments. 'I tried to ring you but, for some reason, I could not get an answer.'

'Bad reception.'

'Ah, indeed.' It was always the same answer. 'So, what progress are you making?'

'I was rather hoping that you would tell me,' said the inspector, ignoring the commander's gesture to take a seat.

'I'm sorry?'

Harris held up the fax.

'Ah, yes,' said Curtis. 'Yes, I was going to talk to you about that. You see…'

'I don't recall sanctioning a press conference.'

'No, I did that.'

'Without asking me?'

'I felt we needed to issue something, Jack. You know how fast word gets round in this place. The Control Room received a number of calls last night and the duty press officer suggested that we had to do something. That's why I was ringing you – or trying to ring you anyway. Since people already seemed to know about the shooting up on the hills, I took the decision in my capacity as…'

His voice tailed off as Harris glowered at him. Loathe to spark yet another row, Curtis made an effort to look more conciliatory, gesturing once again to the chair.

'Sit down, Jack.'

Harris hesitated.

'Please.'

The inspector sighed and sat down, and, arms folded across his chest, eyed the superintendent balefully.

'Perhaps we should start this conversation again,' said Curtis, encouraged that the inspector did not disagree with the suggestion. 'So, might I ask what you would like me to say at the press conference?'

'You?' There was an edge in the inspector's voice.

'Yes. I rather assumed that with everything that has been happening, you would be too busy to talk…'

'And you wouldn't be?' asked the inspector, nodding at the in-tray. 'Surely, there are bits of paper that need signing?'

Curtis looked for a moment as if was about to remonstrate with the inspector but instead he gave the thinnest of smiles.

'Yes, I am sure there are,' he said. 'You do the press conference if you want to.'

'No,' replied Harris, satisfied that his point had been made but also acutely aware that the superintendent was right – there was a lot of work to do. 'No, you do it.'

'So, what do I tell them? Are we assuming that the murder is linked to the attack on these farmers last night?'

'Not sure it is,' said Harris. 'I would have expected Meredith's killer to be long gone so whoever these guys were is anyone's guess. It is possible that they were one of the gangs coming in to steal farm equipment.'

'But guns, Jack? Surely that's OTT for them?'

'I'll grant you that.'

'Which brings us back to the question that we are bound to be asked. What on earth were the farmers doing there in the first place?' said Curtis with a shake of the head. 'One or two journalists are already asking. I thought you made it clear to the farmers that they should only go out when we can provide back-up. And last night simply was not the time to do it. Did you sanction it?'

The question was hard edged.

'I suggested it originally.'

The answer was evasive.

'But surely you knew the pressure we were under last night?' protested the superintendent.

Harris hesitated. Even though he had known the superintendent would hone in on what had happened, he had still not resolved how to play it without landing Matty Gallagher in trouble, something the inspector did not want to do. Gallagher was unsettled enough without something like this persuading him to apply for a transfer. Harris knew that the sergeant had already been keeping an eye on opportunities in more urban areas. He had even mentioned to colleagues that he would not object to a transfer to another force. Such knowledge meant that Harris knew he had to watch his words carefully: irritating though Gallagher was sometimes, he was a damned good sergeant and Harris could not afford to lose such an officer. It was difficult enough to get hold of them in the first place – Levton Bridge was regarded by many officers as a graveyard posting. Even Curtis, he guessed, was only there to advance his career and did not plan on being in the division any longer than necessary.

Harris noticed that Curtis was still eying him intently. The inspector thought quickly: if he was honest with himself, this was not just about protecting Matty Gallagher. Harris needed to find a way of making sure that Curtis did not use the situation to target his detective chief inspector as well. Jack Harris had heard all the stories about Philip Curtis, he had engineered the demise of officers for less.

For his part, Curtis said nothing and let the tension build; conciliation or not, the superintendent was not one to throw away the chance to make the inspector squirm.

'Is there something you want to tell me, Jack?' he asked eventually.

'It was a communications breakdown.'

'Would you care to elaborate on what went wrong?'

'Not really.'

'Well whoever was responsible for it, they need to know that they almost had those lads killed.' Curtis looked hard at the inspector. 'I take it you will convey that point to the person in question, assuming, of course, that we are not talking about yourself?'

Harris said nothing.

'Well, whatever went wrong, make sure it does not happen again,' said Curtis. 'And make sure you get your story straight. We don't want your people telling different versions. There are bound to be questions asked at higher levels.'

Harris stared at him; was it his imagination or was the superintendent trying to be helpful?

'Don't look at me like that,' said Curtis with a slight smile. 'You're not the only one who comes out of this looking bad if it turns out that it was our fuck-up. Anyway, going back to my original point, I need to tell the media something. Can we name Trevor Meredith yet? Have we tracked down any family members?'

'We haven't even formally IDed him. To be honest, Trevor Meredith is a bit of a mystery man – there is nothing to suggest that he even existed before he came here.'

'You've done all the checks, of course?'

'Of course,' said Harris, trying not to bridle at the implied criticism in the question. Normally, he would have been more strident in his approach but, given the incident with the farmers, Harris felt as vulnerable with Curtis as he had felt for a long time. 'One of the theories we are investigating is that he changed his name when he came up here.'

'Any idea why?'

'No.'

'And what about his dog?' asked Curtis, shooting Scoot a dark look as the Labrador wandered into his office and curled up next to the filing cabinet. 'I understand it was torn to shreds. Is whatever did it still roaming the hills?'

Harris shrugged.

'Do we know what the bloody thing is?' asked Curtis. 'People are really worried. We have already had several calls from members of the public wanting to know if it is safe to go out.'

'I'm sure it is. We have had the dead animal examined by a vet – not sure if you know James Thornycroft…'

'Indeed I do,' beamed Curtis. 'A very pleasant man, indeed. He recently joined the Rotary Club. Just the kind of person we are looking for, a respectable young businessman.'

'Yes, well I am reserving judgement on James Thornycroft. We've heard some things.'

The words had hardly come out of the inspector's mouth before he had time to think about it.

'What things?' Curtis looked at him sharply.

Harris said nothing.

'Well? What things?' said Curtis.

'Let's just say he is someone of interest to us.'

'I suggest you focus on the main elements of this inquiry instead of going off on tangents like this,' said Curtis, a new edge to his voice. 'I know James Thornycroft and there is nothing to suggest that he is anything other than a decent member of the community.'

'You can hardly know him that well. He's only been here four mon…'

'I have told you before about stirring up unnecessary trouble. You know what people are like up here. Concentrate on the job in hand.'

Harris glared at him but decided not to argue the point.

'So, what else are you doing?' asked Curtis. 'Because at the moment there is precious little to tell the media.'

Harris sighed. His instinct had always been to keep things away from his superintendent wherever possible because it prevented the commander interfering in investigations. However, on this occasion the inspector realised that he needed to offer his superior officer something that suggested an element of progress, even if it was only an unsubstantiated theory.

'We suspect Meredith may have been investigating dog fighting,' he said.

'It doesn't always come down to animals, Jack.'

Harris groaned inwardly at the comment, realising that he had made a tactical mistake, and decided to try another tack.

'We also know that Meredith was involved in an illegal poker game at the King's Head,' he said in an attempt to divert the superintendent's attention. 'Apparently there's money owed by several of the players.'

'Weak.'

'What?'

'I am not sure I can see a game of pub poker leading to murder, Jack. No, much as it galls me to say it, I prefer the dog fighting line of inquiry at this stage.'

'Really?' Harris could not contain his surprise.

'It sounds feasible and if he was involved, he was taking a massive risk. Knowing him as I do, I imagine he would have been well out of his depth.'

'I didn't realise you were buddies,' said Harris. 'He a member of Rotary as well?'

'Actually,' said Curtis coldly, 'the Club made a couple of donations to the sanctuary.'

'I thought you detested dogs.'

'I do,' said the superintendent, glaring at Scoot who was now licking himself. 'It was someone else's idea. However, if you are right, it might explain this.'

He reached for his in-tray and produced a fax.

'It came overnight from the RSPCA. They want you to go down to Roxham this morning. As you can see, they're bringing in a couple of senior officers from outside the area to talk to us. A woman called Jackson and a Special Investigator by the name of Maynard.'

'I know him,' nodded Harris. 'Good man.'

'In which case,' said Curtis, handing over the piece of paper, 'you might like to ask him why he forgot to tell us exactly what our Mr Meredith was up to.'

Harris scanned the contents of the message, nodded gloomily and got up to go. Five minutes later, chastened by his conversation with the superintendent and irritated that he had been out-manoeuvred into giving away much more information than would normally be his intention, a glowering Jack Harris walked down the first-floor corridor and stalked into the CID office. Only Butterfield was there, sitting at her desk and about to open a large brown envelope.

'You alright, guv?' asked the constable, noticing his expression.

'Am I ever after I've been in with the President of the Rotary Club?'

Normally, the comment would have elicited a chuckle from the detective constable but these were not normal times and Alison Butterfield knew it.

'Are we in trouble over this Farmwatch thing?' she asked.

'Depends who shouts loudest,' shrugged Harris, slumping heavily in a chair. 'The one good thing is that Curtis is as worried about his gonads being squeezed as I am. Has Matty been on yet?'

'Yes, just. From home. Wants to know if you still want him to stay down there and stand in for you at the PM. I think he rather hopes the answer is yes. I don't think he fancies being around Levton Bridge when the flak starts flying.'

'It seems that I will have to go to Roxham after all. And I want you to come down with me.'

'Guv?'

'We have to talk to someone who's got some information about Meredith.'

'Brilliant,' said Butterfield with a gleam in her eye. 'Who is it? One of your gangland informants?'

'Not quite,' said Harris, with a slight smile. 'It's an RSPCA officer.'

Butterfield's face fell.

'The RSPCA?' she said in a hollow voice.

'I knew you'd like it,' said Harris, heading out of the office, his voice coming from the corridor. 'If you're lucky they might let you have a nice puppy to take home.'

Butterfield scowled and glanced down at Scoot, who was sitting in the doorway looking at her – she could have sworn that he was laughing.

'And you can shut up,' she grunted.

As the dog trotted after his master, the constable remembered the envelope in her hand and, still annoyed, ripped it open, using such violence that she tore off the

90

top corner of the top sheet. Cursing her clumsiness, she was about to extract the piece of paper when Harris reappeared.

'Whilst I remember,' he said, 'when I was talking to Dennis Soames last night, he gave me some interesting information. There's a poker ring after-hours at the King's Head. According to Dennis, a couple of the players were Meredith and Thornycroft.'

'Now that is interesting.'

'Yeah, it is,' said Harris, picking a piece of paper out of his suit jacket pocket and handing it over to the constable. 'The DI's back today so I am going to get her to look into it but in the meantime, can you look at this list of names and see if anyone leaps out at you? Leave it on her desk when you've finished. I've got a couple of things to sort then we'll get off to Roxham. I'll see you out the front in five minutes. Be warned, there's a load of journos out there so keep your mouth shut.'

Butterfield nodded and, as Harris disappeared again, Butterfield ran her eye down the list of names on the list, walked across the room and placed the piece of paper on the DI's desk. The constable realised that she was still holding the brown envelope and carefully extracted the documents, fearful of damaging them further. As she read the top sheet, her eyes widened and she fished out the rest of the papers. Scanning their contents rapidly, her eyes glinted.

'Guv!' she shouted excitedly, running out of the room and chasing down the corridor. 'I think you'd better see this. It's the stuff they sent up from Bolton overnight. It could explain why James Thornycroft was playing poker.'

'Now that's even more interesting,' breathed Harris as he flicked through the sheets. 'When we get back, you and I should have a little chat with our friend Mr Thornycroft. I think we can say with some confidence that he may just get himself drummed out of the Rotary Club. Ah, the shame of it, Constable, the shame of it.'

'You'll never be invited to join now.'

'Indeed not,' said Harris.

The detective constable could not remember ever having seen Jack Harris look so happy as he beamed at her and started to walk down the corridor again. As Butterfield watched him disappear round the corner on the way to his office, it struck her that she had never heard him whistle either.

Chapter eleven

Just as the inspector's Land Rover left the market place, heading for the detectives' appointment in Roxham, Butterfield's mobile phone rang. Two minutes later, the detectives had turned round and made their way to the other side of the town and were pulling up outside Levton Bridge Dog Sanctuary, which stood on the outskirts in a field wedged between the last of the new houses and the nearest farm. As the officers got out, they could hear barks and whines of the dogs housed within the complex.

'So was this place going to close or not?' asked Butterfield as they walked up the path.

'You heard Barry Ramsden, he reckoned it was all pub talk,' said Harris as they walked towards the green cabin that acted as a reception. 'I mean, would a politician lie?'

Butterfield grinned. Entering the cabin, the officers were greeted by a fresh-faced young girl wearing a chunky sweater and jeans. She smiled at Butterfield.

'Hello again,' she said.

The constable nodded but did not say anything.

'We are here to see your deputy manager,' said the inspector, flashing his warrant card. 'Jane Porter. She's expecting us.'

'She's sorting out breakfasts,' said the girl, pointing to a door. 'I'll take you down.'

'Thank you,' said Harris.

The girl led the officers out into the sanctuary and between the rundown concrete blocks, their walls chipped and grimy, the odour of urine rank and strong. But the inspector's eye was not drawn to the condition of the buildings, rather the narrow, caged enclosures, each one occupied by a dog. Every type imaginable was there, from Labradors to terriers, Bedlingtons to lurchers. Some came up to the wire and looked hopefully at the passing detectives, others glared and bared their teeth. One or two retreated to the back of their cages and growled when they saw Scoot, who peered through the bars with interest.

'We take them from all over the valley,' explained the girl. 'And even further – we had one in from Carlisle last week.'

'It's a disgrace,' said Harris, visibly moved as he was every time he visited.

'It is certainly heart-breaking sometimes,' agreed the young receptionist as she led them along the path. 'But we do our best to give them a good life.'

She looked at Butterfield, as if seeking her approval of their work, but the constable was eying the dogs dispassionately.

'Do you rehome them all?' asked the constable, sensing that the girl was waiting for her to comment.

'As many as we can.'

'And the rest?'

'We have to put them down, I am afraid.'

'What's the story with that one?' asked Harris suddenly, pointing to a collie staring hopefully at them through the bars.

'That's Archie,' said the girl, pausing for a moment, seemingly fighting back strong emotions. 'I'm sorry, it's just that he reminds me of poor Robbie. It's terrible what happened to him yesterday.'

'And to Trevor,' said Butterfield.

'Yes, yes,' said the girl, nodding vigorously, 'yes, of course, to poor Trevor as well. Of course. Yes.'

But it did not sound convincing.

'So, what's Archie's story?' asked the inspector.

'He belonged to a retired couple. Trouble is…' she crouched down and let the dog sniff her fingers through the bars, 'they were too soft with him, didn't train him properly. One day he jumped up at a pensioner in the marketplace. Archie didn't mean to hurt her but she ended up in hospital with a broken hip so the owners got rid. Brought him here.'

Harris sighed as the dog looked up at him, its tail wagging frantically.

'Tragic,' he said, glancing at Butterfield. 'Absolutely tragic.'

Butterfield shrugged; as a farmer's daughter, she had never been particularly attracted to dogs. They were there to do a job, her father had always said. It was an attitude she had taken into adult life. And for all she liked Scoot, she would never say she cared for him particularly deeply. Indeed, she had been the only one who had declined to sign the protest petition when Curtis tried to ban him from the police station. Not that she had told the DCI, although she was pretty sure that he knew.

'Tell me,' said Harris, 'what was Trevor Meredith like?'

'I'm not sure I should say.' The young receptionist was suddenly guarded. 'I mean, he was my boss.'

'This is a murder inquiry, though,' said Harris. 'I would rather you did not hold anything back.'

The young girl nodded.

'I did not like him,' she said. 'He was not a very friendly man.'

'What do you…?'

'There's Jane,' said the receptionist with relief as she pointed to a thin, dark-haired dungaree-clad woman in her mid-thirties who was approaching them along the path, struggling to balance four dog bowls in her arms.

'Here, let me help you,' said Harris, taking a couple of them.

'Thank you,' she said. 'You must be Detective Chief Inspector Harris.'

'I am. You asked to see us.'

'I did,' said Jane Porter. 'We'll just deliver these bowls then we can talk.'

'The good constable here was just reminding me that there was talk of you moving,' said Harris as they walked along the path between the blocks.

'Yes, there was, a few months ago,' nodded Porter as they stopped at one of the enclosures, inside which sat a couple of miserable-looking mongrels, 'but it didn't come to anything. I did ask Trevor about it but he said not to worry. Will you wait here a moment, please, while I sort their breakfasts?'

Five minutes later, the three of them were sitting in the manager's office back at the main reception, cradling mugs of tea. Scoot was curled up by the door. As Jane Porter took the seat behind Trevor Meredith's desk, Harris looked around him and, mindful of Gallagher's comments the night before, was immediately struck at how impersonal the walls were. No pictures of Meredith's family, no thank you letters from customers, no pictures of Robbie, nothing.

'So, what did you want to tell us, Miss Porter?' asked Butterfield, noting the inspector's reverie and always eager to show herself capable of seizing the initiative when the opportunity arose.

Jane Porter looked uncomfortable.

'Go on,' said Harris, 'I am sure you are not in trouble.'

'I think I might be, actually. You see,' and she glanced at Butterfield, 'I lied to you last night, Constable.'

The detectives exchanged glances.

'In what way?' asked Harris.

'Your constable asked me if I knew of any large terriers that might have gone out in recent weeks.'

Butterfield nodded. 'And you said no.'

'Which was a lie.'

'Go on,' said Harris.

'It was a few weeks ago,' said Jane Porter, her voice quiet now, 'I was working late, down in the bottom block. One of the dogs had damaged her run and I was trying to sort it out. I am sure that Trevor did not even know I was there. If you ask me, he had no idea what happened here after 4pm.'

'4pm?'

'He never stayed after 4pm. Not exactly the hardest of workers was our Trevor.'

'So, what happened?' asked Harris.

'I heard voices. When I came out, I saw them standing further up the path.'

'Saw whom?'

'Trevor and this large man. He was shaven headed and looked really unpleasant so I went back into the block. I did not really want them to see me. To be honest, I felt scared.'

'Do you know who the man was?' asked Harris.

'No, but I did hear Trevor ask him if he had had a good journey up from Manchester.'

'Are you sure about that?' asked Harris sharply.

'Yes, I am. Besides, he talked with a Mancunian accident.' She gave a slight smile. 'He sounded like Liam Gallagher.'

'God help us,' murmured the inspector. 'Then what happened?'

'They were looking at Sabre.'

'Sabre?'

'I know,' and Jane Porter smiled, 'not a great name. I misread the form and for the first couple of days I called him Sailor. No wonder he was bad-tempered. He had only come in a couple of weeks before. He was a bull terrier, a cross-breed – nasty looking thing. He was missing part of his ear like he'd been in a fight.'

'Are you certain?' said Harris sharply.

'Oh, yes, I will never forget Sabre. I love all dogs, Inspector, I really do, but I was dubious about us taking him – you can't trust those kind of breeds.'

'Where did he come from?' asked Harris.

'He was found wandering the streets down in Ingleby. Went for another dog in that little park so the dog warden brought him up here. I assumed that we would arrange for him to be put down as soon as possible.'

'But he wasn't put down?'

'He should have been, you can never rehome dogs like that. He had this wild look in his eye and no one could approach him. None of us went into his run. I am sure he would have gone for us.' She shook her head. 'I have done this job for fifteen years, Chief Inspector, and I have never met a dog which I could not handle but Sabre… Sabre was different.'

'Do you think he was like that because he had been bred for fighting?'

She hesitated then nodded.

'The thought did occur to me,' she said. 'I mean, you do hear stories.'

'Indeed you do. So, do I assume that the man took him away?'

'Yes. I peered through a crack in the door and saw them go into the run and come out with Sabre on a leash and wearing a muzzle. He was trying to get away but the man was stronger than he was. I could not see that well but I think he kicked Sabre a couple of times – I heard the dog cry in pain.'

'Did you not try to stop them?'

'I know I should have,' she said in a voice little more than a whisper, 'but I was too scared. I could not see very well but I am pretty sure that the man handed over some cash to Trevor.'

Harris stood up and walked over to look out of the office window, smiling as he saw the young receptionist taking Archie for a walk down one of the paths, the collie straining on the leash in his enthusiasm.

'So, what happened next?' asked Harris, turning back into the room.

'I must have sat in there for the best part of half an hour until I was sure they were gone. I was shaking. Like I said, I am pretty sure that Trevor did not know I was there because he had locked up and put the alarms on and his car was gone.'

'Did you ever challenge him about it?'

'Yes, the next morning. I had to, the staff were asking where Sabre had gone. I didn't tell him what I had seen but I did ask him why Sabre had disappeared.'

'And he said?'

'He said he had taken him to the vet to be put down. He seemed very calm about it but I never saw any paperwork confirming it. Mind, Trevor was not very good at the paperwork side of things.'

'We had noticed,' murmured Harris. 'What did you make of him as a person?'

'Like I told your constable last night, there was no reason for anyone to hurt him.' She half-smiled at Butterfield as if seeking reassurance – none was forthcoming.

Harris returned to sit down at the desk.

'I know what you said, Jane,' replied the inspector, staring hard at her, 'but what I want to know is what you really thought of him.'

She looked at him for a moment, her face a picture of confusion.

'Look,' said Harris, 'a lot of people are telling us that there was no reason for anyone to kill Trevor but someone did and it really is time that people started giving us answers.'

'I have told you about the dog, surely that is enough?'

'I'm sorry, Miss Porter, but I really do need to know what you thought about him.'

'Am I a suspect?'

The question took the detectives by surprise.

'Should you be a suspect?' asked Harris, fixing her with a stern look.

'No, of course not.' She seemed taken aback by the question. 'I'm just... look, I did not like him, that's all.'

'You did not say that last night,' said Butterfield.

'I'm sorry, I truly am. It's just that I did not want to get involved. This has shaken everyone up, I am sure you can appreciate that. I hardly slept last night, wrestling with my conscience. That's why I rang you this morning.'

'Most commendable,' said Harris thinly. 'Always nice to hear the truth after so many lies.'

She glared at him.

'So why did you not like him?' he asked, ignoring the look.

'There was something about him. I mean, on the face of it, he was perfectly pleasant to everyone, it's just that he never had his picture taken.'

'What?'

'He never had his picture taken,' she repeated. 'If the newspaper came round to do a story about one of our dogs, he would always get someone else to be on the picture. At first, I thought he was just shy or something but then it happened at parties, Christmas, that sort of thing. He always found a way of keeping out of the pictures. I mean, why would someone do that?'

'You tell me.'

'If you ask me, Trevor Meredith was not all that he appeared to be.' She lowered her voice. 'Sometimes when strangers came here, I got the impression that he was a bit – I don't know – a bit nervous. Anxious, that's a better word. Yes, anxious. He tended to keep out of the way unless he really had to meet them.'

There was silence in the office for a few moments.

'Then there were the days off,' said Jane.

'The days off?'

'Yes. Over recent months Trevor had been taking a lot of days off but not telling anyone why. He certainly was not owed as much time as he took. I mean, we all work so hard here and Trevor…' Her voice tailed off again. 'It has become a nightmare, a terrible nightmare.'

'It certainly has,' said Harris, eying her intently. 'Do you know what I think happened to the dog he handed over to our friend from Manchester?'

Jane Porter turned dark eyes on the detectives and nodded.

'I think,' she said quietly, 'that yesterday he tore poor old Robbie apart.'

'I think,' said Harris, 'that you may just be right.'

* * *

Five minutes later, the detectives were back in the car park and walking towards the inspector's Land Rover.

'Bloody woman!' exclaimed Butterfield when she was sure they were out of earshot of any of the staff. 'Last night, she told me that there was nothing wrong with Trevor Meredith.'

'In which case, learn from the lesson she taught you,' said Harris, producing his car keys and opening the door to let Scoot into the back.

'Lesson?'

'The lesson, Constable Butterfield,' said the inspector, climbing into the driver's seat, 'that you should never listen to what people are saying. Always listen to what they are thinking. People can't lie that way. We need to check her out.'

'Surely you don't think she is…?'

'There's too many people keeping secrets, and I don't like secrets.' He started the engine then gave the constable a half smile. 'Apart from mine, of course.'

* * *

Shortly after 11.30am, Jasmine Riley emerged tentatively into the street, clutching her overnight bag. Having stayed in her room as long as possible, knowing that her train was not due until noon, she realised that she finally had no option but to move and expose herself to the dangers of Roxham's streets. Eyes flitting left and right, she stood outside the guest house and nervously scanned the pavements for signs of danger.

Such behaviour had become a way of life in her final days with Trevor Meredith: he had constantly reminded her that someone could be watching. It had become his mantra but, if she was honest, Jasmine's concerns at the time were more for Trevor's state of mind than any reputed threat to their well-being. She had never been convinced that someone was after them. The incidents that had preceded their flight could, she had argued, have simply been coincidences, events onto which Trevor had placed undue significance. The ringing of the doorbell when no one was there that one time, the dog faeces left on the doorstep a couple of days later, these things were the type of pranks played by children, and the local kids knew that he worked at the dog sanctuary, she had said. And, she had added, there had been one or two complaints of youths misbehaving in the area over recent weeks. As for the anonymous phone call late one night, that could have been something innocent, she had told him. A wrong number or one of those automated machines with the funny American voice trying to sell holidays on a cruise ship.

However, Trevor had refused to listen and had seemed increasingly on edge. There had been rows. Irrational rows. Their first rows in ten years together. Imagined slights. Wild fantasies. Was she, Jasmine had started to ask herself, witnessing a man experiencing some kind of breakdown? However, so convinced had he seemed to be that she had agreed they should leave the

102

area, if only for a few days. If only to appease him. Well, Jasmine had said a few days, a short break to recharge the batteries but she was not sure Trevor had seen it that way. His preparations had suggested an air of finality. He had even said that he doubted he would ever see the cottage again.

Trevor's disappearance and his subsequent failure to answer her phone call the night before had changed everything. Now, Trevor's fears seemed only too real, now Jasmine Riley was as frightened as she could recall ever having felt, now she knew what her fiancé had been going through. Seeing few people on the street, she gave a sigh of relief, took a deep breath to regain her composure and started walking briskly in the direction of Roxham's railway station, mind made up. She would not head over to Newcastle, as agreed. No, she decided, it was time to go home, to explain to her mother what had been happening, why she had not been in touch, why she had not returned her calls. To seek reassurance from someone she knew she could trust and could ask for help. Even the thought of home made Jasmine feel better as she walked along the street, enjoying the freshness of the air after the oppressive atmosphere of the storm.

She passed a television shop and stopped to stare in the window. On one of the sets, there was an image of the hills above Levton Bridge and, heart pounding, she walked into the store and over to the TV, leaning over to hear the commentary. 'Police have not yet named the man found in the copse,' said the reporter's voice, 'but have confirmed that his dog died in the same incident. Superintendent Philip Curtis said that it was still early days in the inquiry.' Jasmine clapped a hand to her mouth and gave a slight exclamation as the divisional commander appeared on the screen, standing in front of Levton Bridge police station.

'Are you alright, madam?' asked a young male shop assistant, walking across to her.

Jasmine did not reply but ran from the store and down the street, her view obscured by the tears welling in her eyes. As she ran, she did not notice the man standing in the nearby shop doorway, watching her intently.

Chapter twelve

After leaving the sanctuary, the inspector guided his Land
Rover out of Levton Bridge, the detectives speaking little
as they left the houses behind and the landscape broke into
moorland, the bright morning sunshine and the tatters of
cloud casting darting shadows across the slopes. A mile
and a half out of town, the inspector noticed a quad bike
parked on the roadside with the key still in the ignition. He
brought the Land Rover to a sudden halt.

'What've you seen?' asked Butterfield.

'Apart from a quad bike asking to be nicked?' said the
inspector, getting out of the vehicle with Scoot and
pointing across the moor. 'Someone with a lot of
explaining to do.'

They walked for several hundred metres to where a
man in a fustian jacket and with a flat cap jammed onto his
weather-beaten head was leaning on a shepherd's crook,
watching his dog round up a flock of sheep. The man
started when he noticed the detectives striding towards
him and made as if to walk away.

'Stay where you are, Len Radley!' shouted Harris.

Radley sighed and waited for the detectives to arrive, eying them with trepidation. Scoot disappeared into the bracken.

'I were drunk,' said Radley before Harris could speak. 'I never meant to try to lamp you. I am really sorry, it were stupid but I were in me cups.'

'I don't want to talk about that.'

Radley, whose nose was swollen, looked relieved then his expression clouded over.

'Then what do you want to talk about, Mister Harris?' he asked.

'First off, why the hell is your quad bike sitting there with the keys in it? Do you know, we had three of them nicked last month and all because the damn fool owners left the keys in? Didn't Harry Galbraith give you that crime prevention sheet?'

'I were going to read it, Mister Harris. Just ain't got round to it.'

'Not got round to it! He handed them out six months ago!'

'Aye well, you know how it is.'

'I am afraid I do, Len, I am afraid I do,' sighed the inspector. 'Anyway, that's not what I want to talk to you about either. Why were you and Charlie Myles scrapping in the market place last night?'

'What did Charlie say?'

'He didn't say anything.'

'Then neither will I,' said the farmer firmly.

'Then allow me – was it about your little gambling ring at the King's Head?'

'How do you know about that?' Radley looked surprised.

'Because I'm omniscient, Len.'

Radley looked confused.

'Never mind,' said Harris. 'Tell me, what has been happening at the King's Head?'

'Like I said, I ain't going to say nowt about it.'

Harris glanced at Butterfield.

'I wonder, Constable,' he said thoughtfully, 'if, having reconsidered the events of last night, we could perhaps charge Len here with assault after all? I mean, the magistrates have already said they will treat any such cases of drunken disorder as very serious. A crackdown, I think the papers called it.'

'I think we might well be able to do, Sir. And I could act as the witness. I mean, I did see Len try to attack you. Oh, and maybe Charlie would press charges. It did look nasty, the more I think of it.'

Radley looked at the officers in alarm.

'And,' said Harris, 'did I not hear tell that Len's boss put him on a final warning the last time he got involved in something like this? Said he did not want his shepherd plastered all over the papers again.'

Len Radley had heard enough.

'Alright,' he said. 'Alright, I'll tell you – but it were only a little fun among friends.'

'It didn't look like you and Charlie were having much fun last night,' said the inspector.

Radley said nothing.

'In fact,' said Harris, 'from what I hear, there's not been much fun for anyone. There's a lot of money been lost, I think. Charlie owe you cash?'

Radley nodded.

'I heard a hundred quid,' said Harris.

Radley looked at him in astonishment.

'How the …?'

'Is that what you and Charlie were scrapping about last night?'

'Aye,' sighed Radley; he could see little point in denying what the inspector seemed already to know. 'He said he would bring it yesterday but he didn't have it on him when he turned up. We had a few arguments about it then, when we left, that's when we got to fighting. We'd had a few, mind. I know it were wrong, Mr Harris.'

'Your sense of social awareness is commendable,' said Harris, winking at Butterfield as the shepherd looked bewildered again. 'So who else takes part in these poker games?'

'Some of the regulars – and that new chap, the veterinary.'

'James Thornycroft?' said Harris. 'He a friend of yours?'

'No he ain't! I wouldn't trust him. The man's a crook, Mister Harris. Do you know, he tried to tell me that Roy needed an injection which would have cost thirty pounds.' The shepherd gestured to his sheepdog, which had just rounded up the last of the flock. 'I mean, Mister Harris, does he look like he needs an injection?'

'Who else takes part?'

'That man that got himself killed on the hills yesterday.'

'Anyone else?'

'That posh bloke.'

'Posh bloke?'

Radley nodded.

'Aye, talked right proper,' he said. 'He's called David Bowes. He's not from these parts, mind. He said he were renting a cottage out down in Stonecliffe.'

'What did he look like?'

'Normal like. Short brown hair.'

'Age?'

'I weren't never any good at guessing people's ages, Mister Harris.'

'Try.'

'Forty summat, I would say.'

'Anything unusual about him?'

'He had a scar, Mister Harris.' Radley ran a finger down the right side of his neck. 'Looked like he had been in a bit of trouble in his time.'

'Did he now?' said Harris softly. 'Did he really?'

Chapter thirteen

It was shortly before 10.30am when Harris and Butterfield arrived at the RSPCA's Roxham offices, which were housed in an Edwardian terraced house close to the town centre. On arrival, the detectives were ushered into a large first-floor meeting room, given cups of tea and asked to wait. They had been sitting at the large conference table for the best part of fifteen minutes – with the inspector growing increasingly irritated at what he saw as discourtesy and displaying his annoyance by pacing up and down the room – when the door opened and in walked a grey-haired woman in her early fifties and a balding man in his mid-forties. Both wore uniform.

'Ged Maynard, as I live and breathe,' said Harris, standing up and smiling broadly at the man, his irritation banished by the sight of his old friend. 'Long time no see.'

'Been a while,' nodded Maynard. 'Just before you decided to move to Hicksville, wasn't it?'

'Our super likes to call it a rural policing area,' said Harris, winking at Butterfield as the men shook hands, the inspector noting that his friend's grip was firm but that the palm was cold and clammy.

'This is Helen Jackson,' said Maynard, gesturing to the woman, who had been watching their greetings with a frown at the way the two men were ignoring her. 'Helen is my line manager and has travelled up with me this morning.'

'Mr Harris,' said Jackson in a voice that lacked warmth.

Her handshake lacked warmth as well, the DCI noting that it was cold and limp. He disliked her immediately.

'This is Detective Constable Butterfield,' said the inspector, concluding the introductions as everyone took their seats, detectives on one side of the large table, RSPCA officers on the other. 'She is very keen to learn more about the work of your organisation.'

Butterfield tried not to laugh, Ged Maynard gave a slight smile and Helen Jackson frowned again.

'Can we please get down to business,' she said in an officious tone of voice, reaching into her black briefcase and producing several brown files. 'I would like things resolved as quickly as possible.

'Well,' said Harris, his delight at seeing Maynard again dissipating, 'let's start with the fact that, even though we are all supposed to be on the same side, someone has been keeping secrets.'

'It's not what you think,' said Jackson.

'It is from where I'm sitting, Mrs Jackson.'

'Miss,' she said starchly, 'I'm a Miss.'

'Of course you are,' said Harris. 'However, your marital status matters somewhat less than what the hell has been happening behind my back.'

The RSPCA officers shifted uncomfortably in their seats. The slight pause gave Harris the chance to properly peruse his friend for the first time since the RSPCA officers had walked into the room. Ged Maynard seemed so much older than the last time they had met, not just because the waist was a little thicker and the hair greyer, but because a lot of his old energy seemed to have dissipated. Ged Maynard, Harris concluded, looked like a man who had been backed into a corner and not just by the presence of the detectives. There were clearly tensions between him and his superior officer, Harris decided. The inspector gave a slight smile: he loved situations when those on the other side of the table were at a disadvantage. Still irritated by the way Curtis had controlled their meeting earlier that morning, Harris resolved not to let Helen Jackson do the same this time.

'I mean,' said the inspector, 'the last time we worked together, Ged, I seem to recall that you were only too keen to ask for my help. Call me an old romantic but I had rather hoped that such a situation might be reciprocated. Seemingly not.'

'Your help *was* much appreciated, Hawk,' said Maynard earnestly. 'It really was. We made a good team.'

'Even,' said Jackson, 'if some of your methods were a little, how shall we say it in light of subsequent events, Inspector? Unorthodox? I seem to recall that there was…'

'I am not sure that is relevant here,' said Harris. He fished out of his pocket the fax sent to Curtis. 'Besides, my methods are not as unorthodox as yours because, reading between the lines, it would seem that Trevor Meredith was working for you. An informant perhaps?'

'That's not true,' said Jackson quickly.

'But clearly he was involved with you in some way or else you would not have sent your fax, a touch late since the poor man is dead.'

'The situation was such that we did not deem it your business before the unfortunate events of yesterday,' said Jackson, meeting his gaze across the table.

Harris surveyed Helen Jackson for a few moments. Although her appearance gave the impression of a somewhat matronly aunt, her clear blue eyes betrayed a sharper mind lurking behind the façade. Jack Harris decided that not only did he not like her, he did not trust her either. Abandoning his diplomatic stance, the detective chief inspector was not in the mood to conceal the fact.

'Not our business?' he said in a voice laced with disgust. 'Not our bloody business? You have someone doing dangerous undercover work in my patch and it's none of my sodding business?'

'He wasn't doing undercover work, Mr Harris. We must be clear about that – at no point was Trevor M...'

'Well, whatever he was doing, do you not think it would have been a good idea to let us know?' snapped the inspector.

'Look,' said Jackson, ignoring the detective's cold fury. 'I know that you worked very closely with Ged but might I remind you that the lines of responsibility in these cases are very clearly delineated. These kinds of investigations are the responsibility of the RSPCA, not the police, as I am sure you are well aware.'

'Well, it's my responsibility now, Miss Jackson.'

'Which is why we sent our fax. His death is indeed regrettable, Chief Inspector, but this has been a very complicated inquiry and I am sure you understand...'

'I am sick of this,' said Harris, glaring across the table at her, his voice hard. 'I want to know absolutely everything about Trevor Meredith. Do you hear me?'

'I would not want you to go away from here with the impression that we do not want to help. However...'

'If you try to conceal anything, so help me, I'll charge the both of you with perverting the course of justice,' said the inspector.

Butterfield watched in fascination at the effect the inspector's words had on the RSPCA officers; she loved watching Jack Harris play hardball. Helen Jackson looked shocked, she obviously had not been expecting such a turn of events. Ged Maynard, for his part, stared at his colleague – Butterfield would later describe the expression as beseeching when recounting the event to a fascinated Matty Gallagher – and for a few moments, no one spoke.

Eventually, Jackson gave a shrug and stared out of the window.

'Have it your way,' she said, 'but I have to say that I do not appreciate your methods, Inspector.'

'Look,' said Harris, softening his attitude, 'I don't want this to turn into a slanging match. I know what an important job you and your officers do.'

Jackson looked at him, trying to assess if the inspector was just uttering platitudes, but, deciding within a few moments that he was genuine, her own attitude softened a little.

'Thank you for that,' she said. 'I am sorry that we seem to have got off on the wrong foot. The death of Trevor Meredith has come as a terrible shock to all of us. If we're honest, he was a big problem for us, a real loose cannon. This is exactly what we were frightened would happen.'

'Go on.'

Jackson glanced at Maynard.

'He approached us several weeks ago,' said Maynard. 'Out of the blue. Said he had heard rumours of dog fights being planned for his area and asked whether we would investigate it.'

'And you said?'

'We said yes, of course. We knew that things had become too hot in Manchester and that for some time the dog-fighters had been looking for somewhere else. I don't know if you heard but since you left Manchester there have been several other prosecutions in the city.'

'I did hear,' nodded Harris, 'but you only landed the small fry, I think? Not Gerry Radford, for example.'

'Why do you mention him of all people?' asked Jackson sharply.

'There are some things we like to keep confidential in situations like this,' replied Harris, with the slightest of winks at Butterfield. 'Suffice to say we believe that they were in touch with each other.'

'They should not have been,' said Maynard unhappily. 'We told Trevor it was a dangerous idea. You have to believe me, we really did tell him not to go ahead with it.'

'Go ahead with what?'

'Meredith said he was going to infiltrate Radford's gang.'

'Why on earth would he do that?'

'Said he was disgusted at what was going on.'

'And you said?'

'Said to leave it with us. Things went quiet for a few days then he rang up again, said there was a planned dog fight at Jenner's Farm. Said he was stringing Radford along, had even provided one of the dogs for him.'

'And you let him get in that deep?' exclaimed Harris, his tone of voice one of disbelief. 'You let a civilian get tied up with a psycho like Gerry Radford?'

'Like I said, we tried to persuade him not to.'

Harris looked at him over the table.

'How hard did you try, Ged?' he asked softly. 'How hard?'

Maynard did not reply for a moment or two then he turned dark eyes on the detectives.

'That day in court was one of the most dispiriting of my career,' he said quietly. 'To watch the bastard walk free with a smirk on his face.'

It had been a sensational trial which had run in Manchester Crown Court for three weeks, the jury having heard many hours of evidence against five men charged with organising the dog fight in the warehouse in the east of the city. Much of the evidence about the injuries to the dogs had been deeply upsetting and a number of the jurors had been in tears when shown some of the photographs. The trial had revealed evidence that the event was not an isolated incident, that there was reason to believe that a wide network of criminals from across the North had been regularly attending dog fights at which they wagered large sums of money on the winners. The media had revelled in it and news outlets both local and national had given the case a high prominence, not least because of the involvement of one of Manchester's best known gangland figures.

For his part, Gerry Radford had sat and listened to the evidence day after day with an impassive look on his face, even when Jack Harris took the stand. Radford's lawyer had done everything possible to blacken the inspector's name and there had been a number of heated confrontations during the three hours that Harris gave testimony. Many onlookers felt that the inspector had come off second best: Jack Harris had lost his temper on more than one occasion. Ged Maynard had been subjected to similar treatment by the defence barristers and had come over as anxious and unsure of his testimony. Both men emerged from the experience with their hatred of Gerry Radford intensified.

So, as the final day began, and the jury filed back in after deliberating overnight, everyone in court knew that Gerry Radford would be walking free. Harris and Maynard, sitting next to each other, feared the worst: they knew that the RSPCA had presented enough evidence to secure a conviction against four of the men but the outcome for the big prize, Radford, was more uncertain. The prosecution case against him been further weakened when a number of key witnesses, men within Radford's circle, had failed to attend court to testify. Radford himself had said from the witness box that he did not realise the nature of the gathering and had been horrified when he discovered what was happening. Despite searches by Harris and his team, it had proved impossible to track down the missing witnesses to contradict the story. The men had remained absent from their usual haunts and the rumour was that they had left the city until the trial had ended. Eventually, the prosecuting barrister had to admit to the judge that it was unlikely that they would attend.

As the jury took their seats, not meeting the eyes of the men in the dock, Gerry Radford glanced to his right and saw Jack Harris and Ged Maynard in the gallery. Seeing their glum expressions, he winked at them.

'Members of the jury,' said the judge, 'have you come to your verdicts?'

'We have, your Honour,' said the foreman, a young man, as he stood up.

'Very well, how do you find in the case against Gerald Alexander Radford?'

Radford glanced up at the public gallery where many of his acolytes were crowded in, watching proceedings. He gave them the thumbs-up sign.

'Not guilty, your Honour.'

The gallery erupted into raucous cheers and Ged Maynard closed his eyes and rested his head on the wall behind him. Jack Harris glared at the celebrating Radford as the court ushers tried to restore order.

'After that happened,' said Maynard quietly, 'I determined to do everything within my powers to get a conviction against Gerry Radford. Someone has to bring the guy to book, Hawk, whatever it takes. And sometimes you have to cut corners, you of all people know that.'

Glancing at her boss, Butterfield wondered, and not for the first time, what secrets her superior officer had to hide.

'Granted,' said Harris, 'but that does not include allowing an innocent, and one has to say, a somewhat naïve man, to place his life in danger.'

'I wouldn't be so quick in assuming he was innocent or naïve. Trevor Meredith clearly knew the risks.' Maynard looked puzzled. 'I don't know why but I kind of got the impression that he had done something like this before. And he did come to us, remember, it wasn't as if we took some guy off the street.'

'Yes, but…'

'And what he said made perfect sense,' continued Maynard. 'We have disrupted several fights across the North in the past year – a couple in Cheshire, one in Liverpool and one in Bolton – and we suspected that the organisers had started looking for somewhere where the people were… how can I put it…?'

'Yokels?' asked Harris acerbically.

'No, no, I would not say that, although they clearly did feel that a remote rural setting might allow them to carry out their events unnoticed, that the law enforcement might be… less vigilant.'

'They must be stupid then,' snorted Harris. 'You can't fart in Levton Bridge without someone knowing about it.'

'And yet you had no idea that Trevor Meredith had approached us.'

Harris did not reply at first, acutely aware that news of the poker ring at the King's Head has also been unknown to him. Inwardly, he cursed himself. What was it he always said to his officers? 'This place breeds complacency,' he would say. 'Do not fall into its trap.' The words sounded somewhat hollow now as he looked across the table at his friend. Noticing that everyone else was watching, and sensing that they were waiting for him to speak, he resolved to save what face he could in the circumstances.

'Well, for what's it worth,' said Harris, conscious that, for the second time that day, a meeting was not going the way he had planned, 'I already knew all about the plan for Jenner's Farm.'

'Only because our local chap told you,' said Maynard, 'and he only knew because Trevor Meredith told him.'

Harris scowled.

'And I hate to say it,' said Maynard, 'but we think that your presence in Levton Bridge might have been an added attraction for Gerry Radford. I think he rather liked the idea of staging a fight right under your nose. Your rather strident public comments on the subject down the years made such a prospect almost irresistible for him, I would suggest.'

Harris lapsed into moody silence and Butterfield saw her opportunity to make a mark on proceedings.

'What did you actually know about Meredith?' she asked, glancing at Jackson, wondering if the female connection would ease the tension in the room.

It didn't.

'Not much,' said Jackson. 'Trevor Meredith was less than forthcoming when it came to personal matters.'

'I'm not sure I believe this,' exclaimed Harris. 'When we get a new informant, you can't move for sodding paperwork yet you knew nothing about your guy?'

'Please get this clear in your mind,' said Jackson quickly. 'Trevor Meredith was not an informant, there was no official agreement, nothing at all. There is no paper trail.'

'But you clearly did not object to him doing some freelance investigation on his own?'

'Ok,' she sighed, 'Ok, we should have done more to dissuade him from getting involved. There will be an internal inquiry into what happened and I can assure you that we will take whatever action is required. Lessons will be learnt, of that you can be certain.'

She glanced at Maynard, who returned the gaze uneasily. Jack Harris sat back and crossed his arms, a look of satisfaction on his face: even though he realised that Ged Maynard was in trouble, what really mattered to the detective was that the meeting was swinging back his way.

Which is when it swung back.

'I imagine that the inquiry will be similar,' said Jackson blandly, 'to the internal police investigation into the two farmers who damn near got themselves killed in your area last night. I thought the police were supposed to keep such – what was your phrase, Chief Inspector, innocent and somewhat naïve? – men from getting into trouble.'

The satisfied expression was wiped off the detective's face.

'We all have our loose cannons, Chief Inspector,' said Jackson with a slight smile. 'It's just that yours got lucky.'

'Listen,' said Maynard, leaning forward, eager to avoid another ugly exchange of views, 'what has happened has happened. We should have kept you in the loop and now we want to help your murder inquiry, share what we know.'

'Does that include anything about David Bowes?'

The RSPCA officers looked at him blankly.

'What about James Thornycroft then?'

'What do you know about him?' asked Jackson sharply.

'Ah, that kind of sharing,' murmured the inspector. 'Well, for your information, our colleagues in Bolton were called to a break-in at his surgery at the end of last year. They suspect he faked the burglary to obtain the insurance money. The practice was not doing particularly well financially. They could not prove anything so he was never charged. They think that is why he moved to Levton Bridge. Bolton had his card marked. How come he is of interest to you?'

'We had always known that there was a vet treating dogs injured in the fights,' said Maynard. 'There were reports of several being patched up and a couple being put down. Then, after we broke up a ring in Bolton, we heard that it might be someone from the town. We narrowed it down to James Thornycroft.'

'Yes, but why on earth would he do that?' asked Butterfield. 'He's not the most likeable of human beings but the man is a vet, for God's sake.'

'And Harold Shipman was a doctor,' said Maynard.

Butterfield looked across at Harris, who shrugged and said, 'I take it you confronted him with what you knew, Ged?'

'Yes. I told him that if he co-operated with us, we would keep his name out of it, but he refused. If you ask me, he was more frightened of Gerry Radford.'

'Who wouldn't be? In fact...' The inspector's voice tailed off and he looked at the RSPCA officers with an appalled look. 'Hang on, is there a chance that James Thornycroft could have worked out that Meredith was feeding you information?'

'Why,' said Helen Jackson with a wan look on her face, 'do you think you are here?'

Chapter fourteen

It was just after 10am when, still wearing his pyjamas, James Thornycroft made his way slowly down the stairs to discover that he was alone in the house, his wife having long since left for work. He recalled vaguely that she had tried to rouse him before she left but he had grunted and rolled over in bed. Now, he paused on the landing and stared at his haggard reflection in the oval mirror, wincing as he did so, partly from what he saw and partly because of the jagged pain in his head. Moving in a laboured fashion, Thornycroft headed down the stairs. The couple had only recently moved into the semi-detached house on the new estate in Levton Bridge and had still not managed to unpack all the boxes and, as he walked down the hallway towards the kitchen, he stumbled over one of them, stubbing his toe and swearing loudly.

Hopping into the kitchen, he sat down and examined his foot. As he leaned over, another sharp pain from his head reminded him of the previous night's excesses. Thornycroft made for the sink and ran himself a large glass of water, which he downed in one go. He refilled it then reached into a cupboard for a packet of Aspirin, of which he swallowed two.

'You're a damned fool, James Thornycroft,' he groaned. 'Always have been.'

He sat back down at the kitchen table and turned hooded eyes on the empty wine bottle standing on the sink drainer. Had his wife seen it? Surely, she must have. His mind went back to the events of the previous evening. After leaving the surgery shortly after nine-thirty, he had not felt the desire to go home and face another row with his wife or have to answer her endless questions about the parlous state of their finances. With the wounds of their life in Bolton still raw, Gaynor Thornycroft had turned her anger on her husband on numerous occasions over recent weeks and there had been constant shouting matches. To avoid another one, Thornycroft had bought a bottle of wine from an off-licence near the surgery and had driven around for the best part of an hour and a half before going home.

When Thornycroft arrived home, the house had been in darkness, as he had guessed it would be – his wife always turned in early – so he had sat and downed the entire contents of the bottle. As he sat in the semi-lit living room, his mind had been in turmoil but, as he sat and drank and thought, he had resolved not to do what he had done in Bolton. No, this time he would stay, would face whatever was coming. There would be no running this time. Besides, where was there to run? Into the arms of Gerry Radford and his accomplices? Or the RSPCA and that Maynard fellow who seemed determined to link him to the dog fights? Thornycroft knew co-operating with law enforcement was not an option: he knew that he would not cope well with prison, certainly not given Radford's connections in the inside, but he was even more frightened of the gangster's connections on the outside should word of his involvement leak out. After all, look at what happened to Trevor Meredith, he had reminded himself. Not that he needed reminding. Thornycroft had felt a sudden stab of guilt, knew that he would have to live with

Meredith's death on his conscience until he breathed his last. Eventually, after drinking far too much, he had gone to bed where he lay in the darkness, mind still turning things over and over, until he finally drifted off into a disturbed sleep.

Now, he sat in his kitchen and stared out of the window, oblivious to the bright summer sunshine which had bathed his back garden in golden light. He had been sitting there for ten minutes, sipping his water and wishing that his head would stop throbbing, when the phone rang. Still moving slowly, he walked into the hallway and picked up the receiver.

'Mr Thornycroft?' said a voice.

'Hello, Janice.'

'I am sorry to ring you – I know your wife said you were ill – but Mrs Burns wants to rearrange her appointment and she is most insistent.'

'Tell the old bag to sod off.'

There was a silence at the other end of the phone.

'Tomorrow,' said James Thornycroft. 'Tell her I will be back tomorrow.'

He replaced the receiver and walked back into the kitchen. No running, not this time. Even if it was true that a man could never forget his past, he could at least destroy the evidence that it had ever existed. Thank God for the delete button, thought James Thornycroft. Filled with a fresh purpose, he made himself a cup of strong black coffee and walked upstairs, where he brought down the ladder leading to the loft. Climbing into the darkness, he fumbled for the pull-string to turn on the light. Once he could see where he was going, he walked over to reach behind the water pipes and produce a large box. Opening the lid, Thornycroft brought out a laptop computer and took it down the ladder and into his study in the spare room.

Once the machine had booted up, he searched through his images folder for several moments then pulled up a picture depicting a group of men standing in two rows in front of a veranda, on the edge of jungle. Among the black faces were several white men and, thoughtfully, James Thornycroft stared at his younger self standing next to a bearded Trevor Meredith.

'I tried to warn you, Robert,' he sighed.

Finger hovering over the delete button, Thornycroft hesitated, then, with sudden resolve, pressed down. He opened other files, revealing different images, and started to delete them from the hard drive; stomach-churning images of horribly injured dogs, grainy pictures shot in the half-light of deserted old warehouses and sheds, images of men exulting in the triumph of their combatants and the suffering of the defeated, pictures which would send James Thornycroft to prison if they fell into the wrong hands. Or see him face down in a ditch if Gerry Radford and his acolytes realised that he still had them. Until now, they had been his insurance policy; now, after what had happened to Meredith, they felt more like a death sentence.

'Should have done this a long time ago,' he said as he watched the pictures being swallowed up.

An hour and a half later, the computer was still deleting the files when the front door bell rang.

* * *

As Jack Harris and Alison Butterfield emerged from the RSPCA meeting shortly before noon, the inspector was already on the mobile phone, talking to his detective inspector back at Levton Bridge Police Station.

'How you getting on, Gillian?' he asked.

'Making decent progress,' said the DI's voice. 'We've already talked to a couple of the names on the poker list – the guy who runs the corner shop in Eden Street and that young trainee accountant at the council offices.'

'Anything useful?' asked the inspector as he and Butterfield started walking down the terraced street towards the direction of the town centre.

'They had been waiting for us to turn up. They were really worried; I thought the accountant was going to collapse. Had to get him a glass of water.' Roberts chuckled. 'Old woman.'

'But did they say anything of use?'

'Confirmed your chap's story really. There has certainly been tension over the money being lost. I reckon it got totally out of hand.'

'Which is why we are going to stop it. Did you get anywhere with checks into this chap Bowes?'

'No one seems to know much about him. What's more – and this is a bit funny – I did all the usual checks but can't find any record of him. Odd really, it's like he never existed before he came here.'

'Just like Trevor Meredith,' said Harris, pointing Butterfield in the direction of an alleyway that cut through into Roxham's main shopping street.

'Maybe so, but I'm still not convinced that any of them would kill over a game of cards, guv,' said Roberts.

'I just want to eliminate people, Gillian. Talking of eliminating people, did you come up with anything on Jane Porter?'

'A totally unspectacular woman, guv. Been at the sanctuary for years, no criminal record, no soft intelligence. Unmarried, no skeletons that we can find. Another non-person really.'

'No one is a non-person,' said the DCI, looking over at Butterfield. 'There you are, Constable, your second lesson today from the Book of Jack Harris.'

'You doing your father figure thing again?' said Roberts.

'Something like that. I know you are busy but will you do me a favour?'

'Sure.'

'I know I asked you to leave the Thornycroft interview for us but from what the RSPCA have just said, he was in deeper than we thought,' said the inspector as the detectives emerged onto the shopping street. 'Seems like he might have some distinctly unpleasant little friends. Can you make up some spurious excuse and go and see if he is ok?'

'He in danger?'

'They got to Trevor Meredith.'

'Ok, I'll look in on him,' said Roberts. 'What you going to do?'

'Get some breakfast.'

'Ah, the pressures of life at the top,' said Roberts.

* * *

As he walked down the hallway, James Thornycroft felt his heart pounding. Trying desperately to make out the figure through the frosted glass of the front door, he hesitated, wondering whether or not to turn and escape out of the back of the house.

'Pull yourself together, you daft bastard,' he murmured. 'It's probably only the gas man.'

Partially reassured by the thought, he opened the front door.

'What the…?' he exclaimed as a fist snapped out and caught him full on the face.

Staggering backwards, and before he could react further, Thornycroft was pushed violently into the hallway, his knees buckling as he collided with the telephone stand. As the intruder slammed the door and walked towards his victim, James Thornycroft instinctively threw up an arm to protect himself. He was too late: the man's boot slammed into his gut, knocking the wind out of the vet. Gasping for breath, Thornycroft sprawled across the floor.

'Please God, no!' he cried. 'I did as you said.'

'Gerry reckons you been talking too much to the police.'

With a cry, Thornycroft struggled to his feet and turned to run into the living room. As he did, he stumbled over the cardboard box again, fell forward and hit his head against the edge of the doorframe.

The intruder stared down at his lifeless body.

'Shit,' he said.

Chapter fifteen

Harris and Butterfield sat in the greasy spoon café in a side street off Roxham's main shopping drag, cradling mugs of tea and looking across the table at Matty Gallagher.

'You ordered?' asked Harris.

'Yeah, got the usual,' nodded the sergeant who then looked at the inspector with a worried expression on his face. 'Look, level with me, will you, guv? How much trouble am I in over this Farmwatch thing?'

'Curtis was not desperately impressed – with either of us.'

Gallagher nodded glumly.

'So, what do I do?' he asked.

'You? You keep your head down. The only real problem will come if Curtis decides that this is a way of getting me out.'

'Surely it's not that bad? Not after last Friday? I mean, all that good publicity.'

'Who knows what goes on in the addled brain of Philip Curtis?' shrugged the inspector. 'If he reckons that he has to sacrifice someone for the sake of his career he's capable of doing anything. One thing is for sure, if either of the lads had been killed last night, you and me would be doing school crossing patrol now.'

'Whatever happens,' said Gallagher, 'thank you for trying.'

'No problem.' Harris reached out and lightly touched his sergeant's hand. 'I can't afford to lose good officers even if they are Cockney wide-boys. Anyway, enough of this sentimental shite – tell me about the PM. I take it that Trevor Meredith did not fall on his knife?'

'Certainly didn't,' said Gallagher, relieved that the conversation had moved on; despite his desire to get to know his chief inspector better it always felt uncomfortable when it happened.

'So, what did the good doctor say? Was he able to manage without the expert guidance of young Butterfield here?'

Gallagher chuckled; Butterfield looked gloomily at the chief inspector.

'Reckons the knife had a serrated edge. Thinks it might be a kitchen knife of some kind.' The sergeant glanced under the table to where Scoot was sitting. 'Hardly the kind of thing you would take with you when out walking the dog.'

'Indeed not,' said Harris. 'So, have we got a time of death?'

'Best he can say is mid to late morning yesterday. You were right, the doc says that it is possible that he lived for up to half an hour after the attack. Bled out, the poor bastard. The doc says that the fact that it was cold and wet makes it difficult to be more precise about these things, though.'

'That fits with what we know anyway.' Harris took a sip of his tea and looked at the detectives. 'Not that we know much, mind. However, it does all rather point away from your roving lunatic theory, Matty lad, and towards my hunch that this was a premeditated murder.'

'Maybe,' said Gallagher.

Butterfield's mobile phone rang and she excused herself and went to stand in the doorway. Within a couple of minutes, she was back just as three cooked breakfasts were being delivered to the table.

'So, come on, where are we with all of this?' asked Harris, reaching for the ketchup bottle as the constable took her seat again. 'Is any of this making sense?'

'Not yet,' said Gallagher, through a mouth full of bacon.

'Then maybe I can help,' said Butterfield, picking up her cutlery. 'That call was a friend of mine. Anyone want my black pudding?'

Gallagher reached over.

'So, who is this friend?' asked Harris.

'He runs the vets down in Ramsay, it's the one my dad uses. My friend says that customers had been deserting Thornycroft's place in droves. Not exactly Mr Popular was James Thornycroft. What's more, my friend reckons that his business was in deep trouble.'

'And men in deep trouble,' said Harris, 'will do anything to get out of it.'

'Exactly,' said Butterfield.

* * *

It did not take Gillian Roberts long to drive the short distance to the housing estate on which James Thornycroft lived. She was thoroughly enjoying herself. The previous day, when she had been on a training course at headquarters in Carlisle, she had listened with mounting frustration to the bulletins coming through about the death of Trevor Meredith, desperate to be involved. She had protested when Curtis had informed her the previous week that she had to attend the event and saw the murder of Trevor Meredith as the ideal get-out clause. However, her arguments that she was needed back at Levton Bridge were rebuffed by the fresh-faced instructor; a sulking Roberts guessed he was one of those fast-track university types who had never even done a foot patrol in his life. At one point, he had even suggested that she was 'poisoning the banquet' with her continuous objections. Roberts had given a derisory snort.

The residential course was supposed to run into a second day but that morning, she had got up early and rung Harris, pleading to be released. Harris, who had little time for such activities anyway and had protested when Curtis informed him that he was losing his detective inspector for two days, had readily sanctioned her departure. Roberts had taken great delight in telling the young instructor where he could stick his course. Now, as she cut the Renault's engine outside the detached house, Gillian Roberts was delighted to be involved in the case at last. A mother-of-two in her early fifties, she affected a somewhat matronly demeanour but behind the avuncular façade was an officer as tough and sharp as they came, one who thrived on the challenges of the job. She had once said that having two teenage boys meant that everyday police crises paled into insignificance compared with the challenges presented by her offspring.

She got out of the car and looked at the house. Which was when she noticed that the front door was ajar.

* * *

'So, what was Thornycroft doing wrong?' asked Gallagher, chasing a piece of fried bread round the plate. 'How come he was losing all those punters?'

'Well,' said Butterfield, 'the first thing he did when he took over was push up his prices and put a lid on all the free little jobs that the previous guy did. That's why he and Meredith fell out, if you recall.'

The others nodded.

'What also pissed people off,' continued the constable, 'and this will be no surprise to you, guv, is that people simply don't like James Thornycroft.'

Gallagher looked at her quizzically.

'Thornycroft called him Hawk,' explained Butterfield.

The sergeant winced.

'Ouch,' he said.

'Not everyone dislikes him, though,' said the inspector, taking a sip of tea. 'Curtis thinks the sun shines out of his backside.'

'That's part of the problem,' said Butterfield.

'Curtis is *all* of the problem, Constable,' said the inspector. 'If I teach you nothing, let me teach you that.'

Gallagher laughed out loud.

'What I mean,' said Butterfield with a smile, 'is that Thornycroft gives the impression that he is something special, kow-tows to people he thinks are influential but makes no effort with ordinary folks.'

'Oooh,' said Gallagher with a sly look at the others, 'airs and graces. That's enough to get a man killed oop North.'

Harris scowled. Gallagher chuckled and shovelled scrambled egg into his mouth.

As they talked, none of the detectives noticed the young woman walking quickly past the window, the tears streaming down her cheeks. Or the man who followed a few seconds later.

* * *

Feeling her heart pounding, Gillian Roberts walked up the drive towards the front door of James Thornycroft's house. Instincts screaming out that something was wrong, she wondered whether or not to call for back-up and wait for its arrival before entering the property. With a shake of the head, she dismissed the idea and pushed open the door.

'Mr Thornycroft?' she shouted into the deserted hallway. 'Are you ok, Mr Thornycroft?'

* * *

'However,' said Harris, taking a gulp of tea, 'for all that James Thornycroft might be a dodgy so-and-so, none of this makes him a killer, surely?'

'I hate to agree but I can't see it either,' said Butterfield, reaching for a piece of toast. 'I still reckon that if we find the lads who shot at the farmers then we will be pretty damned close to who killed Trevor Meredith.'

'Which brings us back to the dog fighting,' said Harris.

'Or guys casing out farms to nick stuff,' said Gallagher.

'More likely, given their reaction, that they were friends of Gerry Radford,' said Harris. 'Maybe they were up here casing out Jenner's Farm. The farmers were parked on Jenner's land, remember. Maybe Trevor Meredith set something up after all.'

'They certainly didn't mess around when the Farmwatch lads clocked them,' said Matty Gallagher, hitting the bottom of the ketchup bottle and dropping a ridiculously large dollop onto the remains of his meal. 'Damn it, why does that always happen?'

The others chuckled and watched in silent fascination for a few moments as he tried to extricate his food from the morass.

'Bloody southerners,' said Harris.

* * *

Gillian Roberts stood in the living room and stared down at the motionless man lying in front of her, one leg twisted behind his body, an arm hanging limp and his features battered and bloodied.

'Shit,' she muttered. 'Shit, shit, shit.'

* * *

'So,' said Gallagher, wiping round his plate with a piece of bread, 'if you are right, guv, might it not be time to pay a visit to your Mister Radford?'

'Already in hand,' said the inspector enigmatically. 'Already in hand, Matty lad. Just got to play a bit of politics, first.'

'Brilliant,' breathed Butterfield, eyes bright. 'Absolutely bloody brilliant.'

'Does that mean…?' began Gallagher.

'All in good time. Come on,' said Harris, draining the last of his tea and getting to his feet, 'let's get back up to Levton Bridge.'

Gallagher frowned, the inspector's refusal to elaborate on his thoughts had served as a reminder that, despite what appeared to be recent warming in the men's relationship, Jack Harris remained as secretive and infuriating as ever.

'Right,' said Harris. 'Matty, I want you to go back to the station…'

'Do I have to?' asked the sergeant. 'I was rather hoping to stay down here. Curtis will be absolutely…'

'If Curtis cuts up funny, tell him to talk to me.'

'And where exactly will you be if Curtis goes on one of his rampages?' asked the sergeant, adding acerbically, 'not struggling with phone reception again, I hope?'

'The mobile is always on for you,' said Harris, producing a wallet from his suit jacket pocket and placing a twenty pound note on the table. 'My treat, boys and girls.'

'So where will you be while Curtis is chewing my ass out?' asked Gallagher, following Harris towards the door.

'Myself and the good constable here will check out this David Bowes character – his cottage is just off the main road on the way back. Then we will pay a visit to James Thornycroft.'

As the officers emerged into the street, the inspector's mobile phone rang. Taking it out of his suit jacket pocket, Harris glanced down at the screen.

'Curtis?' asked Gallagher, shooting an anxious expression at Butterfield.

'Hiya,' said Harris into the phone. 'How's it hanging?'

'Not Curtis,' said Gallagher cheerfully.

'Still at Roxham,' said Harris into the phone. 'Yeah, can be. Alright, see you then – oh, and thanks, matey. I owe you one. A big one.'

'Definitely not Curtis,' said Gallagher.

The inspector finished the call and turned to the others with a beam on his face. He was about to speak when the phone rang again.

'Jesus Christ, it's like Piccadilly Circus,' exclaimed the DCI. 'Hello, yes, Harris.'

This time, his expression was different, a grim silence as he listened to the person on the other end.

'Curtis,' said Gallagher gloomily. 'Got to be.'

After a few grunts, the inspector pressed the cancel button.

'What's wrong?' asked Butterfield.

'That was Gillian. I am afraid that our little chat with James Thornycroft will have to wait.'

Chapter sixteen

Shortly after lunchtime, Matty Gallagher was standing in Roxham General Hospital, staring moodily out of the fourth-floor window, across the roofs of the houses to where, when the buildings petered out, the farming flatlands began, stretching away into the distance. The sergeant gave a deep sigh as he watched a mainline train gathering pace, heading south out of Roxham station. He liked south. London was south. Everything he knew and loved was south.

The decision to move north had been the toughest one of his life. The reason for the decision was Julie, the bubbly blonde he had met when both of them were working in London. Gallagher was a detective constable at the time, Julie a nurse, and it did not take long for love to blossom. However, Julie had been born in Levton Bridge and her parents still lived in the area, so it was no surprise to the sergeant when she announced one day that she wanted to apply for a transfer to Roxham General Hospital. He had always known that one day she might want to go home.

The thought of leaving the city appalled Matty Gallagher. As he had gloomily told friends before he left, it was a long way to be able to hear the sound of Bow Bells. However, after deliberating for several days, he put his love for Julie before his love for the bright lights of the capital and, with heavy heart, applied for a transfer, securing a posting to Levton Bridge. Shortly after their move north, the couple had married. For a few weeks, they had lived in a rented house in Levton Bridge until one day, and to Gallagher's immense relief, Julie announced that she had forgotten how claustrophobic the town was. The couple moved an hour's drive down the valley to Roxham, buying a house close to the town centre.

The move had improved things slightly for the sergeant and now, as he glanced down towards the nearby town centre, he resolved, as he always did, to make the best of things, if only for Julie's sake. Roxham might not be much of a place, thought Gallagher as he looked out across the roofs, still glistening with the rain from the night before, but it had a damned site more life than Levton Bridge. Besides, Roxham did have one big attraction and he was watching it disappear from view. Roxham stood on the West Coast railway line, which allowed Matty to get to London in a few hours if he wished to see his family or hook up with friends. Julie never demurred when he took off; she realised that drinking sessions in old haunts were his way of coping with life in the North.

'Penny for your thoughts?' said Harris, walking up behind him and handing over a plastic cup of coffee from the machine.

'Oh, you know… just thinking.'

'Seen the train again?'

'Am I that transparent?' said Gallagher with a rueful smile.

'I want you to stay, you know.'

'Yeah, I know. Don't think I don't appreciate it, guv. Besides, I know I can't change things. Julie is determined to stay up here. I've even toyed with the thought of a transfer to the local nick.' He gestured out of the window towards the nearby communications mast. 'Be easier, we live ten minutes' walk away and Julie works here anyway.'

'I know, and the people here don't get nosebleeds when they get on a train,' said Harris slyly. 'But why transfer? If you're stuck with us woolly-backs you might as well stay at Levton Bridge.'

'Yeah, I know, but Roxham has a bit more happening.'

'Fourteen thousand, four hundred and eighteen,' said Harris.

'What?'

'That's how many people it has. It's hardly a thriving metropolis, Matty lad, and last time I checked we had more murders in our division than they had in theirs.'

'Yeah, I know but...' The sergeant's voice tailed off.

'Besides, you'd hate it down here,' said Harris. 'Take the DI. The man's a complete plonker. We had him at Levton Bridge for a while, you know. Before we got Gillian. I taught him everything he knows. Trouble is, he forgot it all once he got his feet under the desk down here.'

Gallagher smiled.

'And the DCI?' Harris grinned, thoroughly enjoying himself as he warmed to his theme. 'Jesus, don't get me started on Douggie Ramsbottom.'

Gallagher chuckled.

'And as for the divisional commander,' said Harris. 'Think Curtis without the friendly bedside manner.'

Gallagher roared with laughter then, the inspector's rant over, both men lapsed into silence and, seeing the train finally disappear from view, the sergeant felt a sudden urge to change the subject: there was still something uncomfortable about discussing personal matters with Jack Harris.

'Thanks for the coffee,' said the sergeant, looking down at the murky brown liquid and grimacing. 'I assume it is coffee?'

'I'll have it if you don't want it.'

'Why?' asked the sergeant, glancing at the cup in the inspector's hand.

'There's a nasty spot of rust on the Land Rover I want to get rid of.'

Gallagher marvelled at the comment: it seemed that the inspector's uncharacteristically good mood of recent days was holding despite what had been happening. Matty Gallagher wondered why. He knew that the inspector had been delighted with the outcome of the crown court case the previous week but they'd had good results before and he had not responded so cheerfully to them. No, thought Gallagher, staring out of the window again as Harris sipped his coffee, there had to be something else. Something, as ever, that Jack Harris was not telling him. Gallagher decided not to ask.

'Any news on Thornycroft?' he said instead.

'They're still operating but it's touch and go. Fractured skull. I had a quick word with wifey. Reading between the lines, their marriage was in trouble over his money problems. Sounds like the man's life was falling down around his ears.'

'Do we assume that means he was susceptible to getting into things he should have avoided?' asked Gallagher.

'Who knows? Wifey sounded like she did not care what he was doing. Sounds like they had been virtually leading separate lives for weeks.'

'Any word from the DI?'

'She's still at their house. She got young Wayne Howe to take a look at Thornycroft's computer.'

'What, looking for games, was he?' said Gallagher drily. 'That's all he does as far as I can see. You know, I walked past his office the other day and he was shooting aliens or something like that.'

'Well, his knowledge has come in useful this time,' said Harris, craning over as far as he could to watch an attractive blonde walking across the hospital car park. 'You know, Matty, sometimes I wish I were ten years younger.'

Gallagher leaned over as well.

'Dirty dog,' he said.

'Which reminds me, I have had to leave Scoot in the car. I'll have to nip out and see how he is soon. Anyway, according to young Wayne, it seems that James Thornycroft was deleting pictures of injured dogs at the time he was attacked. He's still ploughing through them but he says there are some real shockers.'

'Like you said, find the dog, find the killer.' Gallagher glanced at the inspector. 'You don't look so convinced now, though.'

'It all makes sense. It's just...' Harris frowned. 'I don't know, I can't shake this feeling that we are missing something. Something we saw yesterday but did not see, if you see what I mean.'

'Not really, guv. Too many sees.'

'Indeed,' said Harris, reaching into his jacket and producing a piece of paper. 'Anyway, for the moment our biggest concern is what links Meredith and Thornycroft with Gerry Radford. Our resident computer geek also turned up this from Thornycroft's computer.'

He handed it over to the sergeant.

'Our lot faxed a copy down to Roxham nick,' Harris gave a slight smile. 'It took Roxham a few minutes to work out what the strange buzzing noise was in the corner of the room but they got there in the end.'

'Now, now, they are my esteemed colleagues to be,' said Gallagher then glanced down at the fax. 'Wow, that's good stuff. Looks like I may have to revise my opinion of young Wayne.'

'And there's more where that came from,' said Harris, taking a sip of coffee and grimacing. 'Bye, that's bad stuff, Matty lad. As you can see, Thornycroft and Radford have been in regular contact via email. According to Wayne, they would have assumed that the link they were using was secure but he managed to get into it.'

'Do we know how?'

'I never ask questions like that. The result justifying the means and all that.'

'That one of Curtis's phrases?'

'Ah, no. No, I don't think so.'

'Well, however he did it, this gives a definite link between Thornycroft and this Radford bloke,' said Gallagher. 'Mind, we were lucky that it's the summer holidays. A few weeks earlier and young Wayne would have been in school.'

Harris chuckled.

'So,' said Gallagher, looking back at the fax, 'does this confirm that we reckon one of Radford's heavies did for Thornycroft?'

'Got to be a possibility.'

'Should I get back to the factory?' asked Gallagher, glancing at his watch. 'Sounds like there's plenty to do.'

'We have another little job to do before we go – and one that I would rather Curtis did not know about just yet.'

'Hang on, guv, I don't want to get involved in anything dodgy, particularly given what happened last night. I am not exactly going to be his favourite…'

'Look,' said Harris with an urgency that surprised the sergeant. 'I meant it when I said I do not want you to go. I know things can be a bit tame up here, but maybe I can give you the next best thing to London.'

'What do you mean?'

'I'll tell you in a minute but I have to be able to trust you,' said Harris. 'This case is heavier than either you or Butterfield realise and I do not want Curtis sticking his neb in until I am ready to tell him what is happening. One stupid comment from him and it could blow everything.'

'Bloody hell, guv,' said the sergeant, taken aback by the intensity of the inspector's comments, 'what on earth are you on about?'

'I'll tell you on the way,' said Harris enigmatically, starting to walk down the corridor. 'But first, Scoot will need a wee. Come on, there's some bushes next to where I parked.'

* * *

Butterfield and the two uniforms, a fresh-faced constable in his early twenties and a young blonde girl about the same age, arrived in Stonecliffe shortly before 2pm. The village was like so many of the others in the hills, set against sheer slopes which rose up from houses huddled round a bridge over a stream. It had no more than fifty slate-grey cottages crammed into just three streets, a pinprick on the main road which wound its way up the valley before breaking out into moorland.

'The letting agency reckoned David Bowes rents number twelve Front Street,' said Butterfield, glancing down at her notebook. 'Got a red door.'

'That must be it,' said the young man excitedly, pointing to a cottage in the middle of the terrace. 'Shall we raid it?'

'Well, we'll knock on the front door first,' said Butterfield, giving him an odd look.

'Sorry,' he said. 'Got carried away. This is my first murder inquiry.'

'No kidding.'

Approaching the cottage, the officers noticed that the curtains were closed and that there was a pint of milk on the step. Butterfield peered through the front window, trying to make out the shapes within, then turned her attention to the bottle of milk. She prised off the top.

'Fresh,' she said. 'If he's done a runner, he's not been gone long.'

She reached up and knocked on the door. The officers waited for a few moments but there was no sound within and no suggestion of movement.

'Check round the back will you?' she said to the young constable.

He nodded, jogged enthusiastically up to the end of the street and disappeared round the corner.

'He always like that?' asked Butterfield.

The young girl nodded ruefully.

'Put the blues and twos on for an out-of-date tax disc yesterday,' she said.

The two women stood in silence for a few moments then the young female constable looked shyly at Butterfield.

'What's he like?' she asked.

'Who? Bowes?'

'No, Jack Harris.'

'Why do you ask?' said Butterfield.

The girl hesitated.

'Go on, spit it out,' said Butterfield.

'I wondered if he would take me for CID in Levton Bridge? I've watched our CID at Roxham. I know what they do.'

'I shouldn't say that if you meet Harris,' said Butterfield. She looked the girl up and down. Slim, she thought, a nice figure, curves in the right place but not too many of them, nice face, good hair. Blonde hair. 'But yes, I'm sure he'd love to have you in his team.'

'Really?' The girl looked pleased.

'Yeah,' nodded Butterfield. 'You're just the type of officer he's looking for.'

The male constable reappeared at the end of the street.

'It's all locked up at the back,' he announced, jogging back towards them.

'So, what do we do now?' asked the girl.

'I'm not sure we can force entry without a warrant,' said Butterfield, acutely aware that they were looking at her to make the decision. 'We could ask the letting agency to bring a key up.'

A cottage door opened further down the terrace and a grey-haired woman emerged.

'You'll not find him,' she announced.

'What makes you say that?' asked Butterfield.

'Because this morning he put two bags into his car and drove off.'

'Could have been going on holiday.'

'No, he were definitely leaving.'

'How can you be so sure?' asked Butterfield.

The woman reached into her apron pocket.

'Because he said he was going to ring the letting agency and tell them he weren't going to live here no more.' She produced a key. 'Said something had come up and whether I would give them this when they sent someone up.'

'Excellent,' breathed Butterfield. 'Do you mind if we have it?'

'Be my guest.'

'Thank you. Tell me, what kind of a man was he?'

'Kept himself to himself. Nice enough, he'd talk to you if he passed you in the street. Didn't see him much, mind.'

'He's only been here three or four months, I think?'

'That would be right.'

'Did he tell you what he did for a living?'

'I'm sorry, dearie. I didn't really know much about him.'

'Well,' said Butterfield, taking the house key and turning back to the front door of the cottage, 'maybe it's time that he let us into some of his secrets then.'

Chapter seventeen

'Where exactly are we going?' asked Gallagher as he and Harris left the Land Rover, having locked Scoot back in the vehicle.

'You'll see.'

'Right man of mystery you are.'

'Yeah,' said Harris, 'it's why the women love me.'

Five minutes later, they were walking briskly through Roxham town centre, ignored by the few shoppers who were scurrying past.

'You need to know about Gerry Radford,' said Harris, eventually breaking his silence as they turned off into a deserted side street and were away from other people. 'You need to be under no illusions about who we are dealing with. He's major league. When I was a DI in Manchester, his fingers were all over everything. Drugs, firearms, armed robbery. You name it, Gerry Radford was involved.'

'That does not worry me. When I was in the Met…'

'Now how did I know you were going to say that?' said the inspector with a slight smile as they walked past neatly-kept terraced houses and an off-licence. 'I imagine that when you were with the Met, you had some dealings with the Ferris brothers and the Cavanaghs?'

Gallagher stopped walking and gazed at the inspector in astonishment.

'How do you know about…?'

'Like I have told you before,' said Harris, turning to face him, 'don't underestimate me.'

'Sorry.' Gallagher nodded, it was not the first time he had made the mistake.

'I thought mention of some old names would pique your interest,' said Harris as they started walking again. 'See, Gerry Radford counts the Ferris brothers among his closest associates and there is plenty of evidence to suggest that he has met the Cavanaghs on more than one occasion.'

'In which case, I'm impressed,' said the sergeant, falling into step with his boss. His voice exhibited the most enthusiasm that Harris had heard from his sergeant in weeks.

'Thought you would be.'

'The Ferris boys were the bane of our life down in the Met. So were the Cavanaghs, for that matter. Good old-fashioned villains. We got close a couple of times but…' Gallagher stopped and made a gesture with his hands. 'Poof, witnesses seemed to disappear into thin air. It was like investigating David Copperfield.'

Harris gave a low laugh as they turned into another side street.

'The last time I saw any of them,' continued Gallagher, 'was when there was a raid on a security box place. Got away with a million. We were sure that the Ferris brothers were behind it. Interesting case actually, turned out the place was run by a somewhat shady company from Nigeria. Thought for one moment the DI would send me out there, which would have been good, the furthest he had sent me before was Walthamst… What's wrong? Why are you looking at me like that?'

Harris had stopped walking again and was staring thoughtfully at the sergeant.

'Not sure. Something you said just then.' Harris started walking towards the end of the side street. 'It'll come to me.'

'So, where exactly are we going?' asked Gallagher, following him.

'Here,' said the inspector, pushing his way into a small pub on the corner. 'We're going here. See, I really do think that we will need a bit of help before we tackle Gerry Radford and his mates.'

It took Gallagher a few moments for his eyes to acclimatise themselves to the gloom but when they did, he saw that the dingy little pub was empty save for two people sitting in the corner.

'That's Leckie, isn't it?' he asked, recognising the tall, lean man with thinning black hair and a pronounced five o'clock shadow who was wearing a sharp black suit.

'Sure is,' beamed Harris.

'Who's the bit of skirt?' asked the sergeant as he approvingly surveyed the slim brunette sitting next to Leckie.

Aged, he reckoned, no more than mid-forties, she looked hopelessly out of place in the pub. Immaculately dressed in a pale blue matching jacket and skirt, she exuded class, her clothes expensive, her brown hair beautifully coiffeured, her make-up perfectly applied.

'Surely,' continued the sergeant, 'they haven't given Leckie a secretary?'

'That secretary, my dear boy,' said Harris with a smile, 'is Detective Chief Superintendent Annie Gorman, head of Greater Manchester's Organised Crime Unit, and if she heard you calling her a bit of a skirt she would personally rip off your head and shit down the hole.'

'Really? She doesn't exactly look the type.'

'I'll let you tell her that,' said Harris, grinning as the detectives approached the table and Leckie stood up. The

146

men shook hands. 'Graham, my boy, how the hell are you?'

'Fine, matey,' said Leckie, gesturing to Annie Gorman, who had remained seated and was eying the inspector with a knowing smile. 'I think you know the super?'

'Oh, aye,' said Harris and returned her smile. 'We know each other. Hello, Annie.'

'Hello, Hawk,' she said; the tone of voice was affectionate as she reached out a beautifully manicured hand, which the inspector gently kissed. The fingernails were painted black. 'Long time no see.'

The comment was loaded with meaning and, as he watched the encounter, Matty Gallagher found himself fascinated and wondering. Wondering if they… wondering if in a previous life Harris had… wondering whether or not… everyone had heard the stories about Jack Harris, but someone this classy? The sergeant shook his head to banish the thought.

'Drink?' he said instead.

Several minutes later, drinks started, pleasantries dispensed with, Annie Gorman looked at Gallagher.

'So, Sergeant,' she said, taking a sip of her glass of white wine, 'what's it like working with Jack Harris?'

The question caught Gallagher off guard.

'Oh, it's you know…' he said. 'It's ok.'

'I imagine it's a bit boring after the Met, though,' she said. 'In fact, a little bird tells me that you might fancy a change of scenery.'

'Now, now, Annie,' said Harris quickly, holding up a hand. 'No poaching.'

Gorman inclined her head slightly.

'Always worth a try, Jack, always worth a try,' she said. 'Ok, so you want to go after Gerry Radford?'

'Yeah, I do.'

'I hope this is not because of what…'

'No,' said Harris with a vigorous shake of the head. 'No, it's nothing to do with that. This is purely kosher,

Annie. We think he may be linked to a murder in our patch.'

'Leckie tells me it's the guy on the hills?'

'Not just him,' said Harris. 'We had another guy damn near killed this morning. Radford is linked to that one as well.'

'Evidence?'

'Take it from me, Annie, this has got his mitts all over it.'

'But have you got anything firm?' she asked.

'Well, nothing 100 per cent nailed on yet but I am pretty confident that we will be...'

'Same old Jack Harris,' said Gorman, with a twinkle in her eyes. 'Sure your man wasn't mauled to death by a flock of sheep? Hey, if you catch whoever did it, it would give a whole new meaning to sheepdog trials.'

Gallagher looked sharply at his inspector – he had seen people receive fearsome dressing downs for lesser slights, including himself when he first arrived, you never made that mistake twice – but on this occasion Harris did not sound offended.

'Now, now, Annie,' he said, 'no need to be like that. Besides, we're not some yokel police force in Levton Bridge, you know. We've already eliminated all the sheep from our inquiry. You should have seen the identity parade. People say they all look the same but they don't know what they are talking about.'

Gorman laughed.

'Ok,' she said, suddenly serious, 'if we do help you, and I am not saying we will – this is all very political, as I am sure you can imagine – then I take it you realise what you will be starting? Radford will turn up the heat and he will start by targeting you with the best lawyers he can find. He'll drag everything up again. All that bad history.'

'I know all that, Annie, but I really do need to eliminate him from our inquiry.'

'I appreciate that but do you not have any other angles to work first? I mean, I really will have to do some hard talking to get anyone to even think about your lot going after Radford. Particularly when I mention your name.'

'No,' said Harris with a shake of the head, 'this really is our only lead on this one. Honest.'

Gallagher looked at his boss but said nothing. Gorman thought for a few moments then nodded.

'Ok, Hawk,' she said, glancing towards the bar to make sure the barman could not hear, then leaning forward in conspiratorial fashion. Both Levton Bridge detectives got a whiff of expensive perfume. 'Maybe we *can* work together on this one. As it happens, we've got an op planned for the weekend. Can you wait that long?'

'I have been waiting years for Gerry Radford,' said Harris. 'I guess a few more days will not harm. What's the job?'

'The word is that Radford is bringing in something big – our informant says he is into high quality cocaine at the moment. He plans to pick a shipment up at a service station on the M6 on Saturday night. If I can get clearance from the woodentops, would you like to tag along?'

'Too bloody right, I would,' said Harris, eyes gleaming.

'You might like to bring your sergeant,' said Gorman, with a slight smile. 'You never know, Hawk, it might change his mind about joining us.'

Harris said nothing.

'Alright, I'll be in touch,' said Gorman, downing the rest of her glass of wine and standing up. She gave the detectives a hard look. 'Oh, and I don't want anyone else to know about this. It never fails to amaze me where Gerry Radford has friends. If I find out that word got out from your end, I will personally come back down here and kebab your fucking testicles.'

149

Then she and Leckie were gone, Gorman's heels clicking on the pub's wooden floor.

'Jesus,' said Gallagher with a shake of the head. 'That is one tough cookie. Mind, the idea of her kebbabing my knackers is not an entirely unpleasant one.'

There was silence for a moment.

'Go on,' said Harris, 'you are dying to ask me.'

'Yeah, I am. Did you and she… you know, get up to some kebabbing of your own?'

'You know better than to ask that,' grinned Harris. He rubbed his hands together delightedly. 'Excellent, this really is excellent. I wasn't sure she would go for it.'

'Yeah, but the lovely lady only agreed because you told her a porkie pie.'

'Really?' said the inspector with an innocent expression on his face. 'What was that then?'

'That we hadn't got any other leads. What about the gambling ring? I mean, what if we are wrong about Radford and it's all down to a few farmhands falling out over bad debts? Things have to be bad if Len Radley and Charlie Myles come to blows.'

'Do you know,' said Harris, downing his pint and standing up, 'I clean forgot about that, Matty lad. Thank you for reminding me.'

Gallagher gave a slight smile: having been given the chance to get his teeth into something like this he was not about to argue too much with the inspector over his methods.

'Come on,' said Harris, heading for the door and giving a wave of thanks to the barman, 'we've got plenty to do. Oh, and you heard the lady, I don't want Curtis to know about this, not until I've got everything topped and tailed anyway. He'd only worry. Well, he'd worry me, anyway.'

'Understood,' said the sergeant, following him out into the bright summer sunshine where the inspector was already walking purposefully along the street. 'There was something else I wanted to ask.'

Something in the sergeant's voice made Harris stop walking and turn to look at him.

'And what would that be?' he asked.

'Something the DCI said,' said the sergeant, hesitating slightly as he worked out how best to phrase his next words; good mood or not, you still never quite knew how the inspector would react to some things. 'When she asked why you were after Radford, I kind of got the impression that there was something else to it. Something that you are not telling me.'

'Matty lad,' said Harris, turning and starting to walk along the street again, 'you should know by now that there are always things I am not telling you.'

Chapter eighteen

Later that afternoon, and for the second time in a matter of hours, Matty Gallagher found himself on the fourth-floor corridor at the general hospital. He paused in mid-stride and looked out of the window once more. No train this time.

'Penny for your thoughts,' said a voice behind him.

'You're the second person who has said that to me today,' said the sergeant, turning and smiling at his wife as she walked along the corridor. He looked at her nurse's uniform. 'You're in early.'

'I rang the police station and they said you were down here. Got to grab these opportunities when they arise.' Julie joined him in staring out of the window, leaning her arms on the windowsill and looking out across the roofs. 'You here for anything exciting?'

'This vet fellow who has been attacked.'

'I had a quick word with one of the nurses,' nodded Julie. 'She reckons he is in a bad way. They're keeping him in a coma. Be a while before you can talk to him.'

Gallagher nodded morosely. There was a few moments of silence then she looked across at him with an apologetic look on her face.

'Matty, you know we were going to look at the sofa on Saturday.'

'Haven't been able to think about anything else.'

'Cheeky basket,' said Julie. 'Anyway, you will be pleased to learn that we might have to take a rain check. I've taken a bit of overtime – if we're going to buy the blue one, we'll need the money so I've said I will do days on Saturday and Sunday. One of the nurses has fallen down stairs and broken her arm.'

'That's a relief.'

'I'll tell her. It should speed her recovery. Miles better than a card.'

'You know I didn't mean it like that.' Gallagher grinned. 'It's just that I reckon I'm going to end up working a lot of the weekend as well – I'll be away Saturday night. Maybe Sunday as well.'

'But I've invited Mum and Dad down for Sunday lunch,' she protested.

'I know,' said Gallagher, straight-faced. 'What with missing out on an afternoon in DFS then missing your dad endlessly banging on about darts, it's a pretty grim weekend all round.'

Julie looked at him, noticed his lips twitch slightly, and punched his arm affectionately.

'Sometimes, Matty Gallagher,' she said as he rubbed his arm and gave her a pained look, 'you are insufferable. Tell you what, I'll forgive you but only if you buy me a coffee down in the canteen.'

'Sorry, pet. The guvn'r's got the wife in there.' He nodded to a nearby office. The door was closed. 'Your lot have let us use it to interview her so she's close to her husband. She doesn't want to leave the hospital.'

'I bet she's in a right state.'

'That's the odd thing, she's not. I only saw for a few moments but she looked cool as a cucumber, like she did not care what had happened to her husband.' Gallagher leaned over and kissed her on the cheek.

'What was that for?'

'You know,' said Gallagher, 'just because.'

'You've seen the train again, haven't you?'

'No, it's something else. Julie?'

'Matthew.' Her reply sounded guarded – she knew that tone of voice.

'If I got a job offer from Manchester, what would you think?'

'And have you had a job offer from Manchester?' she said, unable to disguise her consternation.

'Not yet but if I did…' His voice tailed off.

'It's a long way to travel,' said Julie. 'You'd have to live down there, presumably.'

'Unless we moved.'

'I'm not sure I would like that,' she said, looking at him unhappily. 'You know how much I disliked London.'

'So maybe I could get a flat and come home at weekends. It wouldn't be so b…' The sergeant's voice tailed off as he saw her expression. 'Yeah, you're right, who wants to live in Manchester, eh? Dirty old place. Look, forget I ever said anything.'

'We can talk about it later,' said Julie. 'If you want to.'

'No, no need,' said the sergeant, trying to banish her sombre mood and kissing her lightly on the cheek. 'Look, I gotta go, Harris will be waiting for me. See you when you I see you, yeah? Maybe grab breakfast together tomorrow?'

'Are you really serious about this Manchester thing?' she asked.

'No, no, of course not.' He shook his head vigorously. 'Just an idle thought.'

'In which case,' she said, 'breakfast it is.'

'Sounds good to me.'

Julie started to walk down the corridor, gave a coquettish look over her shoulder and blew him a kiss.

'Just think what you be missing if you moved to Manchester,' she said.

'You're just a temptress,' grinned Gallagher and walked the other way down the corridor towards the office – it would be a long time before he could get the image out of his head. Even if it had been her way of taking his mind off the Manchester thing, he wasn't objecting. Uniforms, he guessed as he reached for the door handle, always something about uniforms.

* * *

'I know this is difficult for you, Mrs Thornycroft,' said Jack Harris, trying to sound sympathetic and glancing up as Gallagher entered the room, 'but we really have to get to the bottom of what happened to your husband.'

Gallagher sat down next to the inspector and looked across the table at Gaynor Thornycroft, who presented a picture of control. Her jacket was perfectly pressed, her trousers beautifully ironed: not a crease in sight. Her black hair was well-presented and her make-up was immaculate. Something in her calm demeanour reminded the sergeant of Annie Gorman.

Gaynor sat with her hands resting on her lap and looked silently at the detectives over the top of her dark-rimmed spectacles, almost as if challenging them, as if determined not to give an inch.

'Have you had time to think about what I said earlier?' said Harris, when no response was forthcoming. 'Had anything unusual happened recently which might lead us to whoever attacked your husband this morning?'

'Now let me think,' she said in a voice laced with sarcasm. 'Was there anything unusual? Oh, yes, now I come to think of it, my husband faked a break-in at his surgery in Bolton. I suppose you could say that was unusual. What do you think, Inspector?'

She did not give Harris chance to reply.

'Then it turns out that he was treating dogs that had been injured in illegal fights organised by a bunch of gangsters,' she said. 'I suppose you might also say that that was unusual. It certainly was where we lived. Nice middle-class area like that, what do *you* reckon, Inspector?'

Harris glanced at Gallagher, who shrugged.

'Then we came up here to start a new life,' she continued, warming to her theme. 'And not only is Levton Bridge a shitty little town full of nosey people who want to know everything about your business, but it also turns out from what you say that, in addition to taking on a practice that was virtually bankrupt, my husband's gambling problem has resurfaced.'

She looked at the detectives.

'So, yes, gentlemen,' she said. 'I think you could say that some unusual things had happened. I mean, I don't think we'd do very well on Mister and Mrs, do you? What on earth would Derek Batey say?'

'So I take it things were strained between you?' asked Harris. Her look had him immediately regretting the question.

'Strained?' she said, anger replacing sarcasm. 'Strained? What kind of a fucking question is that? I hate the bastard for what he has done to me. I wish I had never met James Thornycroft and I wish I had never come back to Levton Bridge. I mean, it's not as if I did not know what the place was like.'

A sense of grief suddenly overwhelmed her and she started to cry. The detectives watched the transformation in amazement for a few moments, so rapid and surprising had it been. She reached into the handbag sitting on the chair next to her, producing a handkerchief with which she dabbed her eyes. The make-up had already started to smudge.

'Look,' said Harris when she had calmed down a little, 'I know this is a difficult question but I really do need to ask you if you hated James enough to attack him?'

'No,' she said. With an effort, she stayed the tears. 'No, Chief Inspector, I did not. Don't get me wrong, if I never see him again it will be too soon.'

The detectives glanced at each other.

'No, no,' she said quickly, 'I did not mean it like that. I mean, I don't want him to die.'

'I should hope not,' said Harris.

'However,' she said with a sigh, 'I might as well tell you that last night, when he did not come back, and didn't even bother ringing me to say where he was, I decided to demand a divorce from him. I've had enough, I really have.'

'Did James know about this?'

'No,' she said, shaking her head. 'No, he did not come back until I was asleep. If you ask me, he waited until he knew I had gone up to bed. He's been drinking far too much. Late night. He thinks I do not notice but I'm not stupid. He doesn't exactly hide the bottles well. And this morning, he did not even try to hide it at all. He had a terrible hangover and there was an empty wine bottle in the kitchen. It did not seem the time to tell him about the divorce. I planned to do it tonight.'

She paused.

'I suppose it will have to wait now,' she said.

'I imagine so,' said Harris, not quite sure what to say but feeling that he ought to say something.

'What a scene that will make,' she said, giving a dry laugh. 'There I'll be, the loving wife by the bedside and when he comes round I can hold his hand, ask him how his head is, give him a loving kiss and ask for a divorce. Story of our life really.'

'When did you meet him?' asked Harris.

'Ten years ago this month. I owned a flower shop in Bolton at the time. I have always owned flower shops. I have been looking for somewhere to open one in Levton Bridge. Bring some colour into the drab little place.'

Gallagher chuckled but tried to look serious when Harris glared at him.

'So how exactly did you meet James?' asked Harris.

157

'At a party. He had just come back to the UK. Still had the sun tan.' She gave a mirthless laugh. 'Of course, later on I discovered that, like the man himself, it was all fake. Out of a bottle. The original had long since faded. There's symbolism for you.'

'Where had he been?' asked Gallagher.

'Working for an animal charity in Africa. He wasn't always a selfish bastard.'

Harris leaned forward.

'Africa?' he asked. 'Where was he? And what exactly was he doing there?'

'It was one of these charities that returns monkeys to the jungle. He said they were part of the bush meat trade and the charity rescued them. They ran a sanctuary or something. In Zaire, I think.'

'Can you remember the charity's name?' asked the inspector.

'He did tell me.' She furrowed her brow. 'Something about a chance. Another Chance or something.'

'Now that is interesting.'

'I'm not sure how it can be, it was ten years ago. Surely it can't have anything to do with what happened to him this morning?'

'Did he keep in contact with anyone from those days?'

'Not as far as I know,' she said. 'No hang on, there was one man – I am trying to remember his name. Donald something.' Again, she furrowed her brow. 'Donald Rylance, that's it. He was the man who founded it, I think. James quite liked him.'

'Did he ever meet him back in the UK?' asked Harris.

'Not as far as I know. They wrote to each other for a while but that stopped a long time ago. When I asked James why, he said it was a chapter in his life that was closed.'

'You know,' said Jack Harris softly, 'I would not be so sure of that.'

Shortly after six, Harris stood in David Bowes' cottage – having been called by Butterfield – and let his gaze roam slowly round the living room. Taking his lead, Gallagher and Butterfield did the same. There was nothing to excite their attention, though: an armchair, a sofa, a television, a little bureau, a bookcase with a few cheap hardback romances and a couple of Gerald Durrells, typical fare in a rented house, they thought. Initially, Jack Harris thought the same until he cast his mind back to his early days in CID in Manchester. Not long out of the Army, and thinking he knew it all, he had been mentored by a DCI who was close to retirement. He was the one who told Harris to always read what people were thinking, not what they were saying. He was also the one who taught him to stand back from investigations and let his mind have the space to consider the possibilities. The DCI's words came back to the inspector now. 'Always look for the unusual,' his mentor had also said. The inspector gave a slight smile as he remembered the detective now. He decided that he should ring him when all this was over. See how retirement was treating his old friend.

Perusal of the furniture completed, the inspector turned his attention to the walls. Nothing unusual there, either – a watercolour of a horse in a field, a painting of a little cottage – the cottage they were standing in, Harris assumed – the somewhat crude quality of the brushwork suggesting it was painted by a local artist. But nothing else. No pictures of David Bowes or his family. Nothing unusual until the inspector's gaze settled on something hanging in an alcove in the corner of the room furthest away from the window, almost hidden from view unless you were standing in the right place and even then concealed by shadow. Something unusual. Jack Harris smiled.

'Thanks, Gordon,' he said quietly, his voice so low that the others could not make out what he had said.

The inspector walked over to the alcove, watched in bemusement by Butterfield and Gallagher. As he peered closer, Jack Harris knew what he had been missing, the thing he had seen the day before that had failed to register, the thing that should have triggered his instincts. Yes, he thought, now he knew what he had seen. And knew what it was trying to tell him. Now he knew where the links were.

Harris leaned in closer to examine the shrunken head with the tribal appearance and scraggy hair. It rather resembled a coconut, he thought. It was what he had also thought the first time he had seen one all those years ago. Watched in perplexed silence by the other detectives, he stared at the head, trying to exactly place the memory. Harris reached out a hand and let it rest on the head for a few moments, as if touching it would help. Suddenly, the inspector was a world away, sweltering in the fetid heat as, surrounded by hundreds of smiling African faces, he walked along a busy shopping street, constantly being jostled, trying to battle through the crowd, one eye greedily drinking in his surroundings, the other focused on his own security, unsure how the people would react to his British Army captain's uniform. Encountering only friendliness and excitement – groups of children tugged at his sleeve for attention – he had finally been able to break free of the crowd's attentions and turn into a side street where a small stall caught his attention. Among the many tourist mementoes, Jack Harris found himself staring into a shrunken face and thinking it rather resembled a coconut. Now back in the cottage, Jack Harris remembered the moment and stared deep into the head's dark eyes.

'Kinshasa,' he murmured.

'Guv?' said Gallagher.

'Kinshasa,' repeated the inspector, turning to face the others. 'It's in the Republic of Congo. Mind, they called it Zaire when I was there.'

'Zaire?' said Gallagher. 'Isn't that where Gaynor said her husband worked for that charity?'

'Certainly is.'

'What were you doing in Zaire?' asked Butterfield.

'I was with the Army. Some kind of crappy goodwill visit.' Harris looked back at the head. 'I saw these for sale then. They're made of plaster but the hair is real – well, allegedly. They are supposed to represent a throwback to the early days of Man. I nearly bought one, actually.'

'God knows why,' said Butterfield. 'It's an ugly thing. I would not have it in my house, I can tell you that. It'd give me nightmares.'

'I don't suppose DFS sells them either,' said Gallagher bleakly. 'What you thinking, guv, that James Thornycroft knew this David Bowes character?'

'Hell of a coincidence if he didn't,' said Harris.

'Yeah, but are we sure it's his?' asked Butterfield. 'It is a rented house, after all.'

'Have you got that inventory from the letting agency?' asked the inspector, glancing at Gallagher.

The sergeant reached into the inside pocket of his suit jacket and produced a typed sheet.

'Not here,' he said, scanning it quickly. 'No, I reckon you're right and that it was brought here by David Bowes. Presumably, he forgot it in his haste to leave.'

'Yeah, but so what?' asked Butterfield. 'I mean, I can't see what some crappy head has got to do with what has been happening in Levton Bridge.'

'Then it is time that you did some thinking, Constable,' said Harris, 'because this is the only thing, apart from their love of poker, that links David Bowes with James Thornycroft and Trevor Meredith.'

'Bowes and Thornycroft I get,' said Gallagher, with a puzzled expression, 'but Meredith as well? Sorry, guv, maybe I am being thick but you have lost me there.'

'Think back to last night,' said Harris, walking back into the centre of the room. 'In Meredith's cottage.

161

Remember, you said there was nothing there of the man. But there was something and we missed it. We all missed it. It didn't seem important at the time but it's what has been nagging away at me ever since.'

'The shield!' exclaimed Gallagher excitedly. 'That little shield hanging on the wall in the back bedroom.'

'Precisely. If I am right, it came from Tanzania. I saw them when we were out there the year after we went to Zaire.' Harris looked back at the head thoughtfully. 'I think, guys and gals, that we have been looking in the wrong place.'

* * *

Shortly after 6pm, a weary Jasmine Riley got out of the taxi and walked up the driveway to the semi-detached house on the outskirts of Chester. The door was opened before she even had chance to ring the bell.

'Jasmine!' exclaimed her mother.

'Oh, Mum!' she said, collapsing into her mother's arms. 'Oh, Mum!'

Chapter nineteen

On leaving the cottage, a pensive Jack Harris, with Alison Butterfield in the passenger seat of the Land Rover, started the drive through the hills to Levton Bridge, with Matty Gallagher following a short distance behind in his own car. Not long into the journey, the inspector's mobile rang and he leaned over to read the message on the screen.

'Curtis,' he grunted. 'I better take it. I've ignored him all day and we need all the friends we can get at the moment.'

He reached over to activate the hands-free speaker.

'Sir, how are you?'

'Wanting to know what's happening,' said the superintendent's voice, the irritation clear in its tone. 'I mean, shouldn't you be back here?'

'On our way. Made a lot of progress already, mind. Has anyone said anything about the attack on the farmers?'

'There's a few questions being asked at headquarters but I think I've made it go away,' said Curtis. 'However, it could easily come back if we don't get a fast resolution on this Meredith thing. It is attracting a lot of media attention – they are trying to whip up a panic about this mad dog. Sky Television has been in town most of the day and that damned fool chairman of the parish council even mentioned Hound of the Baskervilles.'

'I did tell Barry that it's not on the loose. Besides, the forensics team have been up there all day and they've not seen anything.'

'Have they found anything useful at all?' asked Curtis hopefully.

'Not much. The rain last night washed everything away. They turfed up Meredith's phone but it was so wet that it's proving difficult to get anything off it.'

'Well make sure we do come up with something,' said Curtis and the line went dead.

'Ah, so supportive,' murmured Harris and he looked at Butterfield. 'Makes you realise what a lovely and fluffy boss I am, eh?'

The constable did not reply. She would not have known what to say anyway. Twenty minutes later, as the two vehicles approached Levton Bridge, the inspector's radio crackled.

'Control,' said a woman's voice. 'Can you proceed out to the car park at Haley's Bank and meet the firearms team there?'

'Why?'

'There's been a report of two armed men walking along the valley.'

'That's all we need,' said Harris, slamming his foot onto the accelerator, the Land Rover's sudden burst of speed startling Gallagher. 'That's not far from where Trevor Meredith was found.'

It took the Land Rover less than fifteen minutes to reach the car park, the inspector sending the vehicle careering round tight corners on little back roads, the sergeant trying desperately to keep up behind him and more than once coming close to putting his car into a ditch. On arrival, the detectives were confronted by several marked police vehicles, a number of uniforms and half a dozen officers, dressed in black overalls and armoured vests, and holding firearms. Harris brought the Land Rover to a halt and leapt out, ordering Scoot to remain in the vehicle as he did so. Butterfield jumped out of the other side and glanced back along the valley road to see Gallagher's car approaching.

'What we got, Andy?' asked Harris, walking briskly up to the firearms inspector.

'The last report we have is that they are within a quarter of a mile west of here.' The inspector turned and pointed to a blue 4x4 on the far side of the car park. 'We think that's their vehicle.'

'Who saw them?'

'The forensic team on its way back from the scene. They were crossing the stream when these two guys emerged from some trees. They have got one of our lads with them in case the dog turns up but he did not fancy taking them on his own.'

'Very wise,' nodded Harris. 'There's a chance they're the ones who fired at our farmers last night. Do we know anything about them?'

'How about a name?'

'Always a nice start.'

'The car,' said the firearms inspector, producing a notebook from his pocket then flipping over the pages, 'belongs to a bloke called Lane, Joe Lane. London address.'

'It's a good job we've got Matty with us then,' said the inspector, turning as the sergeant walked over. 'He can translate from the vernacular. Do you know him?'

'Oh, aye,' nodded Gallagher, 'London is just like Levton Bridge really, one big village. Everyone knows everyone. Of course I don't bloody know him!'

'So, what's the plan?' asked Harris, smiling at the sergeant's comment and turning to the firearms inspector.

'Cut them off on the path. Don't want to spook them with all these vehicles. A couple of the lads went on ahead and reckon they've spotted them somewhere just down the path. A bit of woodland.'

'I know it,' nodded Harris. 'It's ideal.'

It was not long before everything was set, the armed officers having concealed themselves within the woodland, their hiding place giving them a good view of anyone approaching along the dirt track. Harris and his officers stood further back, crouching behind a drystone wall, just able to view the scene if they peered over the top. It was not a long wait and within a few minutes, they saw two figures emerging from a bend in the path. Both wore green Army-style camouflage jackets and green combat trousers and had green caps jammed onto their heads. Each had a rifle, fitted with a telescopic sight, slung over his shoulder.

'Jesus,' murmured Harris, 'it's a coup.'

He heard Gallagher give a low laugh behind him.

The firearms team did not stand on ceremony: within moments the air was filled with their shouts and the two men were lying face down in the mud, still not quite sure what had happened, their guns having been snatched from them and the police weapons trained on their quarry. Harris and the others sprinted out from behind the wall as the firearms team hauled the men to their feet and turned them to face the inspector.

'Which one of you is Joe Lane?' asked the inspector curtly.

The older of the two men nodded. A wiry individual with a weather-beaten and lined face, he looked to the inspector like an outdoor man, one who knew the hills. Instinctively, and he did not know why, the inspector sensed that these were not the men they were looking for in connection with the death of Meredith.

'Me,' said the man. 'I'm Joe Lane and I would like an explanation as to why…'

'And I,' said Harris, 'would like an explanation as to why you and your little pal are wandering round near a crime scene with rifles.'

'We're after the dog,' said the other man, a spotty character in his early thirties.

'Dog? What dog?'

'The mad dog,' said Lane. 'We reckoned there might be a reward for shooting it. Reckoned them sheep farmers would pay up.'

'If the farmers wanted the bloody thing shooting they would do it themselves, and take you with it.' Harris stared at the men. 'Besides, who are you to go out on something that cockamamie?'

'We're big game hunters,' said Lane proudly. 'We heard a radio report about the dog and reckoned you could use our expertise. We're staying in that little town. Levton something.'

'Big game hunters?' said Harris, glancing at his sergeant. 'In Levton Bridge?'

Gallagher laughed but Lane seemed offended by their attitude.

'We just happen to be professionals and you need professionals in these kind of situations,' he said tartly. 'We're expert trackers, been doing it for years. There's a big market for the right animal, you know. We've hunted all over the world.'

'All over the world?'

'Oh, aye, South America, Canada, Africa – shot everything that moves in Africa, we have, antelope, lion, even bagged a gorilla once,' said Lane proudly. 'Big bastard he was.'

'A gorilla?' said Harris sharply.

'Like I said, mate, folks will pay top dollar for the right animal. The Yanks they love it – having an animal head stuck over their mantelpiece. They pretend they were the ones as shot it.'

'And where exactly did you shoot the gorilla?' asked the inspector.

'Congo. Mind, it was called Zaire then. Shot it for a retired American businessman. Some geezer from Tulsa.

Least that's what the bloke who hired us reckoned. Most we'd ever been paid for an animal.'

Harris shook his head, trying to control the distaste he was feeling and battling against the rising temptation to knock the man to the floor. Overriding it, however, was the mention of Zaire.

'And who was this bloke?' he asked. 'This middle man in Zaire?'

Lane suddenly turned cautious, his suspicion aroused by the inspector's interest in the subject.

'I don't remember,' he said, not meeting the detective's gaze. 'It were a few years ago.'

'Pity,' said Harris, glancing at the firearms inspector, 'because we were wondering if there is anything we can charge you with after your little jaunt this afternoon. I mean, do you know much it costs to scramble an armed response team? Got to get our money's worth somehow. It's all budgets, these days, eh Andy?'

'Oh, aye,' said the firearms inspector, latching onto the inspector's train of thought as he lifted Lane's rifle up, 'and I can't help noticing that this has been modified a little. In fact, I reckon it might turn out to be illegal if we got it down to the workshop, Jack.'

Lane looked worried.

'Ok,' he said. 'Maybe I do remember. Some bloke called Garratt. Paul Garratt.'

Harris looked disappointed.

'Not David Bowes then?' he asked.

Both hunters looked at him with blank expressions on their faces.

'Ah, well,' sighed Harris, 'it was worth a go. I don't suppose the name Meredith means anything to you either?'

'Sorry, mate,' said Lane.

'The same for James Thornycroft then, I imagine?' said Gallagher.

'Oh, aye, we know him.'

'You do?' The sergeant looked at the inspector in astonishment.

'Yeah, he was a vet. Worked for a charity in Zaire. Rescued monkeys or something. Run by an old geezer called Rylance.'

The detectives gazed at him in astonishment.

'Mind, we never met him,' said Lane hurriedly, further alarmed by their interest. 'We kept out of their way – old man Rylance did not exactly like our sort.'

'I wonder why,' murmured Harris.

'When he heard that we had bagged the gorilla, he went berserk, apparently,' said Lane, glancing at his friend, who nodded. 'Started offering cash for anyone who could find us, didn't he? He was a good one for taking the law into his own hands was Donald Rylance. Folks said he was one of the good guys but they were all as bad as each other, if you ask me. Jungle law, that's what it was out there, jungle law. We got out of the country pretty damn quick, I can tell you. We ain't seen any of them for years.'

'I don't suppose you know where we can find this Rylance chap, do you?' asked Gallagher.

'Six feet under, mate,' said Lane. 'Got himself murdered a couple of years back.'

'By whom?'

Lane shrugged.

'You got a licence for that thing?' asked Harris, glancing at his rifle.

Lane sighed.

'Ok,' he sighed. 'I get the message. You didn't get this from me but the police reckoned it was this Garratt bloke did it. Mind, it's not as if it's a secret or anything like that. Everyone knows it.'

'And where is this Garratt now?'

'I don't know and I don't want to, neither,' shrugged Lane. 'We don't want dragging into whatever he is up to. You don't cross Paul Garratt unless you have to. We only worked with him because the money was good. Last time we saw him was after we did that gorilla.'

'What'd he look like?' asked the inspector.

'Why so interested?' asked Lane, still uneasy.

'Just idle curiosity.'

'I'm not sure about this,' said Lane, glancing at his partner. 'I really am not sure. Like I said, you don't mess with Paul G…'

'Listen,' said Harris, 'I'll do you a deal. You tell me what I want to know and I'll let you go without any further action – as long as you promise to get in your car and sod off out of my patch once we've finished.'

The two hunters exchanged glances.

'Look, I really don't know about this,' said Lane. 'I mean…'

'Just ask yourself this then, do you really want to spend the night in my nick?'

Lane looked at the inspector's muscular frame and close-cropped hair and shook his head.

'If I do tell you,' he said, 'you got to promise me that Garratt won't find out.'

'Somehow I think we will have other things to discuss than you when we catch up with him,' said Harris. 'So, what does he look like?'

'I reckon he's your age. Brown hair, about average height. Oh, and a scar.' Lane ran his finger along his neck. 'Just here.'

Chapter twenty

'It's all here,' said Matty Gallagher, quickly scanning the contents of the web page on the desk computer. 'Joe Lane wasn't lying about any of it.'

Jack Harris and Alison Butterfield crossed the room to peer over the sergeant's shoulder. It was shortly before eight that evening and they had convened in the CID room at Levton Bridge over a sandwich and a cup of tea. Also present were three detective constables, two men and a young woman, and Gillian Roberts, who was sitting at a corner desk reading through a file.

'This Rylance bloke was at his house in the suburbs of Kinshasa,' said Gallagher, leaning forward to read the news item, running his forefinger over the words. 'June 2007, it was. Someone went in one night and shot him dead. Police ruled out robbery because nothing was stolen. This says they reckon he might have known his killer.'

'Doesn't say it was Garratt, though,' said Harris.

Gallagher did another search.

'But this does,' he said, pointing to the screen. 'This is BBC News three days later.'

Police name suspect in hunt for murder of conservationist, the headline said.

Gallagher turned round in his seat to look up at the inspector.

'You still thinking David Bowes might be Garratt?' he asked.

'Not sure,' said Harris. 'What would a man like that be doing up here?'

'Maybe he was after Thornycroft,' said Gallagher. 'Something spilling over from their time in Africa.'

'I'd happily put a bullet in him,' said Butterfield, quickly adding, on noticing their expression, 'sorry, figure of speech.'

'Hey,' said Gallagher, scrolling down the page, 'they've got a picture of Garratt.'

This time, everyone else in the room crowded round to stare over his shoulder at the screen, gazing in fascinated silence at the grainy image of the man with brown hair and a scar running down the right side of his neck. The image looked as if it was taken from a larger picture. The caption confirmed it was Paul Garratt.

'I reckon that's David Bowes,' said Harris, 'and if he is still in our area, we have to get to him fast. God knows what else he'll do if he's brought some kind of feud here.'

'Yeah, but about what?' said Gillian Roberts. 'And where does Trevor Meredith fit into it?'

'Maybe this will tell us,' said Gallagher, who had been doing another search, this time on the website set up by Rylance's animal charity. 'Ah, that's a blow – looks like it has closed down. The site hasn't been updated for the best part of two years.'

'Yeah,' said Butterfield, pointing to a small box to the side of the screen. 'The charity was disbanded after Donald Rylance died.'

'Is there anything about Thornycroft?' asked Harris.

'Way ahead of you, guv,' said Gallagher, clicking on a section titled The Donald Rylance Story. He took a bite of sandwich while he waited for the page to load then glared at the screen. 'Jesus, it's getting worse. When is Curtis going to stump up for broadband, guv?'

'I'll let you ask him.'

'Ah, no,' said Gallagher, who had been relieved to hear that the superintendent had gone home when the sergeant arrived back at the station. 'No, it probably isn't the best time.'

The sergeant gave another 'tssk' of frustration then leaned forward as the page eventually opened and a photograph slowly emerged showing an elegant white-suited, white-haired man with a goatee beard, sitting on a veranda sipping a cocktail. They could make out trees in the background.

'That must be Rylance,' said Harris.

'Yeah, it is,' said Gallagher, pointing to the caption. 'Looks like his charity had some sort of reserve in the jungle and that's where this was taken. There's another picture down below it. Looks like it was taken at the same place.'

The sergeant scrolled down to reveal an image depicting a group of men beaming at the camera. Rylance sat in the middle of the front row, walking cane in hand, flanked by beaming African volunteers. On the end of the back row stood three white men. One of them was Paul Garratt, the detectives recognising the picture as the source of the image used on the news website following the murder.

'Well, well, well, look who it is,' said Harris, pointing to the man standing beside him.

'James Thornycroft,' said Butterfield. 'I'd know that supercilious smile anywhere.'

'And that,' said Jack Harris quietly as he leaned over to peer at the third person, 'beard or not, is Trevor Meredith.'

'Yeah,' said Gallagher, 'but this says that he is called Robert Dunsmore. Maybe he shaved the beard off so that no one would recognise him.'

'Does it say when the picture was taken?' asked Butterfield.

Gallagher read the small print of the caption.

'Eleven years ago,' he said.

'Which explains why we could not find anything about Trevor Meredith before he turned up here,' said Harris, patting his sergeant on the back. 'Like you said, Matty lad, he was a non-person.'

'It definitely looks like we are on the right track,' said the sergeant.

'Agreed,' said Harris as the other officers returned to their desks, 'but we should not ignore everything else. Gillian, have the background checks on the sanctuary produced anything interesting?'

'All the staff are clean, none of them has so much as a parking ticket,' said the DI, flicking through the file she had been reading.

'What about this rumour of the place closing down? I seem to remember several letters about it in the local rag.'

'Yeah, but a rumour is all it seems to have been, guv. The sanctuary denied it at the time, put out a statement to the newspaper. I left a message for Barry Ramsden to ring me back but he has not done so yet. We'll know more when he does. Not sure if it is important, mind.'

'You're probably right,' said the inspector glancing up at the clock on the wall and reaching for his suit jacket, which he had slung over the back of one of the chairs. 'Come on then, show time.'

The DI nodded and stood up.

'Matty,' said Harris, glancing at the sergeant's computer screen as he headed for the door, 'can you print me out a copy of that picture of our friend David Bowes?'

'Coming right up,' nodded Gallagher. 'What do you want me to do while you're out?'

'Can you drop in on Gaynor Thornycroft at hospital on your way home? I reckon she might know more than she is letting on.'

Chapter twenty-one

'Come on, guys,' said Harris irritably as he held up the computer print-out showing David Bowes' face. 'One of you must know something about him.'

The inspector was standing in the poorly-lit bar, which he had ordered closed to customers; a uniformed officer was standing guard at the front door. The only people allowed in were the men sitting nervously in front of Harris and Roberts now. All had been summoned to the meeting an hour before and those that had proved reluctant to attend had been threatened with a police van being sent to pick them up, lights flashing and sirens blaring. None of them wanted that: they all knew how fast word of such incidents spread in Levton Bridge. Even though all were now here, they still sat saying nothing and resentfully watching the inspector as he paced the room. Perched on a stool at the bar, and wondered if it would be unprofessional to order a gin and tonic, Gillian Roberts watched the inspector's performance as well, but with amusement: it reminded her of a caged tiger for some reason. She had seen him do it with villains enough times to know that the men in the room would be panicking.

At a table on one side of the room were Dennis Soames and Len Radley, the latter deliberately sitting a little apart from Charlie Myles – it was the first time the two men had met since their brawl in the market place the night before. On the other side, and sitting alone, was the trainee accountant, a skinny bespectacled man, and at the next table, the shopkeeper, a large man with a shock of black hair, and two local farm labourers in their twenties. The pub landlord, a ruddy-faced man in his fifties, stood behind the bar, glaring balefully at the inspector but only when he was sure Harris was not looking. Eventually, the landlord could contain himself no longer.

'How long is this going to take?' he said, glancing up at the clock on the wall. 'I'm losing money, Jack.'

'That's DCI Harris to you, Eddie,' said the inspector curtly. 'And it will take as long as it takes. I'm happy to stay here all night if that is what is needed.'

The landlord sighed but said nothing. As Jack Harris walked slowly past each man, fixing them with a stern glare in turn, Gillian Roberts glanced down and double-checked the list provided by Dennis Soames in the canteen the night before: apart from Trevor Meredith, James Thornycroft and David Bowes, the known members of the poker ring were all there. She looked up and tried to read the men's faces to see who, if any, was concealing something, but all she could read was fear. Poor poker players they would make, she thought. Mind, it was understandable, Jack Harris did that to people; like the DCI had always said, administer the odd slap from time to time and you could run any small town in the world. What would Philip Curtis say if he realised the half of how Jack Harris really got things done in Levton Bridge, Roberts wondered. She smiled at the thought.

'Well,' said Harris, glaring at the men. 'I am waiting. What was Bowes like?'

No one said anything.

'Let's start with an easier one then,' said the inspector, holding the picture up a little higher. 'Can you confirm that this is definitely him?'

He turned to the landlord.

'Come on, Eddie,' he said. 'It's hardly a difficult question.'

The landlord nodded ever so slightly.

'I'll take that as yes,' said the inspector. 'If a grudging one. What was he like?'

'I never really noticed.'

Harris turned to Roberts.

'I was only saying to the detective inspector earlier today,' he said, 'that the licensing magistrates would take a pretty dim view of stoppy-back poker games being held at a pub in their area. In fact, am I not right in saying that they closed down the Mitre at Eppleton for something similar a few months back?'

'Yes, they did,' said Roberts. 'Nasty business. The landlord lost his job, of course. Last I heard, he was on the dole. Him, his wife and two small children living in a horrible little bedsit down in Roxham. Doesn't bear thinking about. What's more…'

'Ok, ok,' said the landlord, 'I get the message but I really can't tell you much. He was just a normal bloke who liked his poker.'

'So, whose idea was it?'

More blank faces.

'Come on, gentlemen,' sighed Harris. 'I really – genuinely – do not want to get heavy over this. After all, we have turned a blind eye to things that just about every one of you does from time to time. Take Len, for instance, by rights I should have banged him up for trying to take my head off last night.'

Without realising it, Radley reached up and rubbed his swollen nose, which was now sporting a livid bruise.

'And you, Eddie,' continued the inspector, 'we've been ignoring your stoppy-backs for years. What we did not know about was the poker.'

'I can't see what interest it is to you anyway,' said the landlord with a surly look on his face. 'It was just a bit of fun. It didn't harm anyone.'

'It might have harmed Trevor Meredith,' said the inspector quietly.

He watched the furtive glances between the men and the alarm on the faces of all of them.

'Listen, guys,' he said, his tone of voice softer, 'you know me. I don't care what you do after hours as long as it doesn't impinge on anyone else's life but this time it has, hasn't it?'

The inspector looked at Radley and Myles.

'I mean, last night we had you two daft buggers squaring up to each other in the market square and uniform reckon this place was bedlam yesterday. I think the trouble was all to do with gambling debts, and when two old friends like you come to blows we have to get involved. There really are no options. That's not something I can keep from the Super.'

Radley and Myles looked at the floor.

'And when one of your regulars gets murdered,' continued the inspector, looking at the landlord, 'it becomes even more serious. I am pretty sure that what has been happening here has nothing to do with the murder but I do want it sorted out. I want all debts settled within 24 hours and assurances that the poker comes to an end. In return, I'll smooth things over at our end. Understand?'

The landlord looked at him glumly. No one else spoke.

'So come on,' said Harris wearily. 'I had virtually no sleep last night and I really am starting to get sick of people stonewalling us on this. Will someone tell me what the hell has been going on around here? How did the poker start?'

There was a few moments silence.

'It was Eddie's idea,' said the young accountant eventually. 'Eddie, tell them.'

'Ok, ok,' sighed the landlord, 'yes, it was my idea. We started three or four months ago. I knew it was wrong but business has been so quiet lately I reckoned I could sell a few more drinks. It only started with three or four of us, then the others kind of tagged along.'

'And Bowes? How often did he play?'

'Couple of nights a week.'

'So, do I assume that you remember what he was like now, Eddie?' said Harris.

'He was quite posh,' nodded the landlord.

'Yeah,' said Len Radley, 'he drank white wine.'

'Positively regal,' said Harris, with a smile. 'Who would have thought it in a place like this?'

Eddie scowled at the comment.

'Do we know where he came from?' asked Roberts, the first time she had spoken during the encounter.

'I did ask him once,' said the trainee accountant. 'You know, trying to be friendly but he blanked me. Mind, Trevor Meredith, he was the same. He would never tell you anything about himself either.'

'How did Meredith come to be part of your game?' asked the detective inspector.

'He saw me in the street one day,' said the landlord. 'Said he had heard what was happening and asked whether he could join. Said he liked a game of poker from time to time. That's when it started to go wrong.'

'Wrong?' asked Roberts. 'What do you mean wrong, Eddie?'

'We just played for fun but him and Bowes, they were more serious about it. Liked gambling for more money than the rest of us could afford.' The landlord glanced pointedly at Radley and Myles. 'And some of us got carried away, if you ask me.'

'What about James Thornycroft?' asked the DI. 'How come he was involved?'

'Came with Meredith one night. He seemed to know David Bowes. Mind, so did Meredith. Sometimes, the three of them would go off into the main bar and sit in the dark talking.'

'About what?' asked Roberts.

'I don't know. They kept their voices down and if any of us went close, they stopped talking.'

'So, what about…' began Harris but was interrupted by his mobile phone ringing.

The DCI glanced down at the name on the screen.

'Look after things here, will you, Gillian?' he said, and without further explanation the inspector walked out of the bar.

The detective inspector heard the door into the market place open and could see through the pub window, illuminated by the street lights, the silhouette of Jack Harris pacing up and down, engrossed in his phone conversation. He did not return for fifteen minutes, by which time the DI's interrogation was over and the men were sitting at the bar, nursing pints, and shooting occasional resentful looks in her direction.

'I miss anything?' asked Harris, returning to Roberts who was seated at a table in the corner, well away from the others, a drink in front of her. 'You pay for that?'

'Of course. Who was that on the phone?'

'An old mate of mine in Customs,' said Harris quietly as he sat down. 'This is fast turning into what Curtis would no doubt call a multi-disciplinary operation.'

'How come Customs are involved?'

'When the Africa thing cropped up, I had this hunch. Asked my mate if he could do some digging around for anything on David Bowes.'

'And?'

'He'd never heard of him but when I mentioned the name Paul Garratt, the floodgates opened.' Harris glanced round, keeping his voice low. 'Oh, and he also knew all about Meredith when he was Robert Dunsmore and, believe me, there is a lot to know.'

Before the chief inspector could elaborate further, the officers heard the front door of the pub open and looked up to see Butterfield striding purposefully across the room towards them.

'Guess what?' said the constable excitedly when she got to the table.

'It's a big question, Constable,' said Harris. 'You will have to give me some kind of a clue.'

'Jasmine Riley has turned up!'

'Now that,' said Harris happily, 'is my kind of a clue.'

Chapter twenty-two

'Come on, Gaynor,' said Matty Gallagher as he stared across the interview room table at James Thornycroft's wife, 'it really is time to start talking.'

'Let's start with me saying that I object to being brought to Roxham Police Station, then,' she said calmly. 'It seems an unnecessary thing to do, especially when my husband is so gravely ill.'

'I'm afraid I don't buy the grief bit, Gaynor. Not after your last little performance. Besides, the sooner you answer my questions, the sooner you can get back to the hospital,' said the sergeant, glancing up at the clock; it read 11.45pm. 'Although I remain to be convinced that you really care what happens to him.'

'That's not fair,' she said. For the first time in their conversation, she seemed to be struggling with emotion. 'That is not fair at all. James and I may have had our difficult times but there is no way I would want this to happen to him.'

The comment caught the sergeant by surprise. She seemed to be genuinely upset at the way he had approached their interview. Was it his imagination or were her eyes moist with tears? He could not be sure.

'No,' he said eventually, 'no, I don't suppose that you do. My apologies, Mrs Thornycroft. It's just that the way you talked about him last time led me to think that you and he…'

'Have you ever seen someone fighting for life?'

Matty Gallagher nodded and his mind went back to a darkened hospital room and his mother lying in the bed, struggling desperately for every last shallow breath, her body ravaged by illness yet still fighting for survival. He remembered that helpless feeling of things unsaid, words that she could never hear, of times gone, of times wasted. Noticing Gaynor watching him intently, he nodded.

'Yes,' he said, 'yes, I have experienced that.'

'In which case, how about we start this interview again?'

'Ok,' nodded Gallagher, irritated at the way he had lost control of the situation, 'but all of this does not conceal the fact that we think you might have information that will further our inquiries.'

'I'm not sure what I can tell you.'

'You can tell me about David Bowes.'

'I don't really know the man. I had heard his name a couple of times but that's about…'

'Silly me,' said the sergeant, slapping his forehead with his hand. 'You probably know him better as Paul Garratt.'

Gaynor Thornycroft stared at him in amazement.

'How on earth do you know about that?' she said quietly.

* * *

Feeling weary as his lack of sleep caught up with him, Jack Harris sat in the interview room and stared at Jasmine Riley, who looked down at the table, not meeting his gaze. It was shortly after midnight and she had arrived at Levton Bridge Police Station in a motorway patrol car just a few minutes earlier; the officers who drove her at high speed up from Cheshire said she had spoken little. On arrival, she had spent ten minutes with the duty solicitor who now sat next to her in the stuffy interview room. The only other person present was Gillian Roberts.

'Before we start,' said the solicitor, a sallow faced man, 'I want to make absolutely clear that my client is not under arrest. Is that the case?'

'As far as we know, she has not done anything wrong,' said Harris. 'So no, she is not under arrest.'

The lawyer nodded, he seemed satisfied by the response.

'Please ask your questions then,' he said.

'We would have anyway. You know that.'

The lawyer looked sharply at the detective, who ignored the gesture and instead glanced across at Roberts; he had asked her to help with the interview because he hoped that the female touch would help.

'Jasmine,' said Roberts, taking the cue, 'we really need to know about the events leading up to your fiancé's death.'

Jasmine looked up and nodded; tears glistened in her eyes.

'Then will I be able to go back home to Mum?' she asked.

'Assuming there is no reason to hold you further, the officers are waiting to take you back to Chester. Am I right that your mother declined the offer of accompanying you?'

'She gets car sick,' replied Jasmine and gave a slight smile. 'At least it's not cancer.'

'A pretty awful thing to have told people,' said Roberts.

'I know.' Jasmine looked close to tears again. 'I've done some stupid things. Look, can we get this over with? I really do not think I can take much more.'

'Sure,' said Roberts. 'So, when did all this start? What made you decide to flee Levton Bridge?'

'I'm not quite sure when it started. It was little things at first but over three or four weeks, Trevor went from being a fairly laid-back chap to one who was jumpy, on edge all the time. By the end…'

Her voice tailed off and she looked down at the table. They could see her shoulders heave as she fought back the tears.

'Take your time, luvvie,' said Roberts.

Jasmine straightened up, dabbed her eyes with her handkerchief, and nodded.

'Ask your questions,' she said.

'Trevor's behaviour,' said Roberts, 'it was out of character?'

'You know,' said Jasmine slowly, almost as if the thought had just occurred to her, 'the more I think about it, there had always been something about him. Funny how you only notice these things afterwards. What's that saying, that you can't see the wood for the trees?'

'A somewhat unfortunate phrase to use given the circumstances of his death,' said Harris.

She looked at him sharply.

'Sorry,' he said, but did not sound apologetic. 'What was it about Trevor that made you think things were not quite right?'

'The way he always avoided personal matters.' Suddenly she seemed eager to talk, eager to unburden herself. 'At first I put it down to him being a man. They always shy away from that kind of stuff, don't they?'

Roberts glanced at Harris.

'Sure do,' she said.

'But with Trevor,' continued Jasmine, 'it was more than that. Whenever I asked where his parents were, for instance, he would change the subject to something else. He never ever talked about them – he did once let slip that he had a brother but he said that they did not talk to each other.'

The words were coming in a rush now.

'He seemed to regret mentioning it the moment he had said it,' she said. 'When I asked what his name was and

185

where he lived, was he married, did they have kids, was I going to be an Auntie, that sort of thing, Trevor just would not reply. Said there were some things I should not know. He said it was better that way, that what I did not know could not hurt him. That was one of his favourite sayings.'

'Did this brother ever call?' asked Roberts.

'No.'

'It would really help if we could find him.'

'To be honest, I am not even sure that he even exists.' She looked at them, as if the thought had just occurred. 'The more I think about it, I knew so little about Trevor but you sort of drift into these situations. I mean, I do not even know what he did before he came to Levton Bridge. I would ask him but he would say nothing. Except once. Once, he said he was been in Africa but when I asked what he had been doing…'

Her voice tailed off again.

'Jasmine, my love,' said Roberts, reaching over and touching her hand, 'I think you need to prepare yourself for a shock. Would it surprise you if we said he was not called Trevor Meredith when he was in Africa?'

'I suppose I always knew there was something like that.'

Harris, who had been examining her closely during the conversation and had come to the conclusion that she was genuine, leaned forward, intrigued by her calm response to the question. He had expected more of a reaction: shock, tears, something, but not this. Not nothing.

'What do you mean by that?' he asked.

'It was one night,' said Jasmine, her eyes assuming a far-off expression, 'about eighteen months ago. It had been such a happy day. Trevor had been off work and we'd been out walking in the hills. We'd taken Robbie.'

'So, what happened to ruin it?'

'It didn't ruin it so much, just got me thinking. That night, we were clearing a cupboard out in my house,

186

getting ready for moving in together.' She hesitated, fighting back strong emotions again, tears glistening once more in her eyes.

The detectives let her compose herself.

'I found my birth certificate,' she said eventually. 'We were laughing at my middle name. Trevor said that Jemima was an awful name. Jasmine Jemima, what a mouthful, he said, what were my parents thinking?'

She smiled at the memory. So did the detectives. The solicitor did not react.

'Then?' asked Harris.

'I asked Trevor if he had his birth certificate so I could find out if he had an embarrassing middle name that he had not told me about. It was just a joke, you know – we'd both had a couple of glasses of wine and were mucking about. Suddenly, Trevor changed, had that guarded look about him again.'

'I assume he did not have the passport then?' said Roberts.

'He said he had lost it.' She looked at the detectives. 'What was his real name?'

'Robert Dunsmore,' said Harris.

'I should have guessed Trevor was not his real name,' said Jasmine quietly. 'I am not sure why, but the fact that he did not have a birth certificate really troubled me – I mean, people lose things all the time but the fact that he did not have one sort of made him a non-person.'

'You're not the first to have said that,' said Harris. 'So, if you had all these reservations, why stick with him?'

Jasmine gave the detective a bewildered look.

'I'm not sure,' she said. 'I really am not sure.'

'So, coming back to what has happened over the past month,' said Harris. 'What made him so edgy? We think he might have been investigating dog fighting. Might it have been that?'

'It said on the television that Trevor's dog was dead,' she said. 'Is that true?'

The question caught the detectives by surprise. Harris nodded and Jasmine Riley sighed.

'He was a lovely dog was Robbie,' she said. 'Doted on Trevor. You can trust dogs, you know.'

'Some dogs,' nodded Harris, thinking of Scoot, curled up by the radiator in the CID room. 'We think Robbie was attacked by a fighting dog. I ask again, did you know Trevor was investigating dog fights in the area?'

'He did not tell me that.' She gave a mirthless laugh. 'Now there's a surprise. Mind, he did not have to tell me. I had already guessed something odd was happening – he had been going out at odd times for months. Said he was taking the dog for a walk then he would be out for several hours.'

'I do that with Scoot,' said Harris.

'That's why I did not think too much of it – I know what you men are like with your blessed dogs. Then he was away overnight a couple of times and would not tell me where he'd been. Out, he would say, always just out whenever I pressed him on it. I thought he was having an affair then James Thornycroft told me that Trevor was wrapped up with dog fighting. They'd known each other for years, did you know that?'

'We do now,' said Harris.

'Well, I bumped into James in the shop a few days ago and he asked me to go outside with him. He said that he was telling me as a friend that Trevor was putting himself in danger.'

'Did he say from whom?'

'No.'

'And how did Thornycroft know all this?'

'Why don't you ask him?' asked Jasmine.

'Because James Thornycroft was attacked in his home this morning. It's not certain that he will live.'

She seemed genuinely shocked.

'Did you tell Trevor about what James had said?' asked Roberts.

She nodded.

'How did he react?'

'Just brazened it out. Said that if Thornycroft was going round blabbing lies like that, there would be big trouble. He seemed really shaken.'

'Does the name Gerry Radford mean anything to you?' asked Harris.

'I answered Trevor's mobile on Thursday night,' said Jasmine. 'Trevor had forgotten to take it when he went out with the dog. When I asked the caller his name, he said to tell him that Gerry had called. Gave me a number where he could contact him.'

'We found it,' nodded Harris. 'He'd hidden it in a book. Do you know who Gerry is?'

'Not at first but when I asked him about it the next morning, Trevor said it was this Radford man. I think he regretted it because, after that, he went all quiet. I looked Radford up on the office computer.' She turned dark eyes upon the detectives. 'Do you think he killed Trevor?'

'We are not sure,' said Harris.

'Well, Trevor was certainly frightened enough. He was panicking, saying we might have to leave.'

'Who else did he tell? David Bowes, I assume?'

'How on earth do you know that?'

'Instinct. Did they meet?'

'At the King's Head, I think. They were both part of the poker game there. Trevor had always liked gambling. He always did the online poker, and we went to the races a couple of times. Trevor enjoyed that – we laughed about it because he came out ahead both times.' She smiled at the memory.

'And you think he went to see Bowes about what had happened with Radford?'

'I think so. I got the impression that they had known each other before Levton Bridge. Trevor was delighted when he came to live up here, said he was a man he could trust.'

The inspector leaned forward again.

'Did he at any stage,' he said quietly, 'ever tell you that David Bowes is actually a man called Paul Garratt?'

Jasmine gave him a sad smile.

'What do you think?' she said.

* * *

'So, do I assume that your husband talked about this Paul Garratt fellow?' asked Gallagher, staring intently across the table at Gaynor Thornycroft.

'James said he was a man not to be trusted,' she nodded.

'Why would he say that?'

'I got the impression that James was frightened of Garratt, that something had happened in their past.'

'Any idea what?'

'All I know is that James did not want to talk about him. Whenever I mentioned Garratt's name, James would walk out of the room.'

'And you? How did that make you feel?'

'I was past caring by then, Sergeant. I could see my world crumbling around me. Everything I had worked for over the years, everything I had relied on – my marriage to James, financial security for our future, everything was disappearing.' She hesitated, tears glistening in her eyes. 'I was losing everything, Sergeant.'

* * *

'Who exactly is Paul Garratt?' asked Jasmine Riley.

'Someone we would very much like to talk to. Not only is he suspected of at least one murder, back in Zaire,' said Harris quietly, 'but Customs have been tracking him for years. He's very high on their most wanted list.'

'What the hell are you talking about, Inspector?' exclaimed the solicitor. 'I thought this was about…'

'What I am talking about,' said Harris, 'was Trevor's biggest secret. You see, before he sought the anonymity of life in sleepy old Levton Bridge, Trevor Meredith – or Robert Dunsmore, to use his real name – was in league with Garratt, who just happened to be one of the biggest wildlife smugglers in Africa.'

'But Trevor loved animals!' exclaimed Jasmine.

'People change.'

'Yes,' she said, hope replacing dismay, 'yes, they do. So, maybe Trevor changed. Maybe all this secrecy was because he was ashamed of what he had done and was putting it all behind him, making a new life for...'

'I don't think so,' interrupted Harris. 'Six months ago, Customs were alerted to a container at the docks in Dover. When they forced their way in, it was full of rare birds from Africa. There had been a problem with the ventilation and they had all died on the journey over. Customs re-sealed the container and waited to see who claimed it. The man who turned up the next night was none other than Paul Garratt. Unfortunately, he managed to give them the slip. However, three weeks ago, he turned up at Liverpool docks again, this time with an accomplice. Customs think that they were checking it out to bring something in. They got a CCTV picture. It's not very good but it's good enough.'

Harris reached into his suit jacket pocket, produced a small picture and handed it over to Jasmine.

'I take it,' he said, 'that you recognise the man standing next to Paul Garratt?'

Jasmine stared down at the grainy image.

'It's Trevor,' she said quietly.

'I am sorry, Jasmine,' said the inspector, 'but I think your fiancé's past finally caught up with him.'

'Are you sure about this?' asked the solicitor, looking at Harris as Jasmine started sobbing again.

'Ah, now there's the slight hitch in the scenario. No, I am not. Trevor Meredith was a man of many mysteries, as I am sure you will have gathered by now. Given his recent attempts to investigate dog fighting, it is just possible that he was doing the same thing with wildlife trafficking. Mind, if he was working undercover, he never told Customs about it, which makes me doubt that he was doing anything with official sanction.' Harris gave a shrug of the shoulders. 'Who knows whose side Trevor Meredith was on? And unfortunately, of the two people who can tell us, Paul Garratt has done a runner and James Thornycroft will be unable to speak to us for a long time to come.'

The inspector glanced at Roberts – they had both heard the dismal updates from Roxham General Hospital.

'If ever,' added the DCI.

'So, what was the plan?' asked Roberts, glancing at Jasmine as her sobs subsided and she dabbed bloodshot eyes with her handkerchief. 'When you left the cottage?'

'Trevor said it would look like he was going to work early. He was convinced the house was being watched. He said they would follow him, not me. Said he would shake them off and that I would be ok.' She gave the detectives an anxious look. 'You don't think I was followed, do you? I mean, to my mum's house?'

'Chester Police are keeping an eye on her home,' said Harris. 'No need to worry on that score, Jasmine. She is perfectly safe.'

* * *

'Thank you,' said Matty Gallagher, sitting back in his chair with a look of satisfaction on his face. 'Thank you, Gaynor.'

'It feels good to have told you everything,' she said quietly. 'It's been a very difficult time and all of this has been preying on my mind. I think it is best out in the open, don't you?'

'Always, Gaynor, always.'

'So, what happens now? Will Paul Garratt be charged with attacking James?' she asked. 'And poor Trevor? Will he be charged with his murder?'

'I am sure you realise that I cannot go into those details at this stage. Suffice to say, we would like to talk to him – and there's plenty of other people would like a nice cosy chat as well, if what you have told us is right.'

'It is.' She looked anxiously at him. 'You don't think he will come after me as well, do you? I mean, what if he hears that I have been helping you?'

'My guess is that he will be trying to get out of the country rather than thinking about you. Don't worry, Gaynor, I am sure you are safe. We can provide you with some police protection until this blows over, if you would like.'

'No,' she said, with a shake of the head. 'No, that's alright. But thank you for the offer.'

'You have been very courageous, Gaynor,' said Gallagher, giving her a reassuring smile. 'Very courageous indeed and we are very grateful for your co-operation at such a difficult time.'

'I'm just glad I could help,' she said.

* * *

There was a knock on the door and Butterfield poked her head into the interview room at Levton Bridge Police Station.

'Sorry guv,' she said, 'can I have a word?'

Harris stood up and joined her in the corridor.

'I hope this is good,' he said, rubbing his tired eyes, then running a hand through his hair, 'because I really do want to get some kip after this.'

'I'd better get you a black coffee then,' said Butterfield. 'Chester police have just been on. Jasmine's mum nipped out to see a neighbour and when she got back, a man was ransacking her house.'

'Is she hurt?'

'Not sure. Another neighbour had seen what was happening through the front window and dialled 999. Said she thought the man was armed.'

'Jesus!'

'There's more,' said Butterfield, enjoying the impact her words were having – it appealed to her sense of the dramatic. 'The neighbour tried to warn Jasmine's mum but could not reach her in time and she went into the house just as a police vehicle was turning into the street. A shot was fired, hit the police car and now Mum's being held hostage.'

'Marvellous,' sighed Harris, 'the end to a perfect day. Right, I'll rustle up some transport, you go and put the kettle on.'

'Guv?'

'I might take you up on that offer of a coffee before I go.'

Chapter twenty-three

It did not take Jack Harris long to assemble his team and leave Scoot in the hands of the night desk sergeant who was well used to the task. After a quick chat with the waiting Cheshire Police motorway crew, and summoning a traffic vehicle of their own, the detectives were soon heading south, Harris in the back of the lead car, Roberts, Butterfield and Jasmine Riley in the second vehicle. The DCI's car stopped briefly at Roxham Police Station to pick up Gallagher, the sergeant climbing into the back next to the inspector and regaling his boss with what he had learned from Gaynor Thornycroft.

'Sounds interesting,' said Harris as the vehicle drove fast and smooth on the last of the country roads before the motorway. 'Do we trust her?'

'As much as we can trust anyone. Once she realised that I was not going to be fobbed off, she seemed only too keen to help out.'

'What's in it for her, though?'

'Look at it from her point of view, guv. Her husband is fighting for life in a hospital bed, his friend is dead – I reckon she's terrified of this Garratt fellow. Frightened that he will come after her, maybe.'

'Yeah, I'll buy that,' said Harris as the car turned onto the southbound M6, rapidly picking up speed as it moved into the outside lane. 'There's no telling what he's capable of doing.'

'Do we assume he is the man holding Jasmine's mum hostage?'

'I reckon.'

'He's got to be our main suspect then.'

'Yeah, I guess.'

'Yet even now you do not sound convinced.'

'No, I'm not,' said Harris. 'And I won't be until I get to sit down and look him in the eye and find out exactly what the devil has been happening.'

'Well,' said Gallagher as he peered over the driver's shoulder and noted that the speedometer read 109mph and rising, 'that might be earlier than you think.'

No one spoke much as the two vehicles neared Chester, the cars eating up the miles, headlights flashing to move other vehicles out of the way. For each detective, different thoughts occupied their minds as they approached the city. For Harris and Gallagher, the event brought back memories of crime in the cities, of major incidents and of rapid responses. Of an earlier life which now only existed in seemingly distant memories. For Butterfield, sitting next to Roberts, this was what she had joined the job for and her eyes gleamed as the cars sped through the night. Gillian Roberts' thoughts were on much more mundane matters. Having left her husband caring for her boys, she stared out of the window and wondered whether he would get them enough breakfast. She wondered if she should ring him and tell him about the loaf of bread in the freezer but when she glanced down at her watch, it said 3am so she decided against it.

When the cars entered Chester, the siege had been under way for several hours. On arrival in the quiet residential area on the western fringes, the officers found their vehicles held back at the end of a street of semi-detached houses by a barrier of patrol cars with blue lights flashing. Harris was the first out of the lead vehicle, pulling on his Kevlar vest as he strode past the gaggle of civilians who had gathered to witness the unfolding events and across to a uniformed sergeant to whom he flashed his warrant card.

'I'll take you down, Sir,' said the uniform, 'they're waiting for you.'

'Thank you,' said Harris.

Leaving the others to make their own arrangements, the inspector followed the officer, walking past darkened houses with no sign of life.

'We evacuated them,' explained the constable, noticing the detective's quizzical look. 'The chief inspector said he did not want to take any risk – no telling what this nutter will do. They're all in a nearby church hall. At least two of the old 'uns have already said it reminds them of the Blitz.'

'I'm sure they did. They will be loving this.'

'Reckon you're right. The siege house is at the far end, two up from the junction,' said the officer, pointing down the road. 'The one on the right, with the slightly higher front wall. Our lot are a little further down on the other side. They're using that house with the blue door as their base.'

'Any movement?'

'Nothing,' said the uniform. 'In fact, there's been nothing since it happened. We have got a negotiator trying to talk to the guy but he refuses to say anything. Could be a long night.'

'Not if I have anything to do about it,' said Harris wearily.

A minute later, they were at the house with the blue door and Harris was led down the short drive, past a couple of armed officers crouching in between the neatly trimmed bushes and shrubs, their guns trained on the siege house on the other side of the road. Neither took their eyes off their target nor did they acknowledge his presence. Once into the darkened house, Harris was taken up the stairs and into the front bedroom. Sitting at the window were two men, their features indistinct in the darkness as they stared out at the house across the road.

'DCI Harris for you, Sir,' said the uniform.

The uniformed officer at the window lowered his binoculars, turned in his seat and extended a hand.

'Good morning,' he said. 'Chief Inspector Norris, Cheshire Police. Take a pew. Sorry about the darkness, keeping the lights off in case chummy takes a pot shot.'

Harris sat down on the bed; it suddenly seemed a long time since he had slept in his.

'Hey,' said Norris, 'did I hear Control say that you are from Levton Bridge?'

'Yeah,' said Harris warily; he was well used to the jokes about Sleepy Hollow but they never ceased to irritate him.

'You still got Philip Curtis up your way?'

'Divisional commander.' Harris looked at him for a moment, wondering how best to play it. Was Norris like Curtis, all rules and posturing, or was he another Andy Hulme, the kind of man you could talk to? 'How come you know our glorious leader?'

'I was on a command course with him a few months back.'

Great, thought Harris, another stuffed shirt.

'I assume the man is still a brain-dead fuckwit?' said Norris. 'He must be an absolute nightmare to work for.'

''Fraid so,' grinned Harris and knew they would be alright.

The other person in the room, a sallow-faced, slim man in jeans and a worn brown corduroy jacket, had said nothing during the conversation. Now, he turned round and looked at Harris.

'John Warboys,' he said as they shook hands. 'Official Negotiator. Not that I am doing much official negotiating. Seems like chummy is not in the mood for talking.'

'From what we hear of him, it's not his forte,' said Harris, looking beyond them and out of the window. If he craned his head, he could just make out the siege house, which was still in darkness and silent. There was no sign of movement.

'Been like this since the start,' said Warboys, reading his thoughts.

'When did you last hear from him?'

'We haven't. We've tried everything, ringing the landline, loud hailer, the lot. He does not want to talk, simple as that.'

'Are we sure they are both in there?' asked Harris.

'We got someone round the back straightaway,' replied Norris. 'One of the lads from our patrol vehicle. Got shot at for his trouble. He is pretty sure that neither of them got out, though.'

'So, what exactly happened?'

'When Emily Riley walked into her house, she heard chummy in the living room. By all accounts, she cried out in alarm and he barged past her, knocking her over, then tried to get to his vehicle. That's it, the 4x4.'

The inspector pointed to the black Shogun parked a little further up the road, a patrol car skewed at an angle behind it.

'That's the one that got shot at,' he said. 'It's an armed response vehicle, actually.'

'What, in an area like this?'

''Fraid so. We have had a couple of armed hold-ups at off-licences, one of them not far from here. Double-barrelled jobs. All very crude. We think the gang comes from Liverpool.'

'Yeah,' nodded Harris, 'we get them as well. Just got three of them locked up, actually. This lot were nicking quad bikes.'

'Yeah, well, we're on a big push to get this bunch before they hurt someone. Anyway, we were using the ARV to keep an eye on the vic's house as well, as you requested, and by sheer luck – up to you if you think it was good or bad – it turned into the road just as chummy reached his car. He panicked and let off a shot – handgun of some sort. Smashed a side window of our car.'

'Anyone injured?'

'No, the lads were lucky. Anyway, your guy legs it back to the house, threatens to shoot a couple of neighbours who came out to see what the fuss was about – that'll give them something to talk about at the bridge club – and goes back into the house where Emily Riley was apparently still lying on the floor.'

'Do we know if she is badly hurt?'

'Your guess…'

'So, what do you know about our little friend?' asked Norris, returning his attention to the road. 'I am assuming that he is not your common-or-garden burglar?'

'Not exactly,' said Harris. 'If we're right about him, he is as dangerous as they come. He's wanted for a murder in Africa and another one, and an attempt murder up our way.'

'Africa?' said Norris. 'What's the story?'

'Not sure yet,' said Harris, looking out into the deserted road. 'What we do know is that there may be links to a Manchester gang. Chap called Gerry Radford.'

'Bloody hell,' said Norris with a low whistle, 'he's major league is Gerry Radford. Our drugs boys lifted a couple of his acolytes on the M6 last year. Found fifty grand's worth of smack and a couple of shotguns in the boot. And to think that your chap Curtis said Levton Bridge was a crappy backwater where the people get excited if a cat goes missing. His words, not mine, of course.'

'I am sure they were,' murmured Harris.

'And I hasten to add that I did not agree,' said Norris. Harris could see his eyes twinkling in the half light. 'Plenty of crime, I reckon. Me and the wife stayed in Levton Bridge last summer and went to that tea room in the market place. All the woman needed was a balaclava, the prices she was asking. Daylight bloody robbery.'

Harris chuckled again. Why, he thought, could Curtis not be like this?

'So where does poor old Emily Riley fit into things?' asked Warboys, glancing back to the house. 'I mean, she's hardly a villain.'

'Her daughter is our dead man's fiancée. We are thinking that Garratt tailed her down here for some reason.'

'I dunno,' said Norris with a shake of the head, 'it's always the same – rural areas exporting their armed crime down here.'

Harris smiled.

'Yeah, sorry about that,' he said.

'So how you want to play it?' asked Norris.

'I'd like to talk to Garratt.'

Norris glanced at the negotiator, who nodded.

'Can't do any worse than I have,' he said gloomily.

'Ok,' said Norris and walked over to the doorway. 'Can someone send your gaffer up!'

A minute later, the Cheshire Police firearms inspector walked into the bedroom, gun cradled in his arms.

'What we doing then?' he asked.

'DCI here wants to try talking to meladdo,' said Norris.

'Have to be a loud hailer job,' said the firearms inspector. 'I can't risk you getting too close.'

'I'm happy to take my chances,' said Harris.

'Look,' said the firearms officers, 'I do not want to be disrespectful, Sir, I'm sure you're very good at your job and all that, but do you appreciate just how dangerous a situation this is? It's a bit different to Levton wherever the bloody hell it is.'

'I know,' said Harris with a smile. 'This ain't the Wild West, sonny, you ain't John Wayne and this is not Shoot Out at the O.K. Corral.'

The firearms inspector stared at him, not sure what to make of the comment.

'I was in the Army,' said Harris. 'Specialised in hostage recovery for a while.'

The others stared at him in amazement.

'Then what are you doing in a backwater like Levton Bridge?' exclaimed the firearms inspector.

'Someone,' replied Harris with a slight smile, 'has to take the dog for a walk.'

His mind flashed back to happy days spent tramping the hills with Scoot. As ever, in situations such as this, he enjoyed the rush of adrenaline, felt suddenly more alive, but at the same time he realised that Levton Bridge was where he truly wanted to be. It was just that it took dangerous situations like this one to remind him of the fact. It was one of the contradictions with which the inspector had learned to live.

'Thoughts?' asked the firearms inspector, looking at Norris.

'My concern is for the woman. We have no idea how badly injured she is. For all we know, she could be in need of urgent medical attention.' Norris winked at Harris. 'And if it's a choice between losing an innocent punter and John Wayne here, it'll have to be John Wayne.'

'Ok, I've heard enough,' said the firearms inspector, nodding at Harris. 'Come on then, Sir, let's get this done with.'

'Thank you,' said Harris.

The two men walked down the stairs and, once in the hallway, the firearms inspector checked the DCI's protective vest before giving him a reassuring smile.

'You ready then?' he said.

Harris nodded.

'You be careful out there, yeah?' said the firearms inspector.

'I'll do my best.'

'No shoot out at the O.K. Corral, eh, sonny?'

Harris grinned and the firearms inspector went out into the street, keeping low as he walked up to his officers, who were crouched behind garden walls, their guns trained on the siege property. After a few moments' hurried discussion, the firearms inspector turned back and gave the waiting Jack Harris a thumbs-up signal. Standing in the doorway, Jack Harris gave himself a few moments then, with a sigh, he walked into the street.

'Why do I do this job?' he murmured.

As Harris passed the firearms inspector, the officer handed him a loud hailer and placed a briefly reassuring hand on his shoulder. Then Jack Harris was on his own. Watched by everyone, including his own officers and an anxious Jasmine Riley gathered behind the patrol cars at the end of the street, Jack Harris advanced slowly until he was standing a few doors down from the siege house, his eyes constantly seeking out movement in the darkened windows, his body tensed and ready to move should the man inside decide to shoot his way out. He experienced once more that feeling he had experienced as a soldier, that heightened sense of awareness, that feeling of having never been more alive. Jack Harris liked it. In a strange way, now, in this moment, in this place, it was where he was supposed to be, he thought. The detective raised the loud hailer to his mouth. Suddenly, he realised that he had not thought about what to say.

'This is DCI Jack Harris!' he shouted after a few seconds.

Clicking off the loud hailer, he grinned.

'Now there's bloody original,' he muttered to himself. 'Come on, Jack, get a grip.'

There was no sound from within and no movement.

'Paul Garratt!' he shouted after clicking the device back on again.

This time, an upstairs curtain twitched and Harris tensed as he watched for the appearance of the muzzle of a gun in the darkness. Nothing happened.

'I want to talk to you!' shouted Harris.

There were a few more moments of silence then Harris heard – everyone in the street heard – through the stillness of the night the click of a key turning in the front door lock. The firearms officers tightened their grip on their weapons, sights trained on the house as they awaited the emergence of their quarry. Slowly, ever so slowly, the door swung open and Paul Garratt emerged, the firearm dangling from his fingers.

'Don't shoot!' he cried.

'Drop it!' shouted a voice and firearms officers emerged from their hiding places in the gardens, advancing across the road, guns trained on Garratt.

Garratt crouched down and carefully placed the gun on the ground in front of him, then walked backwards several steps and put his hands in the air. Within seconds, firearms officers had bundled him to the ground and handcuffs were being applied. One of the team pulled Garratt to his feet as others ran into the house.

As Harris walked towards the detained man, Garratt watched him with interest.

'So you're Jack Harris, eh?' he said calmly. 'Heard a lot about you. How long have you known who I was?'

'Not long enough.'

Garratt gave a slight smile. Harris glanced to his right and watched as an ambulance crew jogged into the house. The firearms inspector emerged from the darkened property a few moments later.

'How is she?' asked Harris.

'Not too bad. Nasty gash on the leg, that's all.'

'It was an accident,' said Garratt. 'Honest. I didn't mean to hurt her.'

'Maybe you didn't,' said Harris, 'but the rest wasn't accidental. Paul Garratt, I am arresting you on suspicion of involvement in the murder of Trevor Meredith and the attempted murder of James Thornycroft.'

'Which is odd,' said Garratt, 'because I did not do either of them.'

Chapter twenty-four

Jack Harris arrived at Levton Bridge Police Station shortly after ten the next morning, still feeling weary but having at least grabbed some sleep on his return from Chester. As he parked the vehicle at the front of the station, the inspector's head felt clearer than it had done for the best part of two days: on his arrival back at the cottage a few hours before, he had decided against the whisky, even though the half-empty bottle sitting on the side table had looked inviting, and had instead gone to bed. Now, as he jumped out of the Land Rover, followed by Scoot, the inspector was looking forward to the interview with Paul Garratt, who had spent his night in a cell at Levton Bridge.

Garratt had spoken little on the journey back up from Chester in the patrol car, preferring instead to stare silently out of the window. Sitting beside him, and left alone to his own thoughts, the inspector had found himself troubled by what Garratt had said in the moments after he was arrested. Harris was well used to suspects denying their involvement in crimes – knew it was all part of the game – but the way Garratt had said it had given him the distinct impression that he was telling the truth. The idea had nagged away at the back of the inspector's mind on the journey north and it troubled him now as he made his way up to his first-floor office.

'Jack!' came a harsh voice and, with a sigh, the DCI turned to see Curtis standing at the end of the corridor. 'In my office, please.'

Harris walked with heavy step into the commander's office and sat down in a chair at the desk, looking balefully at Curtis who, for his part, seemed to be struggling to control his emotions. Suddenly, Harris cheered up.

'Met an acquaintance of yours last night,' he said affably. 'Chap from Chester Police. Chief Inspector called Norris. Said he was on a course with you.'

'Who?' Curtis seemed surprised by the inspector's friendly approach, not his usual opening gambit in such situations.

'Norris? Brown hair, greying slightly.'

'I seem to vaguely remember him.'

'He remembers you a little better. You made a huge impression on him, in fact.'

Curtis looked pleased.

'Really?' he said.

'Aye, he asked if you were still a brain-dead fuckwit.'

Curtis looked at the DCI in amazement, mouth opening and shutting, unable to form the words.

'Of course,' said Harris, 'I did not agree with him. It was a terrible thing to say.'

'But did you disagree?' asked Curtis tartly.

'Not sure I remember.'

'For God's sake, Jack!' The superintendent's anger finally exploded. 'Stop messing about! I have had Customs on the phone three times already this morning wanting to interview a man in our cells and I don't even know who he is! Nobody seems to have even the remotest idea about what is happening and when I ring your mobile, well we both know what happens there. It's not good enough, I do my best to work with you and all you can do is…'

'Paul Garratt is wanted by us on suspicion of involvement in the attacks on Trevor Meredith and James Thornycroft, who, incidentally, may be a Rotary Club member but is as crooked as they come. Cheshire want him for a chat about an armed siege in their patch, Customs fancy a talk about his global wildlife trafficking racket, oh, and the police in Congo would quite like him to pop over for a natter about the murder of one of his associates.' Harris beamed. 'All in all, I reckon that Paul Garratt is an excellent catch for a police force in... what was it you called it again when you met Norris on that course? Ah, I remember – "a crappy little backwater".'

Curtis looked at him in astonishment, acutely conscious that Jack Harris had outmanoeuvred him at every step of the conversation and unnerved by his calm delivery of the words.

'Why was I not kept informed?' he asked, but it sounded a weak response and he knew it.

Harris beamed.

'You know how it is,' he said.

The superintendent's desk phone rang and, the relief clear on his face, Curtis picked up the receiver and listened for a few moments, gave a grunt and put the receiver back down.

'That was Control,' he said. 'Another call about the blessed dog on the hills. Some old woman terrified about going to the shops.'

'What?' said Harris with a sly smile. 'In case it jumps out and attacks her in the frozen vegetable aisle?'

'This is no laughing matter,' said Curtis, seizing on the opportunity to regain some authority. 'We've had dozens of journalists ringing up as well. And there was a couple of big game hunters as well. Traipsing round the hills like it was bloody Africa.'

'I know,' chuckled Harris, 'I saw them. Mind, I think you will find that they have gone home now. And if they can't find the blessed thing, perhaps it's not there. I mean, they have hunted antelope in Africa. Sometimes in these situations you need professionals.'

Curtis looked at him gloomily.

'No,' said Harris, 'the dog is no threat to anyone, I am pretty sure of that. You can tell your old dear that she is safe to go to the Co-op.'

'So where do we go now?' asked the superintendent feebly, his defeat final.

'Well I'm off for a bacon sandwich, seems a long time since I last ate.' The inspector stood up and glanced round as Scoot wandered into the room. 'I am sure he would appreciate something as well.'

Curtis did not reply, still finding himself struggling to form the words.

'Then I'll interview Garratt,' said Harris, walking over to the door. 'Trouble is, although everything points to him having something to do with our attacks, he denies everything.'

'Is he telling the truth?'

Harris shrugged.

'Not sure,' he said, heading out into corridor. 'I'll let you know.'

'Now that,' said Curtis bleakly, 'would be a first.'

The comment had Jack Harris grinning all the way to the canteen. Half an hour later, the inspector walked down the corridor to the interview room, Matty Gallagher at his side – Jack Harris liked the feeling and gave a smile to the sergeant as they walked. Gallagher was not sure how to react and gave a half smile in return. When they entered the room, the two officers sat down at the table and Garratt stared calmly at them – his composure had remained unruffled from the moment he was arrested. Next to him sat the duty solicitor, the same man who had accompanied Jasmine Riley during her interview. He watched the detectives warily.

'So, Paul,' said Harris, looking at Garratt, 'I think you have a lot of explaining to do. I take it you are David Bowes?'

'Mea culpa, Chief Inspector. A man with my somewhat unfortunate record needs to be careful and it was a diverting little deception which none of the yokels up here thought to question.'

'I think that a man in your position would be well-advised to show a little more respect,' said Harris icily.

'And what position might that be?'

'Well, let's take your involvement in the attacks on Trevor Meredith and James Thornycroft for a start.'

'I am innocent on that score, Chief Inspector, a point about which I informed you last night.'

'You did indeed but I will need a little more than that. Even we yokels require proof on these matters.'

'In which case, let me tell you a little story.' Garratt gave the officers another mocking smile. 'Are you sitting comfortably, children?'

'Just get on with it,' said Harris.

'Ok. My little story begins twelve years ago when I was in Zaire and became aware of an animal welfare charity called Another Chance – it re-homed monkeys that had been used…'

'We know all about that,' said Harris.

'Oh, very good.'

Harris scowled at the comment.

'Anyway,' said Garratt. 'Your man Meredith was working for them as well – mind, he was not called Meredith then, he was called Robert Dunsmore.'

'We know that as well.'

'You have been a busy boy, Chief Inspector.'

'You're hardly in a position for joking.'

'Au contraire,' said Garratt calmly. 'My position is considerably stronger than you seem to think. In fact, it's just a question of when I get out of this crappy little backwater.'

'Meaning?'

'If you will allow, I will come to that later.'

'Perhaps I need a further consultation with my client before that happens,' said the solicitor quickly. 'Mr Garratt, as your legal representative, I really do think that I should…'

'This is way above your head, sunshine,' said Garratt. 'If I were you, I'd keep your trap shut before you end up looking stupid.'

The solicitor glowered at him and the detectives looked at Garratt with growing unease: there was no doubt about who was controlling the interview and neither of them liked the sensation. Before anyone could speak, Garratt had resumed his story, giving the impression of someone thoroughly enjoying the experience.

'Meredith, let's call him Meredith for convenience sake, was an investigator for the charity, used to find out where the monkeys were being kept, sheds, people's houses, markets, that kind of thing, then take them back. Not always with the owner's permission, might I add. George Rylance was not averse to bending the law himself and he had a group of hired henchmen to make sure the animals were rescued, operating under the command of your friend Meredith. Nevertheless, methods aside, Trevor Meredith was one of the good guys. Well, he was in those early days.' Garratt gave another smile. 'Oh, and before you ask, gentlemen, yes, I was one of the bad guys. As bad as they came.'

'And James Thornycroft, was he a good guy?' asked Gallagher.

'He was then,' nodded Garratt. 'He was the charity's vet when I first came across him. All very idealistic, kept talking about paying his debt to society.'

'And you weren't?' asked Harris.

'I suspect my debt to society is rather bigger than anyone could pay for,' said Garratt. 'In fact, if you allow me to continue, you will see just how big the price will be when we get to it.'

Harris glanced at Gallagher, who shrugged.

'Anyway,' continued Garratt, 'it did not take long to turn Meredith and Thornycroft so that they saw things my way. See, they have always had the same weakness as the rest of us.'

Garratt rubbed his thumb and forefinger together.

'You can have as many ideals as you want but money talks louder than all of them,' he said.

'I am afraid you may be right,' said Harris darkly. 'What happened then?'

'Well, as I said, I had never been into all this noble saving the animals shite. There were plenty of rich people with more money than sense who fancied an exotic animal in their back garden and that's what interested me. I hooked up with a couple of dodgy characters, an Aussie and an American, who reckoned they could get them out of the country – they had good contacts with a bent port manager. Turned a blind eye to what we were doing in exchange for a few readies. However, I still needed someone to source the animals in the first place. When I approached Meredith, he was horrified at what I was suggesting but it did not take him long to come round to our way of thinking. Blame his little weakness, if you like.'

'His gambling?'

'Yeah, his gambling. He used to play with a bunch of ex-pats, sharks the lot of them, and had got himself deeper and deeper into debt. After a few days thinking it over, he asked if he could come in with us. I knew he would.'

'And Thornycroft?'

'He was just a greedy bastard. Once Meredith showed him what kind of figures we were talking about, he fell in line. It was not difficult, mind: old man Rylance paid them both a pittance. I was delighted when he agreed to join us: we needed someone who could anesthetise the animals before shipping them out.'

Harris shook his head, fighting down the rising tide of nausea and anger that he was feeling.

'Anyway,' said Garratt, 'old man Rylance was a bit of a fool so it was easy to hoodwink him. Meredith still found monkeys for him but for every one he handed over to Rylance, we exported another six. It was good money and in time we moved onto other animals as well. Developed a network of people and expanded into East Africa, which was very good for us, recruited a couple of crooked wildlife rangers to help us. Cheetahs and other big cats were big earners for us. We must have shipped a good dozen out.'

'But how on earth do you smuggle one of those out?' exclaimed Gallagher.

'You take the cubs. The sheiks love them, let them roam around the house. They seem them as a status symbol. Nice house, big motor, cheetah sitting on the drinks cabinet.'

Harris shook his head in disgust.

'You may look like that, Inspector,' said Garratt. 'I know you like spouting off about your beloved animals but to us, it was about cash and nothing else. Everything has its price. Always has had and always will. That's the kind of world we live in. Simple as. And if it had continued, we would have all been very rich men, indeed.'

'But it didn't?' asked Gallagher.

'No, someone tipped the Zairean police off and they raided our homes one night. Didn't find anything, we were always very careful, and we paid them off, of course, but Thornycroft got scared. Next thing I know, he's done a runner and left the country. Always was a weak-willed man was our James.'

'And Meredith?'

'Oh, he was all for continuing.'

'But surely he came home at around that time as well?' said Harris. 'He turned up in Levton Bridge around then.'

'Yeah, he did. See, a few weeks later, we got this approach from a guy working for a group of Saudis. Starts talking about gorillas: did we know where to find a couple of juveniles, a breeding pair? Says his client, some oil-rich Arab, wanted them for his private zoo. Show them off to his friends. Well, Meredith knew better than most where to find them in Zaire.'

'Jesus Christ,' exclaimed Harris, 'do you know how endangered those things are?'

'Too right I do – why do you think the price was so high?'

Harris resisted the temptation to jump across the table and strike him.

'Anyhow,' said Garratt, 'Meredith sorts everything out and delivers the animals to the middle man. Trouble is, the guy botches up the shipping side of things and one of the bloody things died on the way over.'

'And the other one?' asked Harris bleakly.

'Died a few days after getting there.'

The inspector bit his lip but said nothing.

'After the second one died,' continued Garratt, 'we got word that the Saudi had sent a couple of heavies to find us. Wanted his money back. Who can blame him – damaged goods, weren't they? Meredith got frightened and fled the country. He always had a yellow streak.'

'And you?'

'Laid low until it was all over. Africa is a big country, Chief Inspector, easy for a man to disappear in. I only went back to Zaire a few years later. Trouble is, I got involved in an unfortunate incident.'

'Unfortunate for Donald Rylance, you mean,' said Harris. 'Apparently, you put a bullet in his skull.'

'Yeah, a miscalculation. I reckoned everything would have long blown over but the daft old bastard confronted me about the gorillas – said he was going to tell the police. I went round to remonstrate and things got out of hand.

You know the rest. I didn't mean to shoot him, just turned out that way. It was an accident.'

'You seem to have a lot of accidents,' said Harris. 'But if you are telling the truth and you did not mean to kill him, why did you not turn yourself in and explain it to the local police?'

'You ever been in a Congolese prison, Mr Harris?' said Garratt.

Harris shook his head.

'If you had,' said Garratt, 'you would understand why I left Africa after Rylance died. Travelled round a bit then a year ago I came back here, hooked up with Meredith and we started off again.'

'Doing what? The same thing?'

'Yeah, all sorts. Rare birds, caymans, exotic insects for the pet trade. Meredith's brother runs a pet shop in Blackpool, he helped us make some good contacts. Like I said, Inspector, money always talks. We did bigger stuff for private collectors as well. Brought a couple of cheetah cubs in for a bloke in Birmingham last month. He's keeping them in his back garden.'

'I find this difficult to believe,' said Harris with a shake of the head. 'I mean, you are clearly as crooked as they come…'

'So kind,' murmured Garratt.

'…but everything we have heard suggests that Trevor Meredith had put all that behind him. Taken up with a nice young girl, getting married, a decent job…'

'Do you know much that dog place pays him?' asked Garratt.

'Not much, I imagine.'

'Exactly, and him with a wedding to pay for. Jasmine had already said she wanted the reception at Ings Hall.'

'Jeez,' said Gallagher, 'that's the most expensive hotel around. Jasmine Riley clearly has expensive tastes.'

'Indeed she has,' said Garratt. 'Trevor told her it was too much but she was adamant, trotted out the "biggest day of her life" nonsense and turned on the waterworks so they booked it. Put simply, Trevor Meredith was short of cash and a man who's short of cash…'

He did not finish the sentence, everyone knew what he meant.

'Did Jasmine not wonder where the money was coming from?' asked Harris.

'He told her that an uncle had died. To be honest, he could have told her that aliens had deposited it in his bank account and she would have believed it. All she wanted was her dream wedding day. Of course, once he realised that no one would question where his money came from, he realised that he could keep on trading in the animals without anyone asking much in the way of questions.'

'And Thornycroft,' asked Gallagher, 'I take it that he was involved in your little scam as well?'

'That was Meredith's doing,' nodded Garratt. 'They had always been friends. Meredith reckoned that since we were moving into larger animals, we needed a tame vet. He knew that Thornycroft's business was in trouble down in Bolton so he fixed it for him to buy the one up here. He knew the old duffer who ran the place had drunk the profits so it was fairly easy to buy him out and Thornycroft was desperate to get out of Bolton. Of course, once Thornycroft realised the extent of the business's problems, he was only too eager to help us. Like I said, gentlemen, when money talks, everyone listens eventually.'

'And you came up here to be close to them both?' said Gallagher.

'Yeah, I reckoned it was out of the way and I was pretty sure that even Harris here would not work out what we were doing so long as we kept our noses clean. We'd got a nice life actually, nights at the pub, bit of poker, walks on the moors, that sort of thing. Could quite get used to this country life. Then, of course, I find out about Trevor's attack of conscience.' Garratt shook his head. 'Crazy, absolutely crazy.'

'Conscience over what?' asked Harris. 'The dog fighting?'

'Yeah. See, Trevor was perfectly happy to ship animals half way round the world but he had always had this thing about dogs. Hated to see them suffering. When we were in Africa, he was always adopting mangy flea-ridden mutts off the street. God knows where he found them. Anyway, a few nights ago, he tells me that he has been trying to stop Radford running the fights. That he's infiltrated his organisation, is stringing him along and feeding the information to the RSPCA.' Garratt shook his head again. 'I was horrified, told him that he was inviting trouble.'

'And he said?'

'Said not to worry, that Radford did not know what he was doing. Said he had even supplied him with a dog – Meredith had agonised about that for days, but reckoned it was the only way to get real credibility with Radford. Trouble is, he told Thornycroft about it as well – and what does Thornycroft do? Goes running to Radford, of course.'

'Why?'

'Said Meredith had become a liability, that he would take us all down. Thornycroft was terrified of going to prison, would have done anything to escape it. He had been treating injured dogs for Radford. I think he hoped that Radford would persuade Meredith to shut his mouth.'

'I take it you knew who Radford was, what he is capable of doing?'

'Oh, aye,' chuckled Garratt, 'I know Gerry Radford. That's where you come into it, Chief Inspector. See, in return for a favour or two from your lot, I might just be able to do you one in return. Give you Radford.'

He gave a slight smile.

'Repay that debt to society, as it were.'

* * *

Half an hour later, Jack Harris was sitting in his office, sipping tea as he mulled over the interview, when there was a knock on the door. Looking up, he saw Butterfield, the young constable hardly able to conceal her excitement.

'They've found the dog,' she announced.

* * *

An hour later, the inspector was standing on the hillside, about a mile from where Trevor Meredith's body had been found, staring at the mangled remains of the bull terrier, lying among thick bracken. The inspector crouched down and gently ran a hand over its bloodstained and scored flank, up to its grizzled head with its numerous bite marks, torn and ripped muzzle and remains of the missing ear.

'Poor old chap,' said the inspector and turned to look at Gallagher, who was standing behind him. 'You were right, Matty lad, Robbie did fight like a tiger.'

'They do,' nodded the sergeant.

The DCI's attention was caught by something which he had not initially noticed, something which had been concealed beneath the congealed blood. Harris leaned over and pushed the blood-streaked fur aside.

'Well, well, well,' he said quietly. 'It would seem to have been a somewhat unfair fight.'

'Why is that?' asked Gallagher, leaning over to look closer.

'Because this,' said Jack Harris softly, 'is a bullet hole.'

Chapter twenty-five

Early the following afternoon, Jack Harris was sitting in his office at Levton Bridge Police Station, trying in vain to concentrate on the report he had been attempting to read for the best part of an hour. From time to time, he would glance up impatiently at the clock.

'Where is he?' muttered Harris, looking down at Scoot who was curled up in his usual spot by the radiator. 'Where the Hell is he, boy? I mean, Roxham is hardly the other end of the bloody universe.'

Scoot gave his master a look and settled back to sleep again. There was a knock on the door and the inspector looked up quickly as Gallagher walked into the room, holding a brown envelope. The sergeant's eyes gleamed.

'That it then?' asked Harris eagerly.

'See for yourself,' beamed Gallagher, sitting down and sliding the envelope across the desk. 'It's all there. She's been playing us for fools. Good job we started looking closer.'

'Thank Paul Garratt for that.'

'Ironic really,' said Gallagher, watching as Harris opened the envelope and carefully extracted the document.

'Ironic why?'

'You proving Radford innocent.'

'Only of this,' said Harris, 'only of this.'

He scanned the contents of the document with satisfaction.

'As far as we can ascertain, it's the only copy,' said Gallagher. 'Which explains why it never turned up in any of our searches. The bank manager was not particularly happy at being brought in on a Saturday morning to open the safety deposit box but a few choice words persuaded him.'

'I'll not ask what they were,' said Harris, reaching the bottom of the page and giving a low whistle. 'Well, well, Matty lad, what do they say in a murder inquiry – always look close to home?'

'Indeed.'

'She still missing, I assume?'

'Yeah, checked on my way back.'

There was another knock on the door and Butterfield walked in.

'You got a minute?' she asked.

Harris nodded.

'I have just come off the phone with Jane Porter,' she said. 'You remember her, the sour-faced woman at the sanctuary?'

'I remember,' said Harris.

'Well, it turns out that your mate Barry Ramsden...'

'No mate of mine,' said the inspector.

'Well you'll like this then. Seems he turned up at the sanctuary half an hour ago, getting all aerated and demanding to know why we were there this morning.'

'Yeah,' said Harris, glancing down a scrap of paper on his desk. 'He's rung here seven times now, demanding to talk to me as well. Even rang Curtis at home but he was out playing golf. The pressures of life at the top, Constable.'

Butterfield grinned.

'But,' said Harris, standing up and reaching his jacket down from a peg on the wall, 'I suppose he is right and that it is time to talk to the good burgher. Somehow I think I am going to enjoy this.'

* * *

Ten minutes later, Harris and Gallagher strode up the front drive of a semi-detached house on the edge of Levton Bridge. Harris rang the bell and the detectives stood on the front step and listened to the sound of barking dogs from the sanctuary which stood at the end of the estate, beyond a row of recently planted trees. After a few moments, the parish council chairman opened the door.

'Jack,' he said, 'where the Hell have you been. I have been ringing the pol…'

'Yeah, sorry about that. Can we come in?' said Harris. The detectives walked into the hallway without waiting to hear the answer.

Ramsden followed them in, his face betraying his anger at their behaviour.

'I really must object to the way you have ignored my calls,' he said. 'And don't tell me that you weren't in because the desk sergeant told me…'

'Nice house,' said Harris, glancing approvingly along the hallway. 'Will you be moving into one of the new ones?'

Ramsden stared at him.

'Well?' said Harris. 'Will you?'

'It's not what you think,' said Ramsden quietly, his bluster dissipating in the face of the detectives' solemn looks. 'We had the best interests of the dogs at heart when we decided to…'

'I wonder how many people will agree with that when they hear that you are going to pocket all that money?'

'We're going to build a new sanctuary,' protested Ramsden. 'We will make sure that the dogs are ok. That's

221

why we didn't want word to get out until everything was sorted. People would only jump to the wrong conclusion.'

'I am sure they would. I mean, I can see that people might easily misunderstand about the bit being creamed off the top. What do you think, Sergeant?'

'Oh, aye,' nodded Gallagher. 'People just would not understand that.'

Ramsden stared at them in horror.

'Particularly,' said Harris, 'when they find out that it cost Trevor Meredith his life.'

'Oh, God,' said Ramsden, going pale and leaning against the wall. 'Oh, dear God.'

Chapter twenty-six

'So, is your chap right?' asked Annie Gorman.

'I hope so,' said Harris. 'I can think of better ways of spending my Saturday nights.'

'*You* hope so,' said Gorman, giving him a sly look. 'Besides, as I recall, spending a Saturday night with me was one of your more pleasant pastimes.'

It was shortly before midnight on Saturday and they were sitting in the darkness of an empty first-floor office on the fringes of a small business park in Manchester. They had been there for two hours, binoculars trained on an industrial unit on the other side of the road. Because it was a warm summer's night, both wore jeans, T-shirts and light jackets. Jack Harris was acutely conscious of Gorman's perfume. The building in which they were sitting had been empty for the best part of a year but, although the air was thick and musty with damp and neglect, all he could smell was Annie Gorman. Memories stirred for him.

'Missed your chance, Jacky boy,' she said.

He gave a rueful smile.

'Yeah, I heard you got married.'

'And happily.' She chuckled. 'So keep your lecherous thoughts to yourself.'

Harris grinned and resumed his vigil out of the window. The building had been chosen because of its proximity to the flat-roofed red-brick workshop standing on the other side of the only road through the estate. Both officers had been watching for signs of movement but it had remained deserted and in darkness.

'I'm still not sure about this, you know,' said Gorman.

'Relax.'

'You can't relax with Gerry Radford. You of all people know that.'

Harris nodded, his mind going back to the scene outside a Manchester warehouse, no more than three miles from where he sat now.

Suddenly consumed by fury, and with the shrieks of the dogs still ringing in his ears, the inspector jumped to his feet and, spotting a familiar face among the group of arrested men being taken out to the police vans, he strode rapidly outside.

'Wait a minute,' he said to one of the uniformed officers, pointing at a burly dark-haired man in his late thirties. 'I want to talk to this one.'

Harris walked up to the man until their faces were but inches apart.

'Gerry Radford,' he said in a soft voice laced with menace, 'I am going to make sure you wish you were never born.'

'In your fucking dreams, Harris,' said Radford with a mocking smile.

The DI's fist caught him full in the face and for a few moments, Radford swayed, his eyes registering his shock, then he slowly, elegantly, slid to the floor. Watched in stunned silence by the other officers, Jack Harris turned on his heel and walked back into the warehouse.

'Radford's complaint could have gone either way,' said Gorman. 'Your suspension could have been permanent.

Why do you think I have had to fight long and hard to get you along tonight? Some people around here have long memories. Balls this up, Hawk, and…'

Her radio crackled and she reached down to pick it up off the floor, flicking dust off it with her manicured fingers before putting the device to her ear.

'Gorman,' she said.

'Still no show,' said a man's voice. 'The service station is pretty quiet.'

'Ok, stay there a bit longer.' Gorman put the radio down and glanced at the inspector. 'Maybe you're right after all. Maybe the drugs drop is a blind.'

Harris nodded and peered along the road as it ran further into the estate where he knew several unmarked cars were parked up behind one of the other workshops. Sitting in them were a mix of police officers and Customs investigators. Harris let his gaze slide to the small factory unit next to the target workshop; Gallagher and two Manchester detectives had been sitting in a parked vehicle behind the building for the best part of two hours. Glancing back towards the main road, Harris saw a stationary box van, its paintwork rusting, the windows grimy. He knew that Alison Butterfield was sitting in the back of the vehicle with several armed officers; he also knew that the young constable would be loving this.

'Your man Gallagher,' said Gorman suddenly, breaking into the inspector's reverie.

Harris gave her a sharp look.

'Ok, ok,' said Gorman, holding up a hand, 'I know I'm out of order but I'm hearing good things about him.'

'He is good,' said Harris, looking at her fiercely, 'but good and mine so you can keep your hands off him, Annie.'

'Don't worry. Besides, even if I did offer him a job, there's no way he would come and work for me.'

'Yeah, he's got his eye on a transfer to Roxham,' said Harris gloomily.

'Actually, he's got his eyes on you, Jacky my boy. I had a long talk with him earlier. Back at the nick. Yeah, ok, I was poaching, mea culpa, but, like I said, you have nothing to worry about: Matty Gallagher says you are the most infuriating senior officer he has ever worked with.'

'Doesn't exactly put my mind at rest.'

'Ah, but it should do because he loves working for you, you curmudgeonly old bastard. God knows why. There's no way I could prise him away even if I wanted to.' Gorman looked at him gently. 'And I don't want to, Hawk. Losing me and a damned good sergeant in one night would be too much for any man to bear.'

Harris was not sure what to say.

'Look after him,' said Gorman and looked out of the window again. 'Still no movement. Are you sure this is not a set-up as well? Is your man reliable?'

The inspector's mind went back to his last encounter with Paul Garratt the previous day when, after 48 hours of intense negotiations which had seen Harris and Curtis spending many hours in meetings and on the phone, he had been able to secure for Garratt the deal that he wanted.

Armed with the agreement, Harris walked into the interview room at Levton Bridge that final time to be greeted by a hopeful look from Garratt. His expression clouded over when he saw a man he did not recognise following the inspector into the room.

'Who's he?' he asked curtly.

'Customs,' replied Harris.

'Eric Stabler,' said the Customs man, sitting down and taking off his suit jacket to reveal rolled-up shirtsleeves. 'None of this happens without me.'

Garratt looked at Harris.

'He's right,' said the inspector. 'Customs investigator trumps woolly-back cop on this one.'

'Ok,' said Garratt. 'Do I take it you have got my deal then?'

'Yes, but you had better deliver your side of the bargain, mind,' said the DCI, glancing at Stabler. 'This has gone all the way up to the Foreign Office. No one is entirely happy about this. You're a pretty good catch yourself and no one is entirely comfortable with letting you go.'

'Yeah,' said Stabler, 'so if this is a piss-take...'

'It isn't,' said Garratt. 'So, what's the deal, Harris?'

'All charges dropped. Things smoothed over with our Congolese friends, a new identity, safe passage to the border then we stick you on a horse and you fuck off into the sunset, never to return.'

'I've always fancied South America,' said Garratt. 'Too wet here. And too many sheep.'

'So, start talking then,' said Harris. 'Where does Gerry Radford fit into the picture? You reckon he's moved into wildlife trafficking?'

'Big time.'

'You will have to do better than that,' said Stabler. 'Our information is that he is relatively small fry.'

'Was,' said Garratt. 'Was small fry, Mr Stabler. See, Gerry Radford has got a new hobby and it's making him huge sums of money.'

'What is it?'

'Caged birds,' said Garratt. 'Caught all over the world and shipped over here.'

'It's a massive racket,' said Stabler, glancing at Harris.

'It is,' said Harris. 'So where do they go after he brings them back here, Paul?'

'The illegal pet trade in the UK or moved on to the Continent. Oh, and a lot go over to the US. The Americans can't get enough of parrots and the like. Anything pretty-coloured. They'll pay top dollar, particularly for the rarer species, and with the US getting tougher on legal imports, the black market is on the up and up. It's much less risky than trafficking drugs.'

'But not for the birds,' said Harris, his disgust undisguised. 'Surely, many of them will die on the way over?'

'Maybe they do,' said Garratt and gave a slight smile, 'but, as I have tried to teach you before, the fewer there are, the higher the price

227

on the ones that survive. Don't look at me like that, Harris. Everything is a commodity.'

Harris scowled at him.

'We'll need names,' said Stabler. 'You're going to have to work for this.'

'Give me a pen and a piece of paper then.'

Twenty minutes later, once he had finished writing, Garratt handed the paper over to Stabler, who scanned the list and gave a low whistle.

'Thought you'd like it,' said Garratt.

'You said you could deliver Radford as well,' said Harris as he looked at the list handed to him by Stabler. He placed it on the desk. 'His name is not on this.'

'And so I can. Tomorrow night, he is bringing in something that I think will interest you. Be warned, he knows that someone inside his organisation is grassing him up to the police and has put the word out that a delivery of drugs is coming in at a service station. That's a red herring to keep the cops over there tied up. The real one is coming to a workshop he uses to store stuff.' He reached for the piece of paper and scribbled something. 'That's the address. Third building on the left. Look inside the truck and you will find everything you need.'

Garratt sat back in his chair and stared expectantly at the chief inspector.

'Ok, Harris, I have kept my side of the bargain. When do I get to go?'

'Now. You'll go with Mr Stabler here,' said Harris. 'He'll arrange things. I think he will want a further conversation with you before you do your disappearing act.'

Stabler nodded and Garratt stood up.

'Oh, one thing before you do go, Paul,' said Harris. 'How do you know all this about Radford?'

Garratt gave a slight smile.

'Who do think fixed tomorrow night's little operation for him?' he said. 'The birds come from a bent dealer I know in Ghana.'

'Sit down,' said Harris.

Garratt hesitated.

'Sit down,' repeated Harris, his voice harder edged this time.

Garratt sighed and took his seat again.

'What's this about, Jack?' asked Stabler. 'I don't want you doing anything that will wreck our arrangement.'

'There's something I need to clear up first, though, I still have an unsolved murder,' said Harris. 'Paul, did Meredith know about you and Radford?'

'I was going to tell him the night I found out what he was doing but when he told me that he was grassing up Radford, things suddenly got a whole lot more complicated. Never shit in your own nest and all that stuff.' Garratt chuckled. 'A nice bird analogy, I think.'

Harris scowled.

'Come on, Inspector,' said Garratt, 'lighten up. You have got what you wanted out of this.'

'Not quite. See, we have a witness who says that you were involved in Meredith's murder and the attack on James Thornycroft. I did not believe that until now but now I am thinking that you had a good reason to see him dead.'

'I imagine we are talking about Thornycroft's wife? The lovely Gaynor?'

'I can't reveal…'

'You don't need to. She has always hated me. Blames me and Meredith for leading her husband into bad ways. However, you can rest assured that she's lying about me. I know for a fact that Radford sent a couple of his own heavies after Meredith and Thornycroft. Bloke called Lennie Ross, shaven-headed guy – and another chap, don't know his name, evil-looking bastard. They're the ones who shot at your farmers. Mind, I did hear that they are adamant that they didn't kill Meredith.'

'Yes, but did you?' asked Harris. 'I mean, you've got plenty of motive if you thought he was threatening to screw things up with Radford. Or maybe you were worried that he was going to grass you up? You are already wanted for the murder of Rylance, it's not like you have not got a track record for this sort of thing.'

'Not my style these days,' said Garratt with a slight smile. 'Jesus, I can't ransack some old bird's home without being caught.'

'Yeah, what were you doing there? Weren't you taking a bit of a risk?'

'You are right about one thing. I had gotten kinda jumpy about Meredith. When he disappeared, I started to wonder if he was informing on me as well, cutting a deal. I tried to get into his home, see if he had anything on me, but you had a police guard on it. I wondered if you had taken him into protective custody. I don't mind admitting, I was crapping myself. He knew where all the skeletons were buried.'

'So, when you found out that Jasmine had done a runner as well, you decided to see if she had taken anything with her?' said Harris.

'Something like that. Once I got thinking about it, I reckoned that he would not be so stupid as to leave anything at his place so Jasmine was the obvious person to trust with it.'

'And did you find anything at her mum's house?'

'No.' Garratt gave a smile. 'Ironic really. Honour among thieves and all that.'

'Oh, before I forget,' said Gorman. 'I should thank you for the tip-off about Radford rumbling our informant.'

'You got him out of there alright?'

'Yeah.'

Gorman's radio crackled.

'We got movement,' said a man's voice. 'Truck turning into the industrial estate. And a car behind it. A Jaguar.'

The officers watched both vehicles cut their lights and drive slowly down the road, towards the detectives' hiding place. Truck and car pulled up out outside the workshop. The back doors of the lorry were flung open and half a dozen men jumped out.

'Radford,' said Harris, with a gleam in his eye as he pointed to another man getting out of the Jaguar's front passenger seat.

'Ok,' said Annie Gorman into her radio. 'Show time.'

As the two officers ran down the office block's stairs, there was a squeal of tyres and the police cars careered out onto the road and drove towards the workshop, tyres squealing. The back doors of the surveillance van were thrown up and more officers spilled out on the road and sprinted towards the startled gang members. Within seconds, the air reverberated to the sound of shouting as the officers quickly overwhelmed their targets. Jack Harris ran towards the truck just as a shaven-headed man jumped out of the driver's side. For a few moments, the two men eyed each other then Lennie Ross turned and started to run back towards the workshop. Harris sprinted after him and hurled himself into a flying rugby tackle, bringing the man to the ground where he struggled for a second or two, shouting profanities as the inspector twisted his arms behind him and snapped on a pair of handcuffs. Then, realising that they were partially concealed by a low wall and having glanced round to check that no one could see them, Jack Harris grabbed hold of the man's shoulders and slammed his face into the tarmac. The man gave a squeal of pain.

'That,' said Harris through twisted lips, 'is for a couple of farmer pals of mine.'

He dragged the dazed man to his feet and led him back towards the others. Gorman viewed the man's bloodstained features but said nothing. Handing Ross over to one of the other offices, Harris scrambled into the back of the truck, where he was confronted by a large number of bird cages. Wrinkling his nose at the acrid smell, he glanced inside the first few and saw a wide array of brightly coloured birds, some unconscious, others barely alive, some clearly dead and lying in their own faeces. Harris scowled and returned to the back of the van, jumping down onto the road.

'Where's Radford?' he asked.

Matty Gallagher appeared from round the back of the van, holding a struggling Gerry Radford by the arm.

Jack Harris walked up to the gangster and smiled sweetly.

'Gerry Radford,' he said in a soft voice laced with menace, 'I am going to make sure you wish you were never born.'

Chapter twenty-seven

'I take it the idea of the strong-arm stuff was to keep their mouths shut?' said Harris, looking hard at Lennie Ross.

It was shortly before ten the next morning and Harris and Gallagher were sitting in the interview room at Levton Bridge, staring across the table at the arrested man's battered and bruised face, one eye swollen and livid.

'I ain't saying nothing,' said Ross.

'Listen, Lennie,' said Harris, 'I've already told you that your mate Radford is going away for a long time. There is no way he is going to get out of this one – there's already three countries want to extradite him for trafficking offences. He can't get to you.'

'He's got a lot of mates has Gerry.'

'The amount of trouble they're in, I don't reckon that some hired meathead will be much concern to them,' said Harris. 'They are already running for the hills.'

Ross hesitated.

'Do yourself a favour,' said Gallagher.

'Ok,' said Ross eventually. 'I admit that Gerry Radford sent me up here to put the frighteners on, but what happened to Thornycroft was an accident. The idea was to rough him up, make sure he kept his mouth shut, but he fell and hit his head.'

'I am prepared to believe that,' nodded Harris. 'But not sure you are going to be able to wriggle out of Meredith's murder so easily.'

'I did not kill him, that's the God's honest truth, Mr Harris.'

'But you did go after him?'

Ross nodded.

'Yeah,' he said. 'Gerry was sure that if we scared him enough, he'd refuse to talk to them RSPCA investigators. Garratt told Radford that if you turned the screw enough, Meredith took fright. Said he had a yellow streak. I'd been watching the house for a couple of days and when I saw him leave, I followed him to sort it out.'

'Why the pit bull?'

'Thought it might help scare him. It was a mean bastard was that dog and he'd sold me the bloody thing so he knew how crazy it was.'

'And the idea was?'

'To follow him out of town and run him off the road. Listen,' said Ross, looking increasingly anxious, 'I may have done some bad things in my life but I did not kill him.'

'I believe you,' nodded Harris. 'See, we know about the woman.'

'You do?' Ross looked relieved.

'Yes, we do.'

'She was driving behind Meredith's car. When he broke down she drove past. I thought nothing of it at first but just as I was about to pull in, I noticed that she had done the same thing a bit further up the road. Something did not seem right so I went past her car all innocent like then backed into a gateway round the corner. By the time I got going they were both out of sight. Took me ages to catch up.' He gave a slight smile. 'I'm not exactly the fastest of walkers. Not really my scene.'

'But you saw them both later?'

'Not together. I saw her coming towards me. Hid in the trees until she had gone. I noticed that she was carrying a knife and I guessed what she had done.'

'And then?' asked Harris.

'I went up to the copse and found Meredith. He was still alive. His breathing was very shallow, mind, and he kept making this gurgling sound. His dog was standing next to him and the bloody thing takes one look at me and goes berserk. Starts growling and snarling then it goes for my dog. Fought the bloody thing to a standstill.' Ross shook his head in admiration. 'Fought like a tiger. He would have been magnificent in the ring.'

Harris scowled.

'I assume it was you that shot him later?' he asked.

'Yeah, he was too badly injured to go on. Seemed like the kindest thing to do.' Ross gave a half smile. 'You've got to show them some kindness, haven't you?'

Harris looked at him bleakly.

Chapter twenty-eight

Shortly after four that afternoon, a woman in dark glasses approached the booking-in desk at Manchester Airport. The two Customs men standing nearby watched in silence as she stood for a few moments, glancing nervously about her as she waited for the queue to advance. Unseen by the woman, one of the officers took a faxed photograph out of his pocket and studied it for a few moments. He looked across at his colleague and nodded, and together they walked slowly towards her.

'Would you accompany us, please, madam?' said one of the men, taking hold of her arm.

'Why?' protested the woman as other passengers turned to watch the confrontation. 'I have done nothing wrong. You have...'

'Please do not make a fuss,' said the Customs officer calmly. 'Let's do this nice and quietly, shall we?'

'I don't know what...' began the woman angrily but her voice tailed off as she saw a figure emerge from behind the check-in desk and walk along the queue towards her.

'Hello, Gaynor,' said Harris, glancing down at her luggage. 'A strange time to be going on holiday with your husband at death's door, is it not?'

With a cry of anger, Gaynor Thornycroft wrenched free from the Custom man's grasp and started to run across the hall, heading for the nearest exit, but found her way blocked by Gallagher. She veered to her left and started to run towards the other exit only to see a couple of uniformed police officers emerging to stand between her and safety. Whirling round, she saw Matty Gallagher walking over to her.

'Now where,' said the sergeant, 'would you be going?'

* * *

It was shortly after seven that evening and Harris and his sergeant were sitting in the interview room at Levton Bridge, Gaynor Thornycroft eying them from the other side of the desk, the duty lawyer sitting alongside her with a glum look on his face. He had experienced enough run-ins with Jack Harris over recent days to view the forthcoming interview with anything but dread.

'This had better not take long,' said a furious Gaynor. 'I did not kill Trevor Meredith and when I get out of here…'

'The United States is a long way from Roxham hospital,' said Harris calmly, glancing down at the airline ticket lying on the desk.

'I had to get away. I could not stand it any more. Do you know what it's like being cooped up like that?'

'I take it that James was not aware of your little plan?' asked Harris.

'Plan? What plan?' she snapped.

'Please do not take me for a fool, Gaynor,' said Harris, his voice hard-edged now. 'There's enough people tried to do that over the past week. Besides, Barry Ramsden has confirmed what's been happening. Positively eager to help, he was, wasn't he, Sergeant?'

'Certainly seemed to be once he realised what we knew. That's civic duty for you, I guess. I think it's called damage limitation.'

Gaynor Thornycroft looked at them, her face a mask of confusion.

'I really do not know what you are talking about,' she said, glancing at the lawyer. 'None of this is making any sense at all.'

'Do you plan to charge my client?' asked the solicitor. 'Because at the moment I am not quite sure why she is here.'

'Then let me enlighten you,' said Harris, glancing down at another document lying on the desk. 'Five years ago, a new housing estate was built on the edge of town. The one on which Barry Ramsden now lives, oddly enough. Very pleasant it is, too. Mock-Tudor some of the houses and people tell me that the most expensive ones there go for the thick end of £350,000.'

Gaynor Thornycroft eyed him uneasily.

'Several months ago,' continued Harris, 'the same developer, a fairly small firm from Roxham actually, decided that with the housing market starting to pick up, it would like to expand the estate. However, to make that happen, it needed to buy the adjoining land. There was a problem, though, because the dog sanctuary stands on the site in question. Doing ok so far, Gaynor?'

She stared down at the desk but said nothing.

'So,' said Harris, 'they made an offer to the directors of the company which runs the place. They were all for it. Why would they not be? See, they realised pretty quickly that constructing a new sanctuary elsewhere would not cost much more than a million and the land was worth what, Sergeant?'

'Two and a half mill.'

'So?' protested the lawyer. 'Surely none of them would benefit because under the rules of the not-for-profit company they cannot receive payouts.'

'Indeed they can't,' nodded Harris. 'Which is why they established a secret fund into which the additional money would be paid. Everyone won, the town got a new sanctuary, the developer got his site and they got a nice payback for all their commitment to the dogs down the years. And who knows – it might even be lawful in the hands of a clever solicitor.'

'All very interesting but what does this have to do with my client?'

'Ah, well,' said Harris, leaning forward in his chair, 'that is when it gets interesting. You will recall that some months ago, a rumour started circulating that the sanctuary was to be closed. The directors were horrified and stamped it out pretty quickly, a denial in the local paper, putting right anyone they heard spreading the gossip, that sort of thing. Trouble is, one of the people who heard the story was Gaynor Thornycroft.'

'So?' asked the solicitor.

'During one of our interviews with Gaynor, she let slip that she had lived here as a child. I did not remember her and we did not really pick up on the significance of it at first. A lot of people try to pretend they don't come from here.'

Harris glanced at Gallagher, who gave a rueful smile.

'When we checked her background, we discovered that her father was a man called Matthew Grainger,' said the inspector. 'Then I remembered him. He used to run an antiques shop in East Street. You might remember him as well.'

Harris looked at the solicitor.

'I bought some stuff at Grainger's,' nodded the lawyer. 'Nice man, a bit old school. A real gentleman, mind.'

'And a successful one to book. However, in time he decided that Levton Bridge was too small for his ambitions.' Harris glanced at Gallagher. 'A lot of people feel that. Anyway, he relocated to Liverpool. A big city centre shop. Unfortunately, the move was a disaster. The recession hit, his health failed and the business went bust.

Matthew Grainger died a poor man. Am I still right, Gaynor?'

She nodded, tears glistening in her eyes.

'However, he did leave one thing of value, didn't he? Or rather, you thought he had.'

She said nothing.

'I will answer that for you as well, then,' said Harris. 'It turns out that Matthew had always loved dogs and when he lived up here, he heard about the idea to create a rehoming centre and wanted to be involved. His business was doing well in those days, very well indeed, and he donated some money to help buy the site where the sanctuary stands. When his company eventually collapsed, Matthew managed to keep this arrangement secret from his creditors so no one tried to make a claim against the sanctuary. Honourable to the last. His wife having predeceased him, any claims to the land passed down to his daughter. The only thing he was able to leave you, Gaynor, a little nest egg. How I am doing?'

She said nothing but they could see her battling the tears, her shoulders heaving with the effort.

'So,' said Harris, 'when she heard the rumour that the land might be sold, she saw her chance of bailing herself out of her own financial difficulties. She approached the directors demanding a cut of whatever they made from the sale.'

'Have you got any evidence of this?' asked the lawyer.

Harris held up the document.

'We didn't have until the good sergeant here persuaded the bank manager down at Roxham to open his safety deposit box this morning,' he said.

Gaynor looked at the inspector in shock.

'That's confidential,' she protested.

'In a murder inquiry, nothing is confidential,' said Harris.

'What is it?' asked the lawyer.

'It is a letter written by Matthew Grainger shortly before his death and given to his daughter. In it, he chronicles what he claims was a verbal agreement with the directors that he, or his heir in the case of his death, receive a cut of the sale. How am I doing, Gaynor? Still right?'

She glowered at him.

'During the discussions that followed,' continued Harris, 'the directors initially refused to acknowledge the letter but when Gaynor said she would go public, they backed down pretty quickly. None of them wanted to be seen as money-grabbers. All except one of them – our friend Trevor Meredith, who refused to acknowledge the validity of the claim and said they should not give in to blackmail, a stance which he refused to soften. One can only guess at his motives but one imagines that the last thing he wanted was Gaynor stealing part of his share. Am I guessing right, Gaynor?'

She said nothing.

'Anyway,' said the inspector, 'a week ago, the developer loses patience with the delays and says that he's going to look elsewhere. In desperation, the directors make a final approach to Trevor. He says they can go ahead and sign the deal but that he will not countenance Gaynor getting any of the money. Our Gaynor could see her money disappearing. How much was it, as a matter of interest?'

'I would have made half a million pounds,' she said quietly.

'A tidy sum but none of it would happen without Trevor agreeing – according to Barry Ramsden, the directors were prepared to reject the offer for the land rather than be unmasked as moneygrabbers. Standing in the community, it's a terrible thing. However, there was a get-out clause in all of this. You knew, because your husband had told you, that Radford was after Meredith and that gave you an idea. I assume there was a deadline for the sale of the land?'

'The developer gave us until tomorrow morning,' said Gaynor. 'The contracts were ready and the money would have been paid over on Tuesday.'

'Which got you thinking. You realised that if Trevor were to die, the problem would be solved. And because James had told you what was happening, you knew that there were plenty of people who would like to see Meredith dead. Even if he was murdered, everyone would simply put it down to Radford's doing – he's got plenty of form for such things, after all – or maybe a falling out with our friend Garratt, a man with a record of violence and even murder. Who would suspect a respectable woman like you, and a grieving wife to boot? And by the time anyone had worked it out, you and your money would have been long gone anyway.' Harris glanced down at the airline ticket lying on the desk. 'To Los Angeles, no less. Very nice.'

Gaynor glowered at the detectives.

'We even know why you did it,' said Harris, taking a document out of his jacket pocket. 'Your husband was about to be declared bankrupt. You would have lost the new house, the one thing you had left. You needed money and you needed it fast, Gaynor, and I suspect that by that stage, it did not really matter who got in your way.'

'Trevor Meredith was a bastard,' said Gaynor in a voice infused with anger, surprising the detectives with the sudden vehemence of her response after listening in virtual silence. 'Everything bad that ever happened to us could be traced down to that man. He was the one who introduced James to wildlife trafficking in Zaire, he was the one who got him gambling, he was the one who persuaded him to buy that crappy vets practice up here and he was the one who persuaded him to get back into smuggling the animals again. Trevor Meredith ruined my life, Chief Inspector, ruined it, I tell you.'

'I really must...' began the solicitor but she waved away his attempts to speak.

'Now here he was doing it again. Threatening to take away the only security I had, the one thing my father left me.' She was battling with emotion now. 'He was a decent man, Inspector, it never even crossed his mind that they would not honour his agreement if the land was sold. Do you know my father's last words before he died? "Be happy." With that money, I could have been happy, started a new life, a fresh start, without my feckless husband. And Trevor Meredith? Trevor Meredith was going to ruin it all. And for what? Greed, that's what.'

'Pot or kettle?' said Harris.

She did not reply but sat there, trembling slightly as silence settled on the room for a few moments.

'So how did you kill him?' asked Harris.

'Look,' said the solicitor. 'I really do think...'

'No,' said Gaynor. 'Let me tell him. He knows anyway.'

The lawyer shrugged and sat back in his seat.

'I could never have imagined how easy it was,' said Gaynor with a slight smile as she regained her composure. 'I followed him when he left his house. My plan was to get ahead of him and pretend to break down so he would stop and help me. Then he pulled off the road and I decided to follow him over the hills. I followed him to the copse. Gave him a final choice, change his mind or face the consequences. Showed him the knife but all he did was laugh in my face.'

'So you stabbed him?'

She nodded.

'When he saw I was serious, he tried to get the knife off me and we struggled for a few moments. Then his bloody dog went for me so I stabbed Trevor and got out of there as fast as I could.' She gave the detectives an odd look, her eyes flashing anger. 'And do you know what I felt when that knife went in?'

Harris shook his head.

'I enjoyed it, Inspector. I enjoyed killing the bastard.'

Suddenly, Jack Harris felt very tired.

Epilogue

Two days later, shortly after eleven in the morning, the inspector stood in the graveyard of Levton Bridge's parish church. Sun filtered through the trees and the birds sang as the mourners drifted away after the body of Trevor Meredith had been lowered into its grave. Matty Gallagher walked across to where the inspector was standing.

'Strange occasion,' said the sergeant. 'Poor old vicar did not know what to say.'

'What can you say?'

'I suppose.'

The detectives watched as Jasmine Riley detached herself from a group of mourners and walked across the grass towards them, supporting her mother who was walking with the aid of a stick.

'How's your leg, Mrs Riley?' asked the chief inspector.

'It's getting better. Thank you for what you did.'

'It was no trouble.'

'Will that awful Garratt man be sent to prison, Inspector?'

'It's a long story,' said Harris.

For a few moments nobody spoke then Jasmine looked at the inspector.

'I'm glad Trevor didn't die alone,' she said. 'I'm glad Robbie was there.'

Harris nodded. There was another silence, then Jasmine looked at him.

'Can I ask you a question?' she asked.

'Sure.'

'Trevor did try to stop the dog fighting, didn't he? I mean, he was genuine about that, wasn't he?'

'Who knows what his motivations were?'

'But it's possible,' said Jasmine. 'I mean, it is possible, yes?'

'I suppose so,' said Harris.

'So, do you think he was a good man, Inspector? I mean, at least in some way?'

Harris looked at her, saw the hopeful, almost pleading, expression on her face, and knew what he had to say to ease the suffering of a woman struggling to come to terms with what had happened. Even if what he said helped only a little, Jack Harris knew the right thing to say. Knew what she wanted to hear.

'No, Jasmine,' he said instead, 'on balance I don't think he was.'

As the inspector turned and walked away, Jasmine shot a distressed look at Gallagher but the sergeant simply shrugged and followed his boss. As Harris walked out of the graveyard and towards his Land Rover, his mobile phone rang. Looking down, he saw the name Ged Maynard on the read-out and frowned.

'Ged,' he said, taking the call. 'How's it…?'

'I hear you got Radford.'

'Yes, Ged, yes we did. Word is they are going to throw the book at him. Apparently, there's guys falling over themselves to save themselves by stitching him up.'

'Good.' Maynard hesitated. Harris could hear him fighting to control his emotions. 'They've fired me, you know. Said I handled the Meredith thing unprofessionally.'

'I know,' said Harris. 'And I'm sorry.'

'Not your fault, Hawk.' There was another pause. 'Listen, keep in touch, will you?'

'Yeah,' said Harris. 'Yeah, of course I will.'

But he knew he wouldn't.

An hour later, Jack Harris, Scoot trotting at his heels, walked into the cabin at the dog sanctuary to be greeted by the young receptionist.

'Hello,' she said.

'Thought you would be angry with me,' said the inspector. 'Because of me, the sale is not going ahead and you won't get a new sanctuary.'

'No, I'm not angry,' said the girl. 'It would not have felt right knowing what has been going on. Besides, there's talk that the new directors are going to put some of their own money into this place. And they're starting a fundraising campaign. They've already had a thousand pounds pledged.'

'Make that a thousand and ten,' said Harris. 'No, hang it, make it fifty.'

'Really?'

'Least I can do,' said Harris.

'That's very generous.' The girl went to pick up the phone on the desk. 'Are you here for Jane? I think she's…'

'No,' said Harris, 'actually I came to see you.'

'Me?'

'Yeah, you. I wonder, does Archie still need a new home?'

The girl beamed.

'Do you know,' she said. 'I think he might well do.'

THE END

List of characters

Levton Bridge Police:

Superintendent Philip Curtis
Detective Chief Inspector Jack Harris
Detective Sergeant Matt Gallagher
Detective Inspector Gillian Roberts
Detective Constable Alison Butterfield

Other characters:

Trevor Meredith – a hill walker
Jasmine Riley – Trevor Meredith's girlfriend
Detective Chief Superintendent Annie Gorman – head of Greater Manchester's Organised Crime Unit
Graham Leckie – a uniformed constable with Greater Manchester Police
Eric Stabler – Customs man
Lennie Ross – Chester villain
Chief Inspector Norris – Cheshire Police
Joe Lane – a hunter
Paul Garratt – a criminal
James Thornycroft – a Levton Bridge vet

248

Gaynor Thornycroft – his wife
Julie Gallagher – Matty Gallagher's wife
David Bowes – rents a cottage in the Levton Bridge area
Helen Jackson – Senior RSPCA officer
Alec Hulme – RSPCA inspector
Dennis Soames – Farmwatch member
Harry Galbraith – Farmwatch member
Bob Crowther/Mike Ganton – mountain rescue team leaders
Jane Porter – deputy manager, local dog shelter
Barry Ramsden – parish councillor
Len Radley/Charlie Myles – Levton Bridge pub regulars

If you enjoyed this book, please let others know by leaving a quick review on Amazon. Also, if you spot anything untoward in the paperback, get in touch. We strive for the best quality and appreciate reader feedback.

editor@thebookfolks.com

www.thebookfolks.com

Made in the USA
San Bernardino, CA
28 September 2017